Michael Franks is a writer who enjoys building stories that involve a wide range of human emotions. He has a wealth of life experience having spent many years in military service around the world and holds a BSc in Psychology. His aim in his writing is to touch the senses of the reader and enable them to experience the emotions of the characters in the story.

To my darling wife, Marion, for her perseverance and unswerving support.

Michael G Franks

MARELLE

AUSTIN MACAULEY PUBLISHERS™
LONDON * CAMBRIDGE * NEW YORK * SHARJAH

Copyright © Michael G Franks 2023

The right of Michael G Franks to be identified as author of this work has been asserted by the author in accordance with sections 77 and 78 of the Copyright, Designs and Patents Act 1988.

All rights reserved. No part of this publication may be reproduced, stored in a retrieval system or transmitted in any form or by any means, electronic, mechanical, photocopying, recording or otherwise, without the prior permission of the publishers.

Any person who commits any unauthorised act in relation to this publication may be liable to criminal prosecution and civil claims for damages.

This is a work of fiction. Names, characters, businesses, places, events, locales and incidents are either the products of the author's imagination or used in a fictitious manner. Any resemblance to actual persons, living or dead or actual events is purely coincidental.

A CIP catalogue record for this title is available from the British Library.

ISBN 9781035800551 (Paperback)
ISBN 9781035800568 (ePub e-book)

www.austinmacauley.com

First Published 2023
Austin Macauley Publishers Ltd®
1 Canada Square
Canary Wharf
London
E14 5AA

Chapter 1
France, 1944

The two children were huddled together in a darkened closet. They had been put there by their parents who, once again, believed they were about to be taken by the German soldiers. The town of Sedan in north eastern France had been occupied following the German invasion in 1940 and since that time, many of the town's Jews had been taken away to concentration camps in Poland or Germany. The Germans continued their attrition against the Jewish people and anything remotely Jewish.

The children's parents always ushered them into the hiding place whenever a German patrol was near. A large wardrobe would be slid in front of the closet door to conceal its entrance. Up until now, the Germans had not entered the house and Emily and Bernard Wilder had kept extremely low profiles, only ever leaving the house when there was little or no soldier activity.

The Wilder's knew that sooner or later the soldiers would come for them, so they agreed that their priority was to save their children. The closet was well stocked with dry rations and the eldest, Angelique, was given strict instructions of what to do in the event that the soldiers came. She had awareness of what was happening; she was eleven years old although seemed much older than her years.

Anton, who was six, still didn't understand the danger his family faced and he was very afraid, especially when he and his sister were put in the cupboard and told to keep very quiet.

'You must not make a sound whilst you are in here, not one sound, do you understand me? This is very important.'

'Yes Mother,' they would both say in unison.

'If you hear soldiers in the house, you are to stay here and not come out until at least one hour after they have gone. Do you understand me?'

'Yes Mother,' the two very frightened voices replied. They had listened to their mother's instructions many times before but could only obey whilst not fully understanding. They listened once again to the scraping of the wardrobe being pushed over the doorway to their little hideaway and once again they were locked inside, cold, frightened and silent.

The children never considered how they would remove the obstacle that would enable them to open the door if they had to. Nor had they ever considered the possibility that their parents would not be there to do it. It started to dawn on Angelique that the food supplies and other essentials like blankets and heavy coats were preparations for their future survival—without their parents.

Up until now, they were never in the hideaway much longer than an hour and most of the times much less than that. Although she was afraid each time the process took place, Angelique was always sure that her father or mother would soon be back to let them out.

During the daytime was best because the closet backed on to an outside wall of the house and there was a small crack out of which she could see the road and people walking by. She would sometimes let Anton look out on the promise that he wouldn't make a sound, it helped to calm him.

Angelique heard the rumble of vehicles stop near to the house and the clatter of soldiers' boots coming closer and closer. She peered through the crack in the wall, could see the German soldiers marching towards the front door and then heard the door being burst open.

Anton almost screamed but Angelique, recovering quickly, covered his mouth with her hand. She whispered in his ear.

'Quiet Anton, please keep quiet.' He started to shake and she held him close to her.

There was much shouting in German.

'Look in there, search that room.' The leader then turned to Bernard.

'Your papers,' he commanded, holding out his hand. A soldier came into the room and spoke to his Officer.

'There are signs of children here Sir but we cannot find them.'

Bernard, in an attempt to distract the Officer from his children, reached into his jacket pocket and handed over his identity card.

'Now, I wish to see your birth certificates and I will also want to see your children.'

Trembling, Emily Wilder went to a side table drawer and removed a folder of papers; she knew that there was now no escape and handed the sheaf of documents to the Officer, who spent time examining them.

'I see that you were both born in Sedan but you Mrs Wilder, I believe, have Jewish parents, is that not so?'

'Yes, my parents are Jewish but they are very old and live many miles from here. My children are being looked after by them.'

The Officer spoke slowly and quietly.

'I have no immediate interest in your parents Mrs Wilder, what I want to know is why you have not registered as a Jew at the registration centre and why you have disobeyed the strict rules we have set. Fortunately, there are some people in your town that are very helpful to us in finding those of you who wish to hide from the truth. You will be moved from here to a work camp as is the case with all Jews in the town.'

The Officer nodded a silent instruction to two of his soldiers who stepped forward and took hold of Emily by each arm.

Bernard shouted, 'What are you doing? You can't take her, she is a French citizen.'

The German Officer looked squarely into Bernard's face.

'You and this town are under command of the Army of the Third Reich, Mr Wilder and your French citizenship counts for nothing. Take her away.'

Emily was struggling to free herself but the guards held on to her tightly. Bernard lunged forward and tried to drag his wife from her captors, pleading.

'Let her go, please let her go, she has done nothing wron—' Before Bernard could finish, a single shot rang out and Bernard fell to the floor. Emily screamed as the soldiers dragged her past the lifeless body of her husband.

The Officer in charge holstered his pistol as he casually stepped over Bernard's body and followed Emily as she was virtually carried to the waiting truck outside. She resisted the desire to shout out to her children, knowing that it would certainly expose them, there was nothing she could do.

One thing was certain; she trusted Angelique and knew that she would look after herself and Anton. Emily wept not for her own situation but for what her children would have to face alone.

Angelique heard the Officer in charge asking the questions and realised that this was what her parents had been preparing for. Then she heard the gun shot noise and her mother screaming.

'Bernard, no—please God, not him.'

Her Mother's voice faded as she was dragged outside. At the sound of the gun shot, Anton went into some sort of fit and Angelique struggled to keep him from crying out, using all of her weight on top of him to stop him from kicking the door and making a noise, he then suddenly became very still. Angelique was unsure what had happened but for now, he was quiet.

She used the opportunity to look through the gap in the wall only to see her mother being dragged and pushed into the truck that was parked outside the house, which was full of other people just like her mother and father. All of them had the same haunted look in their eyes, a look of fear, despair and hopelessness.

As instructed, Angelique waited one hour before attempting to get out of the closet. She tried to move the door but the wardrobe at the other side was too heavy. She was worried about Anton, he hadn't moved at all since the fit stopped. She touched his face and listened for his breathing which was all right, he just seemed to be in a deep sleep.

The hideout was colder now, somehow less safe and she felt more isolated than she had ever experienced before. She thought it must be nearly two hours since the Germans left, so she was about to try again when the wardrobe started to inch slowly away from the door.

There was now a significant gap that allowed her to apply leverage with her feet to push it open further for her to squeeze out into the room but before she did so, she realised that she had no idea who had moved the furniture in the first place.

'Papa, are you there, is that you?'

There was a muffled reply.

'Come quickly princess, you need to help me.'

After struggling to move the wardrobe and using all of her strength, Angelique emerged to find her father propped up against the wall, his face and clothes covered in blood. There was a trail of blood from the centre of the room to the closet door.

'Papa, Papa, what have they done, please don't die, we need you.' She held his hand and tried to put her arms around him but he held her away.

'You must listen very carefully, Angelique,' he gasped and gulped in air, 'there isn't much time,' his breathing was laboured, his speech slurred. She was finding it difficult to hear him, as his speech was almost a whisper. 'You must look after each other now, go out only at night and make sure there are no soldiers around. As soon as you are able to,' there was a long pause as he tried to gather his strength, 'seek out Mrs Vignon and tell her what has happened here. You must both stay in the closet, do not turn on any lights; Mrs Vignon will see that you have food. If there are bombings, go down into the cellar and wait un—' Bernard sucked in a gulp of air and shuddered as his head rolled to one side and his eyes closed.

'Papa, Papa, wake up, wake up, you haven't finished.' She shook him gently, then a little firmer, 'wake up, please Papa.' She realised that he was not going to wake up. Oddly, she stopped crying just as Anton emerged from the hideaway. The young boy looked around, trying to absorb what he was seeing but didn't speak.

Angelique wiped the tears from her face and suddenly adopted a very adult posture.

'Are you alright Anton? I'm afraid our Papa has been very badly hurt.' Anton didn't answer he just stared at his father's body.

Angelique ushered her brother back towards the closet.

'We must stay in here Anton until after the bad people have gone away. Do you understand?'

He just nodded his head and crawled into the corner of the closet. Angelique closed the door and wrapped a blanket around him.

'I must be strong for Anton, I must be strong,' she said to herself and fell asleep.

When she woke up, she remembered that the wardrobe was now positioned at an angle from when she and her father had moved it away from the cupboard door. This would be a clear giveaway to their hiding place. Also, her father's body now lay by the side of the door and a trail of blood stretched from the other side of the room.

Anyone coming into the house would immediately be directed to where Angelique and Anton where hiding. She remained calm but tense and strained to listen for any sound, a door opening, footsteps, voices, anything that would warn her of someone approaching. She decided that she would need to move her father's body back to where he had originally fallen.

Then she would have to clean the blood stains from the wall and floor that pointed ominously to their hiding place. Angelique knew she could do nothing about the wardrobe except push it away from the cupboard door and back to its original position, which would be the only way she and her brother could enter or leave their hideout.

Anton was fast asleep, so Angelique steeled herself for the task of moving her dead father. It was an undertaking that no child of eleven years of age should be expected to carry out but Angelique was brave and now more grown up than her eleven years and she had promised to take care of her brother. She had taken on the mantle of mother and father.

It was dark in the house when Angelique emerged from her hiding place. She crept quietly to the kitchen and obtained the cleaning materials she needed, then went back to where her father lay. She kneeled by his side and gently stroked his forehead.

She wanted to dip the cloth in the basin of water and clean his face but she knew she couldn't give any indication that someone had been here after the shooting. She spoke to her father as though he could hear her.

'I'm sorry Papa but if I wash you, then they will know that Anton and I are here. So, I must try and move you now. I'll try not to hurt you.'

She put both hands under his arms and turned him, so that he was now horizontal on the floor. The girl needed all of her strength to slide him across the wooden floor as she edged his body slowly inch by inch to where she thought he had fallen. It had taken nearly an hour and she was exhausted.

The next task was to clean up the trail of blood that led to the hideout. Another hour passed by and Angelique could only guess whether the room was back to the state it was when her father was killed and her mother taken away.

Although it was nightfall, a bright moon gave some light through the large bay window, a shaft of light lit up the centre of the room and Angelique could see her father's face clearly. She sat quietly by his side and held his hand as Anton emerged from the refuge, rubbing his eyes against the bright moonlight.

'Come and kiss your Papa goodnight Anton, he's sleeping now.'

Anton didn't speak and just shook his head before running back into the hideout.

Angelique followed him and asked, 'What's the matter my little brother, can't you just say goodnight to your Papa?'

Anton once again just shook his head and lay down on the blanket with his back to Angelique. She would let him be for now and decided that she would seek out Mrs Vignon tomorrow because they would need to find somewhere else to live. She had no idea why Anton wouldn't speak and hoped Mrs Vignon would know what was wrong with him.

Suddenly, the night air was filled with the deafening noise of loud explosions, some of them quite close by. Angelique was unaware that the D Day landing assault had started and bombs were those of the British and American forces. What she was certain of was that she was afraid and could not stay here and so, remembering her father's instruction, she grabbed Anton who was trembling and crying but no sound came from his mouth.

She took as much as she could carry and headed for the cellar just as her father had told her. The noise got louder and one very close by explosion made the whole house shake. Windows were shattering all around them as they made their way to the cellar, Anton clung on tightly to his sister as she made her way carefully down the stairs deep into the bowels of the house.

Whistling noises preceded the explosions and each time Anton's small body convulsed and jerked with fear. Angelique tried to soothe him by holding him close to her and stroking his face. With each blast, dust and plaster would fall on their heads and Angelique was afraid that the house would collapse on them. Walls shook and between the bombs, the children could hear the bricks crashing to the ground. The bombing went on for just under an hour and eventually stopped, leaving an eerie silence.

'It's alright Anton, it has stopped now and we're not hurt.' She brushed the dust from his hair and lifted his chin, which was buried tightly into his chest. 'It really has stopped. We're alright now.' Anton continued to tremble and tears were pouring down his face but there was no sound. Angelique became puzzled by Anton's silence. 'Say something to me, little brother.'

Anton looked at her, opened his mouth and tried to say something but nothing would come out. He just shook his head and mouthed the words, 'Maman, Papa'.

Angelique did not understand what had happened to Anton but she knew she needed to find out how she could communicate with him.

'Do you need a drink of water, Anton?'

He nodded his head vigorously.

'Then you must wait here while I go and see if I can find something for you to drink.'

He grabbed her arm as she got up and shook his head ferociously.

'Then you must come with me but be very careful, we don't know what has happened to the house.'

They walked gingerly up the now rickety wooden stairs towards the entrance to the house. On opening the door, all that could be seen was utter devastation. The roof had almost collapsed, one side of the house was completely open to the outside and there were no windows or external doors.

The children clambered through the rubble towards what was once their kitchen. The house had not been directly hit but had been severely damaged. Water spewed out of an exposed pipe, so Angelique searched for a container to capture some of it.

Anton continued to cling on tightly to his sister's arm, which didn't help her in her quest. But eventually, she found a large ceramic jar and promptly filled it. She instructed Anton to cup his hands and drink from the running water pipe. She decided that she must try and recover the rest of the rations from the hideout if she could.

When she approached what was the front lounge where they had taken refuge, it was unrecognisable. The roof was gone and one wall had completely collapsed. The pile of bricks and rubble had totally covered her father's body. She quickly turned away and taking the hand of Anton made her way back to the cellar. She would look again in the daylight.

Chapter 2

Three months before the D Day landings, Sergeant Andy Miller was captured by the Germans and held in a POW camp close to the French German border. He was in the company of other allied soldiers, some of whom had been held there for several years. Most of the inmates were airmen and were there as a result of their aircraft being shot down or some sort of mechanical breakdown forcing them to land in enemy territory.

The Germans liked to separate their captives into military categories, Army in one, Air force captives in another, a special camp for officers and another for "other ranks" and so on. This practice was gradually stopped as soon as the Gestapo became more involved in the running of the camps but for now, the Luftwaffe ran the camps based on values and principles that differed considerably from that of the Gestapo.

Andy was quite tall for an air crewman and it was sometimes very difficult operating in some of the small spaces of an aircraft. He could have been mistaken for the archetype German with his blond hair and blue eyes. He was an experienced navigator and had flown many missions and early in 1944 was eventually hit by enemy fire after a bombing sortie in the industrial heartland of Germany.

As far as he was aware, he was the only survivor and managed to parachute away from the damaged bomber uninjured. German soldiers were quickly upon him where he was taken away for interrogation and imprisonment.

Andy had made several attempts to escape but was recaptured quite quickly each time. Every failed attempt prompted harsher treatment from the camp commandant who was rapidly losing patience, brought on mainly by the increasingly severe reprimands he was getting from his superiors. Once again, Sergeant Miller was to face his captors.

Oberst Franz Miltz, a career officer in the Luftwaffe stood with his back to his office door and stared out of the window. His posture was ram rod straight with his hands clasped behind his back, his knee-high black leather boots gleamed beneath his immaculately ironed breeches. He remained gazing out of the window as Sergeant Andy Miller was pushed and roughly manhandled into the centre of the Colonel's office.

There was a long pause then the Colonel spun around and faced Andy.

'You have once again abused my hospitality, Sergeant,' the Colonel said in his very good but clipped English. He slammed his clenched fist into the desk. 'This is the fourth time I have had to waste my time chasing and recapturing you. You are increasingly becoming a major nuisance to me.' Andy smiled inwardly but remained po-faced. The officer continued, 'I have tried to make you and your colleagues comfortable here and treated you all fairly, have I not'? The question was rhetorical and not expecting an answer. 'I hoped you would sit out this war, which I believe will end soon.' His face saddened as he slowly, wearily, sat down at his desk.

Franz Miltz had indeed treated his prisoners fairly and with great respect, the Luftwaffe were generally honourable men and rigorously applied the rules of war under the Geneva Convention. He knew first-hand how brave the pilots and air crew were on both sides and held a deep respect for them.

Franz understood which way the war was going and knew the end was not too far away but he also valued his own survival, so he therefore played the good, loyal German soldier game. Habitual escapees like Andy Miller only brought the Gestapo, an organisation that he despised passionately, closer to Franz's door. He knew that any dissent or perceived disloyalty meant a long stay at the eastern front or worse, so his true feelings were kept to himself.

There was a long period of silence and Andy tried to assess what his punishment would be. Could it be that this time he might be taken away and executed, his thoughts raced through his mind? He studied the Colonel's face for clues but saw nothing except a sort of tired resignation. Franz suddenly looked up at Andy and said, 'Are you aware that the Gestapo now have full responsibility for the running of Germany's prisoner of war camps? I will be frank with you Sergeant; when they become involved here, then I cannot guarantee that you will walk away from another escape attempt such as this with just a reprimand. Do you understand what I am saying?' Andy nodded but remained expressionless. The Colonel continued, 'can I have your assurance that you will cease the foolish notion that you can escape from this camp?'

Andy straightened his back even further and said, 'I have a duty to continue my attempts to escape from wherever I am held by the enemy and return to my unit to fight against you for my country, I will continue to do so until I succeed or you kill me. I consider myself a soldier fighting for my country. I am sure you will understand that is what I have to do.'

'You're a very brave man Sergeant but also very foolish. I do not intend to witness you throwing your life away nor indeed do I want to go through the trauma of having to make excuses about why my prisoners are escaping. When the Gestapo arrive here in three days' time, they will ensure one way or another that you do not escape again and believe me, that experience will not be pleasant.

Therefore, it is my intention to ship you and some of your colleagues out of here to a camp further north in Germany where I know escape is virtually impossible and more importantly, where you will be someone else's problem. In the meantime, you will be held in solitary confinement until the arrangements have been finalised.'

He turned to the guards at each side of Andy and commanded, at the same time waving his hand dismissively.

'Escort the prisoner to the detention cell until further notice.' The camp Commandant returned once again to gaze out of the window as Andy was hauled roughly out of his office.

Throughout the next three days, Andy considered his next escape. The solitude of the small dark cell he now inhabited was good for thinking things through. He was convinced that there would be an opportunity on the way to wherever he and his fellow prisoners were being taken, that meant that the next escape would be opportunistic rather than planned, of that he was sure. For now, he would reflect on his single-minded need to escape and get back to fighting the Germans.

For the following hours and days, Andy slipped in and out of sleep and in between these periods of slumber and wakefulness, he maintained his fitness by exercising as much as he could in the confined space he now occupied. In the short periods when he was neither asleep nor exercising, he lay on the straw mattress that separated him from the cold concrete floor and would remember a time in 1940 some four years earlier. His stomach churned when he relived hearing the words "Andy, Wing Commander wants to see you urgently". He drifted back to that moment.

****

Sergeant Andrew Miller was based at a bomber command unit in Norfolk and his unit had carried out many successful missions deep into Germany but they had also lost many pilots and aircrew. In 1940, the Germans had been pounding London relentlessly.

Day and night, the drone of the German bombers could be heard; the ominous sound of sirens and the noise of buildings being hit together with the hurrying crowds scampering to the nearest shelter were frequent occurrences. Fire fighters fought bravely to keep more fires than they could manage under control and at night, the London skyline was a blaze of dancing flames.

He was glad that his wife and two children were able to get away to the country through the evacuation programme but still didn't know where they had been re-housed. He remembered lying on the bed in his billet waiting for his next sortie call out. Instead, the door opened and an orderly entered.

'Andy, Wing Commander wants to see you urgently,' he promptly left to let the Sergeant prepare for his urgent meeting.

Andy, got up, looked in the mirror, paused momentarily and saw how much this war had aged his forty-three-year-old face; now the smoothness of his blue eyes and blond hair had become more rugged.

'Why would the boss want to see me urgently?' He wondered. He straightened himself up, placed his cap squarely on his head and made his way to the Wing commander's office.

The orderly ushered him into the office and he marched smartly towards his Commander's desk and saluted.

'You wished to see me, Sir?'

'Yes Sergeant, please sit down.'

Andy looked towards a chair and then saw the Squadron Padre sat to one side. His heart started to pound; he knew instinctively something was terribly wrong.

'Sergeant Miller, I'm afraid I have some very bad news to give you and I am so sorry.' The colour drained from Andy's face. He wanted to shout "what, what is it, tell me for God sake" but no sound came out of his mouth.

'Yesterday evening, your family home in London received an indirect hit during a German air raid. The house was totally destroyed.' The wing Commander paused momentarily.

Andy had recovered slightly on the news that it was just his house, *just bricks and mortar*, he thought. He was relieved.

'I'm not bothered about the house Sir, at least my family are safe in the country, although I'm still not sure where.'

The wing Commander held his hand up to interrupt him.

'I'm afraid your family were in the house when the bomb struck the house next door Andrew, your house collapsed and there were no survivors, I'm truly sorry.'

'That can't be, they were evacuated weeks ago to somewhere in the country away from London. There must be a mistake, Sir.' Andy was shaking his head and trembling with rage at the thought that the authorities would make such a mistake.

'There is no mistake, Andrew, I wish to God it was but I have to tell you that their bodies were recovered last night and identified by your wife's mother, the children's grandmother. We don't know why they were not evacuated.'

Andy slid off the chair to his knees and sobbed uncontrollably. The Padre rose quickly, went to Andy's side and knelt with him, placing a comforting arm around his shoulders. He gently helped him back into the chair.

'There is little I or anyone else can say that will help you at this time Andrew but I and the Padre will be available at any time, day or night if you need us. Take some time out now, go back to London, you will need to make arrangements. I have asked the Padre to go with you to provide you with any material as well as spiritual support. Once again, I am deeply sorry for your loss.'

Andy, still trembling stood up slowly and said, 'Thank you, Sir and Padre. If you don't mind Sir, I would like to leave immediately.'

'Yes, of course you must Sergeant; take as much time as you need.'

Andy and the Padre left together.

****

The pain of remembering what followed in London during the next two weeks in 1940, the funeral and all that went with it awakened Andy from his daydream. He knew though that it wasn't a dream; in fact, it was a nightmare that engulfed his every moment.

Even after almost four years, he had not got over his loss, the picture of his daughter Katie aged eight and son Charlie aged six started to form in his mind and he saw them chalking their hopscotch map out on the street in front of their house.

He fondly remembered how much they enjoyed their simple game and smiled as he recalled how they would argue over whether a heel had touched the line. At that time, they were so happy.

'Come on Dad, you can play too,' they would shout excitedly. They would laugh heartily as they watched their father with his comparatively big feet repeatedly step on the lines as he attempted to join in the game.

****

He sat bolt upright, shaking his head in an attempt to get rid of the agony of those memories, an agony that dominated his life. He often wished he could savour just the joy he experienced whenever he saw his family in his mind's eye, instead that joy soon turned to anguish and pain as he remembered seeing them laying lifelessly next to their mother at the makeshift mortuary.

That he would hear them laugh no more broke his heart and so, he replaced that heartache with a burning desire to escape and wreak havoc on the enemy that had destroyed his family.

Each escape took him closer to getting back to a fighting unit, to a position where he could hit back but he had made mistakes, which was why he was now in the "hole" for the fourth time. He was learning from those mistakes, in future he would travel only at night and stay away from populated areas, trying to mingle with the German civilians was one of his first errors, travelling during daylight was another. He had worked out what his next strategy would be and when the opportunity came along, he would make sure that this time there would be no mistakes.

After three days, the cell door swung open and he was ordered outside, he hadn't seen daylight in that time and had difficulty opening his eyes. The guard barked an order at him to move and coupled this with a sharp thump in his back with a rifle butt.

He was ushered to a line of four other prisoners who were gathered at the tailgate of a truck, presumably one that would transport them to their next residence. He knew a couple of them only vaguely but he was sure that all of them had made several attempts at escaping.

Colonel Milzt stepped out of his office and approached the prisoners.

'It is not my intention to wish you a pleasant journey—in fact, I believe that where you are going will not be pleasant at all and you can only blame yourselves that the regime you will encounter will be a great deal harsher than anything you have experienced here.' His clipped English gave emphasis to his words. He turned away smartly and walked back into his office.

The guards immediately shouted at the prisoners to get into the truck. Two armed guards accompanied them and took up positions at the tail gate, their weapons firmly trained on their captives who were now gathered at the front of the vehicle behind the drivers cab.

The open top lorry slowly moved out of the compound and headed north. Andy made a point of picking out landmarks and ground features along the way that might help him if he managed to escape. It was a really pleasant day and the German countryside was quite breath-taking in places.

Andy made the most of taking in the fresh air. He studied the faces of his fellow escapees and wondered who would make it through this war and who would not, *the odds of any of us getting out of this mayhem alive are pretty small*, he thought.

They were driving for almost an hour before anyone spoke. The soldier sat next to Andy suddenly held out his hand and introduced himself.

'Rick, Rick Frederici, I've seen you around the camp a few times especially when they've brought you back.' The soldier spoke with a broad American accent that Andy found difficult to follow.

Andy extended his hand.

'I'm Andy Miller, nice to meet you.'

One of the guards shouted for them to keep quiet.

'Schweigen!'

Andy leaned towards his neighbour.

'I think he doesn't want us to talk.'

'Schweigen,' the guard shouted again, this time levelling his rifle towards the pair.

Andy held his hands up Okay Fritz, okay, keep your helmet on.' The pair remained silent for the next thirty minutes, when suddenly Andy saw a fighter plane coming in low from behind the truck. The pilot had a good look at the vehicle as he flew over the top.

'It looks like a Mustang; it's one of ours,' Rick shouted excitedly.

The fighter plane went on and then suddenly banked hard right and started back towards the truck. The pilot had obviously decided he would take out a soft target on his way home.

The German truck driver brought the vehicle to an abrupt stop, throwing its passengers in the rear on top of each other, he and his passenger threw themselves onto the road and took cover in the ditch. The two German soldiers in the rear of the truck were catapulted into the bodywork of the back of the driver's cab at the same time, crashing in to the three POW's that were in their way.

Andy and Rick didn't hesitate and jumped clear as the Mustang opened fire with his 12.7mm machine guns, raking the lorry from front to back. The fuel tank exploded as the Mustang turned for home, accompanied by the sound of rounds of ammunition exploding in the truck. The three POW's and the two guards in the rear of the vehicle had no chance to escape.

If they weren't hit by the machine guns, then they certainly would not have avoided the ball of flame that followed. The lorry was ablaze as Andy and Rick cautiously emerged from the ditch from where they had taken refuge. The German driver and his passenger did likewise from the other side of the road.

As the group faced each other, there was a long silence as they both assessed the situation. None of them had weapons; they had been left in the truck and were now just melted, twisted lumps of metal.

The German driver stepped forward and pumping out his chest said, in English.

'You are still prisoners of the German Army and it is my duty to escort you to the nearest town, where we will obtain alternative transport to continue our journey.'

Rick stepped forward and said, 'Is that right, Fritz? Well, we're nobody's prisoner.' In a flash, he rammed his fist into the soldier's jaw, who was sent flying backwards crashing his head onto the concrete road and was either dead or completely unconscious. The remaining German, who was rather short and tubby, decided he was now outnumbered, turned tail and ran off.

'That was a pretty mean right hand Rick, where did you pick that up?' Andy was impressed.

'In the Bronx where I was brought up, that's how you survived. A strong right hand and get it in there first,' Rick replied as he crouched, sparring, boxing style.

Andy jokingly said, 'Remind me not to tangle with you then. By the way, where is the Bronx?'

'New York. Hell man, don't you know the Bronx, it's in the greatest city in the world.'

'Uh, I don't think so. London already has that title. But we should avoid any disagreement, let's say we come from the two greatest cities in the world.'

Rick shrugged his shoulders.

'Okay buddy, I'll go with that. So, what next?'

'Well, we came north for about fifteen minutes, then we headed North West for an hour, then we travelled west until we got hit. I think we were heading for Luxembourg. So, I suggest we carry on heading west.'

'Whoa, whoa there partner, what's all this North West, West shit? You got a map in your pocket or something? I think we should head South man, because the good old United States of America's Army is on its way from that direction and I think we should meet them on the way.'

'Okay, if that's what you want to do, be my guest but I'm going west. Firstly, South is where we came from, so the likelihood is that we will bump into the Nazi's who will be looking for us before we see your fifth cavalry. Second, if we go north we'll just go further into Germany and the same would happen if we went east.

So, heading west will get us into France quicker where we'll have a better chance of meeting up with the French resistance. And by the way, I am a navigator, so I've a good idea of how to get where I want to go even without a map.'

'Wow, partner, I'm impressed. I'm with you all the way. Let's go.'

'Okay, first thing is we get off this road and into the forest. We travel at night and rest under cover by day, okay?'

'Fine by me, so let's get moving.' Rick started to step out into the wooded area when Andy stopped him.

'West is that way,' he said pointing to the other side of the road.

'Yeah, Yeah, I knew that,' Rick said in his broad Bronx accent, smiling ruefully.

Rick's full name was Lucianno Frederici. He was an American Italian with typical swarthy Italian looks, good-looking but plenty of evidence that he had learned to take care of himself on the streets of the Italian quarter in the Bronx. Rick decided to enlist when one of his three brothers had been killed in action in Italy. His motivation was similar to that of Andy's-he needed to fight back.

It was something that had been ingrained into his psyche on the harsh streets of the Italian district he lived in. "someone hits you, you hit them back harder" he would say. He was an airborne infantryman and had been in the European warzone for about a year.

He had seen some action in Italy but was being dropped in the south of France on an advance reconnaissance mission when something went wrong and the drop zone was missed. He was captured and ended up at the same POW camp as Andy. He had tried escaping on two occasions but had been recaptured each time.

'The smoke and flames of the truck can be seen for miles, so we should get away from here as quickly as we can. There will be German patrols in the area any minute soon,' Andy said, 'Yeah I guess so but I think when they find the burnt out truck, they'll hopefully think everyone on board including us bought it.' Rick announced and his companion agreed.

'Nevertheless, we should get well away from this area. And don't forget, the driver may have survived and his co-pilot certainly did. They will use dogs once they're told that we escaped.'

Rick acknowledged, 'Yeah, I forgot about the two krauts that we left behind.'

Fortunately, one was rendered unconscious by Rick and was unlikely to come to for some time, if at all. The other had a long walk to the nearest town. So, they had a good head start.

The two men stepped out briskly and threaded their way through the trees westwards. It was now getting dark, so they used the time to put as much distance between them and the burning vehicle as they could. The night air was barmy and there was a bright moon, which left them a little exposed but they pressed on.

They had heard explosions and anti-aircraft fire going on in the distance to the east and concluded that it was their boys but Andy was a bit surprised that a raid would be carried out in such bright conditions. Aircraft would be sitting ducks for anti-aircraft batteries. He guessed that such a risky bombing sortie could only be for a special reason and if he were right, then he had made the right decision to head west.

Andy estimated they had travelled throughout the night for about twenty miles through the forest. They decided to rest. They were still under cover of the forest but were now feeling extremely hungry and thirsty. As day light approached, they saw that they had been climbing to high point for the last mile or two and were not too far from the edge of the woods. The two men edged forward cautiously and found themselves looking down towards a small town on the banks of a quite wide river.

'Where do you think we are then, navigator?' Rick asked. Andy sensed he wasn't being sarcastic by calling him navigator. Rick was genuinely impressed by Andy's navigational assessment.

'I can't tell exactly but we're too far west for that river to be the Rhine, so I think it's the Moselle, it makes sense if we were heading towards Luxembourg. How far south or north we are, I don't know. Whichever river it is, we have to cross it at some point and as you can see, there's a lot of military activity down there.'

The roads appeared crammed with military vehicles heading in both directions. Crossing at the bridge would be out of the question, so they needed to find another way. They also needed food and water soon. Both men decided to forage for whatever food they could find.

After feasting on some wild mushrooms which, thankfully Andy was able to identify them as edible from a survival course he had attended, neither of them therefore, suffered any ill effects, so now they would take cover and rest until nightfall.

****

Angelique and her brother spent a cold night in the cellar of their ruined and now derelict home. They had a little food and some blankets she had gathered from their previous hiding place. At least the bombing had stopped and Anton was sleeping peacefully. The next morning, Angelique crept out of the cellar while Anton was still sleeping.

She wanted to see what it was like outside and whether Mrs Vignon's house had escaped the bombing. She peered out of what was the front door onto the street and was shocked to see the devastation in front of her. Mrs Vignon's house was completely obliterated. All she could see was smouldering, blackened buildings that were no longer habitable.

Occasional flames licked up into the air from some of the ruins. She spotted an army patrol vehicle slowly picking its way through the rubble and scampered back to her cellar. Anton was awake and distressed. He still made no sound but clearly he was crying. Angelique became extremely worried, not knowing what was wrong with her brother.

It was now impossible to find a doctor and anyway, the risk of being seen by the soldiers was great. *Something horrible could happen to us*, she thought. They had enough food for several days if they were prudent and so she decided she would make the cellar home for the time being. Anton was shivering but she didn't think he was cold.

'I know,' she said, 'let's play Marelle Ronde. I'll clear a space on the floor and we'll draw the map. I'm sure there are some pieces of coal we can use to mark it out.'

Round hopscotch was Anton's favourite game and Angelique hoped it would help him speak again, especially if his mind were taken off whatever caused it. The game was similar to the hopscotch children in England played but this variation was drawn in the shape of a snail's shell and was sometimes called Escargot. It was ideal for a confined space such as that they occupied now.

Anton's face brightened when they started to play and he laughed when Angelique lost her balance as she hopped on one foot, falling over into a heap. She was so relieved that Anton had found his voice.

'That was very funny Anton I know but I could have hurt myself, you should be ashamed of yourself.' She scolded him jokingly.

He laughed but didn't speak.

'Do you feel better now, Anton?' She asked, trying to encourage him to say something. He opened his mouth and made lip movements but there was no sound. Angelique started to cry on the realisation that her little brother couldn't speak. She held him close to her and prayed for her mother and father to come back.

The two children spent the next two days working in the cellar, making it as liveable as possible. There was sufficient food if they were careful and also plenty of running water, so Angelique was not concerned about their survival in that regard. Angelique frequently went upstairs, looked out into the street and saw that there was surprisingly little activity.

What she was unaware of was that the main body of soldiers had been moved to Reims to reinforce the garrison there. Nor did she know that the Allies had landed in Normandy and were fighting to liberate France. She occasionally saw one or two German soldiers but that was all. Most of the people had left the devastation of their town and homes behind and gone away to relatives or friends elsewhere. Sedan was a desolate place.

Angelique decided that she and Anton must get to her grandparents who lived in Givet but it was a long way away, about forty miles to the north and she had no idea how she would get there. She resolved to get Anton and herself to their grandparents one way or another. For now, she and her brother would rest and play Marelle Ronde.

Chapter 3

At nightfall, Andy and Rick edged down the hill towards the river. They were about two hundred metres north of the bridge where there was a lot of military traffic activity and fortunately, they had sufficient tree and bush cover to prevent them being seen from the bridge. As they approached the water's edge, Rick excitedly pointed to a spot on the riverbank, about one hundred metres upstream towards the bridge.

'Look, down there, a rowboat. That will get us across.' A small skiff type boat was tied up on the bank.

'Don't you think it might be a bit close to the bridge and we will be spotted? And anyway, there's probably no oars, I can't imagine the owner just leaving his boat complete with oars for anyone to take,' Andy said doubtfully.

'We'll only be borrowing it and we'll leave it on the other side nicely tied up. As for being spotted, just look at the traffic over there. They're in a hurry to get somewhere fast, so I don't think they'll be too bothered about two fishermen out for a late bite. So, do we go, yes or no?'

Andy carefully weighed up the risks before he answered. He wasn't going to be captured again if he could help it.

'Okay but we keep low and if the boat is usable, we stick close to the bank and head downstream, away from the bridge before we attempt to cross. Are you okay with that?'

'Yep partner, let's do it.'

They slowly edged their way towards the rowboat, making sure that their profile wasn't exposed against the night's moonlight of which there was fortunately very little. Rick was first to reach their potential transportation for crossing the river. He pointed to the belly of the boat and smiled with that broad Italian grin of his.

'We're in luck, my friend. All we need to do now is learn how to drive it,' he said jokingly as he spotted the oars.

Andy was constantly looking up to the bridge, waiting for a possible sound of an alarm. The small boat was straining on its tether as the swift waters wanted to break it free. He hauled in the rope, so that the boat was close to the riverbank and put a single loop onto the mooring post. Both men gingerly stepped into the dinghy. Andy held the vessel in place as Rick fitted the oars into the rowlocks. He nodded to Andy that he was ready.

'When I let go of the rope, Rick, the flow of the river will take us downstream and away from the bridge but I want you to keep us close to the bank for as long as possible. If we drift into the centre, we will be easily spotted and within rifle range. We don't know it but there could be a curfew here, so they wouldn't expect to see any civilian activity.'

Rick was as strong as an ox and fought against the current of the river that wanted to turn the boat in swirling circles and take them into midstream. But he kept in control and let the stream move them quickly away from the bridge. Andy thought they were now far enough away, out of sight, and suggested they should stop for a short rest.

It would be a chance to assess their options for crossing the river. Rick steered the dinghy into the bank close enough to a low overhanging tree branch. Andy grabbed it and loosely tethered the boat to it. Rick let out a sigh of relief and stretched out his arms, which were starting to cramp.

'I'll take over when we're ready to cross. I think this is going to be as good a place as any.' Andy felt a little more relaxed now that they were a good distance from the bridge. They could hear the rumble of vehicles crossing the bridge in the distance and other than that, the night was quiet apart from the sound of the water lapping by.

'Ready?' Andy asked.

'Whenever you are, navigator.' Rick stood up very carefully and changed places with Andy, who positioned himself centrally facing Rick at the rear.

'Untie her, Rick, and let's get across as quickly as possible. Keep low and watch out for any movement on the other side. It wouldn't be good for us to have a welcoming party waiting for us.'

The dinghy moved away from the riverbank as soon as Rick let her loose but before it went too far under its own steam, Andy started to pull on the oars with a good rhythm. He could feel the pressure of the river current pushing the vessel sideways and downstream but he wasn't too concerned about that. It would just mean a diagonal traverse of the river rather than the more direct route.

The river was about sixty metres wide at this point and because of the downstream current, the actual distance to row would be closer to one hundred metres. Andy was strong but after travelling about halfway and fighting to direct the craft towards the opposite bank, he started to tire and Rick was quick to see that his buddy was losing the battle to cut across the river and instead was heading downstream.

'I'll take it from here buddy, so let's change places, eh?'

Andy wasn't in the mood to argue, he was not only tired but also hungry. They had drunk some of the river water, which didn't taste at all bad and was quite refreshing but they needed food.

'Okay but let's be careful we don't turn this thing over, I don't fancy swimming the rest of the way.' They carefully swapped places but not without a few wobbles and they had lost some momentum, so were a lot further downstream. Rick soon picked up a rhythm and having rested, he put in some strong strokes and quickly reached the riverbank.

They decided to let the boat go rather than tie it up, which might have given away their landing point. There was a slight slope on the riverbank, which was well covered with shrubs and vegetation. It gave them some cover from the road above them.

'We should rest here for a short time, get our breath back and I'll try and figure out which way we should take the road that's just above us. It runs parallel to the river, which travels south to north therefore, so does the road.' Andy was thinking out loud rather than expecting an answer.

'If we go south, then it'll take us back to the bridge and the town we saw earlier. If we go north, then we will head further into Germany. So, I think our only option is to head due west, avoiding the roads. What do you think, Rick?'

'You're the navigator my friend, I'm following you. You've got us this far up to now and we're still free, so I aint going to rock the boat, if you get my drift.'

'Okay, we'll have ten more minutes here, then we should head out and make the most of what's left of the night.'

The two men lay on the riverbank, looking up at the night sky. The occasional break in the clouds opened up a vista of a calm and peaceful glistening sky, which was in sharp contrast to the mayhem that was happening on the ground beneath it.

They were both lost in this moment of tranquillity when they were alerted to the sound of an approaching vehicle. Both men looked at each other with a sort of "what do we do" look. Andy held a finger to his mouth and indicated that they should keep very still and quiet. To their horror, the vehicle came to a stop just a short distance away from where they were laying.

Whoever they were, they were heading north. They could hear voices but only two. Andy and Rick staying flat to the ground, crawled up to the edge of the road but still under cover. They could see an open top car with a Swastika badge on the side door, which was open.

There was also a pennant flying on the bonnet; a driver sat behind the wheel. The passenger who was wearing what looked like a high ranking officer's uniform stood at the side of the road relieving himself.

Rick whispered very softly.

'That's a jerry officer and he's taking a piss. We could take them out if we're quick.'

Andy whispered back.

'They will be armed and we're not.'

Rick picked up a large lump of a fallen tree branch, which he held in both hands like a baseball bat and smiled his Italian smile.

'We are now.' As quick as flash, he was up and within ten paces was upon the unsuspecting Germans. The Officer was adjacent to the driver with his back to the vehicle and was struggling to fasten his trouser fly buttons. The driver sat impassively behind wheel.

Before the Officer could react, Rick took a full blooded swing of his club hitting the Officer on the side of the head and knocked him to the ground. He bounced off the wing of the car before hitting the ground unconscious. The driver turned quickly towards Rick and attempted to reach for his holstered pistol when Andy coming from the other side, slammed the driver's face into the steering wheel.

Andy didn't see Rick deliver another blow to the Officer, who was now dead. He then smashed his club into the back of the driver's head. Andy shouted, 'No, there's no need to kill them. We could have just tied them up and left here.'

'You're a good navigator, Andy and you're used to fighting this war from the air but I'm used to fighting it on the ground and it's either kill or be killed, trust me on this. If I had left them alive here, then there would have been a posse tracking us down like dogs as soon as they were discovered. Have you seen the uniform on this guy?' He said, pointed down to the dead German Officer. 'He must be at least a Colonel. So, they would be really pissed when he told them that two escaped POW's knocked him out and took his car.'

Andy paused for a moment realising that there was nothing fair about this war and he struggled still, despite his own tragedy, with the sheer brutality of it.

'You're right Rick, it would have been stupid to have left them alive. By the way, looking at his insignia I'd say he was a General, so we have hit the jackpot and his troops are going to be sending search parties out for him once they find him missing.'

They dragged the bodies to the side of the road and pushed them into the undergrowth. Andy had gone through their pockets and apart from the pistols with a few rounds of ammunition, there were some useful items; a packet of salted biscuits which they munched into straight away, there was a watch and a compass and some cigarettes and a lighter.

They next searched the car and it turned out to be well stocked with all the essentials that a high ranking officer in the German Army would need; bottles of wine, a box of rations, toilet paper, a first aid box, a torch and binoculars and most importantly, a map. How much of all this they could take with them was debateable but the torch and map, binoculars and some food, they decided, was a must.

Andy had been studying the map for some time, occasionally looking around at the terrain and then back at the map.

'I believe I know where we are.' He beckoned Rick over closer to see the map. Andy pointed to a river and a town called Schengen, 'that's the Moselle River we've just crossed and that's the bridge that we avoided. If we cut due west across country, we will go through Luxembourg and then into France and if we travel only at night, it will take about three nights.'

Rick was excited by the idea that crossed his mind. He picked up the General's cap, set it jauntily on his head and said, 'Why don't we take the uniforms, get in their car and drive to where we want to go?'

'Are you crazy? We'll be blown to kingdom come as soon as we're spotted.'

Rick passed the German Officer's cap to Andy and put the driver's forage cap on his own head.

'Not if they see there's a blond, blue-eyed German General being driven by his loyal German servant, footman and generally all-round good guy driver.' Rick smiled with what was now becoming his trademark smile. His gleaming white teeth set against his swarthy complexion and his shock of thick wavy black hair exaggerated the grin and turned it into a beaming smile.

Andy was beginning to warm towards the American. At first he thought he would have been happy to go off on his own, the GI looked like trouble waiting to happen. Now, he felt it was probable that he wouldn't have got this far on his own.

Rick waited for an answer.

'Well? If we pull this off, then we can be well into France in no time. And don't forget, we can carry everything we need in the car.'

'Okay, let's do it.' Andy studied the map again and decided that they could turn west before Schengen, which would avoid all that military movement there. 'We should get going as quickly as possible and make as many miles as we can during darkness.

We should hit the Luxembourg border before sunrise. The only problem is that there will undoubtedly be a checkpoint at the border and that is where the "kingdom come" is likely to happen. Get the Jerry topcoat off the General and the jacket off the driver while I stow the gear.'

Rick returned wearing the German soldier's jacket, which wasn't a bad fit and the topcoat of the General over his arm.

'May I, General sir?' Rick said holding the topcoat out in man servant fashion.

Andy put on the coat and the cap and sat in the back of the car. Rick got in behind the wheel and started the engine.

'Hell, how am I supposed to drive this thing?' He said as he fiddled with the gear stick and various other controls.

'First thing you have to do Rick, is turn this thing around, it's pointing the wrong way.'

The gears grinded and the car jerked to and fro in spasms as Rick tried to maintain control.

'Don't worry Herr General; I'll get there in a minute or two.'

Despite the desperate risk they were taking, Andy laughed out loud and as Rick finally turned the car about, he also laughed heartily. Andy became serious.

'Rick, drive steadily, don't divert your attention away from your driving. If we pass a patrol, ignore it; I will acknowledge any salutes I get and I'm hoping they will know from the pennant that the car is carrying a very important person, so I suspect that there will be much clicking of heels and Nazi salutes, it should also be the case when we reach the border. Okay, let's go'.

'Kingdom come, we're on our way,' Rick shouted.

The pair had eaten some of the rations and the car sped onwards towards Schengen.

'Take the next turning on your left Rick, it's before we get to the bridge.' They had been passed by military vehicles going in the opposite direction but up until now, they did not appear to have raised any suspicions. Dawn was approaching and Andy was keen to get to the Luxembourg border before sunrise. There would be less chance of their cover being blown whilst it was still dark. However, dawn was starting to break, so a little light was coming through the darkness.

Andy spotted the checkpoint at the same time that Rick shouted, 'Up front, see it?'

'Yes, I can see it. Rick, approach the barrier slowly as though you are expecting them to open it. I'm hoping they spot the pennant and let us through.'

As Rick got closer, he put his left hand out of the car and started to make an upward motion with it.

'Open it; open it, you stupid Nazi bastards,' he said to himself.

Andy was sitting bolt upright in the rear of the car, giving the guards a good view of him. He said, 'If they don't raise the barrier, drive straight through it and keep your head down, this may well be our "kingdom come" moment.'

It was at a critical moment as Rick was about to hit the gas pedal when a guard came out of the sentry hut and shouted instructions to the barrier guard.

'Schnell erhohen die barriere, schnell, schnell! Raise the barrier quickly,' he urged frantically.

Rick kept a stern face and looked straight ahead as he increased his speed through the checkpoint. Andy returned his raised right arm salute in response to the group of German soldiers who stood rigidly to attention. Their leader, probably an NCO Andy thought, shouted Heil Hitler at the same time snapping his heals together as they passed under the raised barrier. The car sped its way through the checkpoint until it was out of sight.

Rick asked, 'Okay to stop for short time? I need to get my breath back.'

'Yes, let's take some time out. We need to figure out our next move. To carry on or wait till nightfall is the question. Pull over when you find a place with a bit of cover and we can talk about what we do next.' Andy needed time to think.

In the meantime, Rick was breaking into a very good French wine, courtesy of the General. Andy spotted the wine and said, 'Take it easy on the juice Rick, you may have some difficult driving ahead.' Rick responded glumly and put the cork back into the bottle. He knew Andy was right.

Chapter 4

The cellar in the parental home being made of stone and concrete with bare brick walls was naturally cold and even though it was early summer, Angelique and Anton lay close to each other for warmth. She had gathered as many blankets and coats as possible that she could find, then made up an improvised bed.

Angelique had lost count of how many days and nights they had spent here but what was certain was the fact that they were running out of food and she knew she would soon need to risk going out to search for more supplies. Anton had still not spoken and whenever Angelique spoke to him, he would either shake his head or nod for yes or no.

Anything that required more than a monosyllabic answer was met with a shrug of his tiny shoulders. When he was thirsty, he would point to his mouth and mimic pouring a drink. When he was hungry, he would rub his tummy. Angelique understood most of what he indicated but despaired that he didn't appear to want to speak anymore.

Both Angelique and Anton were of dark complexion with black hair and round dark eyes, which betrayed their Jewish and Gallic background. The darkness around the eyes that now showed, however, was deep and hollow; borne out of stress and anxiety, particularly for Angelique who had hardly slept since her father was killed.

She worried constantly for her brother and for their future. Her prayers were almost totally for the safe return of her mother.

'Please come back Maman, please help us,' she would softly sob each night when Anton was asleep.

The water supply that she obtained from the broken pipe had started to dry up and was merely a trickle. So, now her concern was not just food. She gently woke Anton up.

'Come, little brother, it's time to get up. I will see if we have any food left to eat.' He was silent as he rubbed his eyes and pointed to his mouth, indicating he wanted a drink. 'We have very little water left, Anton. I will have to go out and see if can find another tap or leaking pipe. I also need to find us some food, so I want you to promise me you will stay here while I do that. I will get you some water before I go but that is all there is, so I must go out and find some more.'

Anton was furiously shaking his head and grabbed her arm to prevent her from leaving.

'No Anton, you cannot come with me and I can't stay here, I must find food and water, otherwise we will get very sick. Do you understand me?' Anton continued to grip Angelique's arm and shake his head from side to side but now he was crying. His small frame juddered with each sob. Angelique could contain herself no longer; she screamed at her brother.

'You must stop this instantly Anton, I cannot take you with me and that is final. If you do not do as you are told, I will leave here and not come back, is that what you want?' The young boy looked at her with sad pleading eyes and slowly let go of Angelique's arm. He sat with his back to a wooden post that supported the cellar roof and quietly continued to sob.

'I know it is hard Anton but I have to look after you now and so you have to help me by doing as I ask. It would be too dangerous for us both to be outside, I don't want those bad men hurting you. So, I will now get you some water and then I will leave to search for some food. I promise I will be back quickly.'

Angelique returned with the water jug with not much more than a mouth full of water. She was herself very thirsty but was certain that she could find another source outside. Anton in the meantime, drank the water and had calmed down a little.

'I shall go now, Anton, you must be the man of the house and look after everything until I get back okay? You must not go outside—do you understand me?'

Anton nodded his head and wrapped a blanket around his shoulders. He popped his tiny hand through a gap in the blanket and waved his hand to his sister as she turned to leave. She ran back to her little brother and gave him a big hug. Angelique's resolve was weakening up until that moment but seeing the sad face of her brother and him being very brave, despite knowing the sheer terror he would be feeling of being left alone—gave her renewed strength.

After kissing him gently on the forehead, she made her way up the rickety staircase into the daylight of their derelict and roofless home. She ran quickly from one mound of debris to another and found herself in a house that was only partially destroyed. There were no windows, of course but a couple of rooms still had doors and the roof was still intact.

It appeared to her that the occupants had left because there was little evidence of anyone living there. It seemed that many, if not all, of the town's people had gone. There was an eerie silence about the place. She was acutely aware that the German soldiers could appear at any time, so she decided that her first priority was to find a hiding place in the event that they did.

She found a small cupboard inside the first room and was satisfied with that. Then Angelique entered a room at the rear of the house that turned out be the kitchen, which was relatively unscathed. Cupboards were well stocked with tinned food such as beans and canned sardines, jars of rice and packets of various dried herbs.

There was a large lump of cheese, which was looking a bit stale around the edges but she managed to find a knife to cut out much of the bad bits. In one of the drawers, she found a table cloth and immediately started to wrap as many things as she could carry. All that was required now was water.

She looked at the taps and wondered whether there could still be water coming through. Putting her makeshift knapsack down, she approached the taps at the kitchen sink as if they might run away if she moved too quickly. Then, turning one of the taps on, she waited for what seemed an age and following a great deal of clanking and spluttering, water started to flow.

She cupped her hand under the tap and tasted it, gingerly at first then gulping great mouthfuls. She swilled her face and dried it on a surplus piece of her knapsack. Now, she was having second thoughts about carrying all this over to the cellar.

Why not, she thought, *bring Anton here? I will take a little food for today and then I will bring Anton here tonight.*

Through the broken kitchen window, she spotted a German vehicle patrol again winding its way through the rubble in the streets. They didn't appear to be in a hurry and it was strangely odd that this was only the second time she had seen any soldiers at all. She scampered off to her hiding place and waited for about an hour before coming out.

Throughout her time in the small cupboard, she prayed that Anton would not dare venture out of the cellar, especially now. Angelique was sure that the patrol had moved away from this area, so she gathered what she needed for the rest of the day, wrapped the goods up in the tablecloth and made her way back to her brother.

Anton heard the footsteps on the wooden staircase and quickly hid under the blankets, scared that it might not be Angelique.

'Anton, where are you?' Angelique asked even though she knew exactly where he was but wanted to make a game of it. She could see him shivering under his camouflage. As soon as he knew it was his sister, he threw the blankets back and ran to her, folding his arms around her as tight as he could.

'I have a surprise for you Anton. We are going to move to a new home tonight. It is warmer than it is here and we have a kitchen with water that comes out of the taps. There is plenty of food there that will last us until I find a way of us getting to Grandpapa's house. There are not many of the bad people here now but we will still have to be very careful.'

Angelique couldn't tell whether Anton understood what she said but would soon know when they moved tonight.

'Here's another surprise,' she said giving him a large portion of the cheese she had brought with her. His eyes lit up and he promptly filled his mouth. For the moment, the rest of his worries were relegated.

****

Andy and Rick had travelled about halfway through Luxembourg without any mishaps. Most of Luxembourg was under German civilian administration at this time, so encounters with the German military were rare. On the occasions that they were passed by a military convoy, they were given a full German salute and recognition. The two escapees knew that it would not be long before the German General and his driver's bodies were found.

Andy was certain that a full manhunt would follow, so they couldn't push their luck too far in carrying on with their charade. The car and the uniforms would soon have to go. How soon depended on the outcome of what was about to happen as they approached the western border checkpoint.

'Let's do exactly as we did before Rick, slow down and hope they spot who they think I am and raise the barrier.'

'There are only a couple of men out at the barrier. Do you think there's anymore?' Rick asked.

'There could be one or two more in the hut but I don't think many more than that.'

Rick started to slow the vehicle down and waved his hand up and down as he did before. The guards saw the car and after a short scrutiny, realised who might be approaching. They started to raise the barrier and Rick accelerated. As they passed through the barrier, the guard commander came running out of the guard hut shouting:

'Halt, halt.'

Rick raced on and Andy maintained his superior posture in the back of the car. The guard commander was shouting furiously at his guards who were manning the barrier.

'Stop that car, shoot them.'

He drew out his pistol and started to fire at the General's car, which was out of range for small arms fire. The guards just stood there, looking totally bemused. They couldn't understand what they were being asked to do. *Shoot at a General's car, has our sergeant gone mad*, they thought. It was only after Andy and Rick were well out of sight that the guard commander was able to tell his men what had happened.

'You idiots, they were two escaped prisoners of war who have hijacked the General's car and probably killed him. Orders to shoot them on sight had just come through when they went through the barrier.' There was a long pause as the guard commander gathered his thoughts. 'In future, you dolts, when I give you an order, I want you to obey me without question, do you understand me?' He shouted, the veins in his neck bulging. His men stood rigidly to attention and quivered as he berated them.

'I will now inform our commander that the escaped prisoners had got through the barrier before we got the message. At least they will know the area to start searching for them. If the Oberleutnant finds out that we allowed them to escape, we will be lucky if we are not sent to the Eastern Front or worse.'

The guard commander picked up his field telephone and rang his headquarters, he swallowed hard as the voice at the other end said, 'Ah, Feldwebel, have you managed to detain the escapees?'

'No, I'm afraid not Oberleutnant, the car had already gone through the barrier some time before I received your message. My men on the barrier said they saw the General's car pennant and could see a General sitting in the car, so the vehicle was not stopped.'

The officer was apoplectic; he screamed and yelled down the phone at the guards' Sergeant who had to hold the phone away from his ear.

'Do you realise that these prisoners have probably killed our General? There will be hell to pay for this, Sergeant. I will send a search and destroy party out after them as soon as we have some air reconnaissance reports. At least if they just drove through your control point, then they won't be aware that we are on to them, so they should be still on the road. That will be easy for air reconnaissance to detect them. You should hope that they do just that Feldwebel, for your sake.' The Officer slammed the phone down; the guard commander winced.

Rick had driven a further twenty miles when the car started to splutter, he stopped it quickly.

'We're running out of gas, so I guess that all we have left is enough to get it off the road and under cover.'

Andy had been expecting this.

'They will be after us now Rick; the guards on that barrier must have just got the message when we went through. Let's get rid of the car, carry as much of the rations that we can and make our way on foot again. I suspect we're not far away from the town of Sedan.

There's plenty of forest cover, so we don't have to go through it; we can probably skirt around it. In the meantime, we should find a place to rest up under cover until dark. See if you can see somewhere to dump the car, so that it can't be seen from the air.'

Rick had pulled up at the side of the road under a canopy of trees either side of the road, so while they were hidden from view from the air, they were still vulnerable to a chasing road patrol. He got out of the car and walked into the wooded area. Andy was busy picking the equipment and rations out of the car and stuffing them into his pockets.

Fortunately, there was a large canvas backpack in the car that they could use for the bigger items. Rick got to the edge of a tree clearing and saw quite a steep drop in the ground in front of him. He reckoned that he could get the car here through the trees and then it would be just a matter of pushing it over the edge.

The wrecked car wouldn't be seen from the road and it would be extremely difficult for it to be spotted from the air.

Ideal, he thought and hurried back to Andy and the car. He explained what he had seen and Andy agreed it was a good idea.

The two men guided the car slowly between the trees and shrubs. The ground was firm, so the wheel grip was good but the car spluttered and coughed as the last drops of gasoline were sucked into the engine. About twenty yards from the lip of the ravine, the car engine stopped. They would need to push the car the rest of the way.

They just needed to move it to the lip of the rise and thereafter, they could roll it down the other side to its final resting place. It was a heavy car and Rick and Andy needed all of their strength to budge it. Rick used his back against the rear of the car and dug his heels into the ground; Andy positioned himself with his shoulder to the rear quarter. Both men counted, 'One, two, three, push.' The car edged forward eventually creeping up to the where the incline became a decline. Just before the top of the ridge, Rick lost his footing and couldn't maintain his hold and the car started to drift backwards despite their extra efforts to try and hold it. Eventually, the car came to an abrupt halt when it was prevented from going further by a tree.

It wasn't a great distance lost but nevertheless, they had to start all over again. They heaved and strained every muscle in their bodies until the last push saw the car's front wheels edge over the ridge and the nose of the car tip forward rendering the effort being applied by the men suddenly unnecessary. The German Staff car gathered speed as it hurtled towards the gorge toppling over several times before landing on its roof, its wheels still gently rotating. Rick stood to attention and saluted.

'Thank you Adolf for the loan of the car, sorry but it might be a bit bent when you get it back.' The two men laughed as they collapsed, totally exhausted. They lay down by a nearby tree to regain their strength. It was still daylight, so they decided they would rest there until dark.

Andy had studied the map and said, 'If the Allies were ever to invade France, it would have to be through Normandy because I don't think they would try Dunkerque again. Of course, I could be wrong. I just hope that if we can keep heading west, then we will eventually meet up with the British or American forces pushing their way east. The big problem will be running into the Germans defending their ground.'

'Or hightailing it back to the Fatherland.' Rick added.

'Either way Rick, we'll be in the middle of it.'

The two men lay back and rested, watching the blue sky through the gaps in the trees.

Rick asked, 'you have any family back home, Andy?'

'No, I don't.' Andy responded sharply, he did not want to be reminded of his wife and children right now.

'Hey man, just making conversation,' Rick replied defensively. He was puzzled by the aggressive tone Andy took, so decided to talk about his own family, 'I have a whole Italian brood, my mother,' which he pronounced mudda, 'my pop, he has a little coffee shop and makes the best espresso outside of Italy and I have, no, had two brothers.' Rick's face suddenly saddened.

'There were three of us until Johnny, my older brother got killed in Salerno,' Rick's face brightened 'and I have a beautiful girl waiting for me. She is a knockout babe and if anything is going to keep me alive in this goddamn war, it's the thought of getting back to her. Surely you got someone; you're a good looking guy. Come on man, you holding out on me?'

'Just leave it out, Rick; I don't want to talk about it, okay.'

'Yeah, sure, whatever you say.' Rick was puzzled but didn't pursue the subject.

The two men lay in silence until dusk descended.

'Right, let's move out then,' Andy said as he rose to his feet. He held out his hand and helped Rick stand up. 'Look Rick, I'm sorry about being short with you earlier and I'm sorry to hear about your brother. I know exactly how you must feel. I promise I will tell you about my family but not right now, okay.'

'Not a problem navigator, you talk when you want to talk, I'll listen and I'll try not to bug you with how gorgeous my broad is back home.' The American smiled in his inimitable way.

There were not too many lights coming from the town up ahead and that puzzled Andy. What little lighting they could see, flickered in the distance. They stood on a high point overlooking the town and noted very little movement. Occasionally, they could see the headlights of a small vehicle slowly moving through the streets and guessed it would be a military patrol.

That together with the small amount of lighting gave it an almost ghost-like quality. The men discussed the possibility that if the town wasn't heavily garrisoned, then they might be able to find another vehicle. But there was an obvious risk; they would not know for certain just how many Germans were there until they got closer. Then it might be too late.

The biggest attraction for Andy was that the town may have a French Resistance group that can help them. Rick was all for going into the town and taking a look. Andy was unsure.

'Let's wait for another hour and see if we can spot any more troop movements.'

They sat down and it was beginning to get a little cold in the night air, so their motivation to keep warm by moving, cut the waiting time to shorter than the hour planned. In just fifteen minutes, they stepped out to get closer to the town.

Keeping as close as they could to the unlit areas, they edged closer to the town and quickly realised the extent of the devastation.

'I'd be surprised if anyone survived this,' Andy whispered. 'We should try and find some shelter for the night and let's just hope we don't run into any German patrols, although I suspect there's not much of the place left for them to defend.'

The pair picked their way through the rubble, making sure they kept in the shadows. Their movement was slow, deliberate and above all watchful. They at least were armed and could put up a fight if they had to. Not many of the houses were fit for habitation, which explained why they had not seen any townspeople. About one hundred yards away, they suddenly caught sight of a dim light coming from a building. Rick very quietly asked, 'You think it's townspeople or Krauts?'

'I don't know, can't see any vehicles but they might be out of sight,' Andy replied 'do you want to find out?' Andy winked at Rick as he asked the question.

'Yeah, why not.' Rick smiled his usual smile.

The two men carefully picked a route towards the building and as they got closer, their pulse rates pounded and adrenalin raced around their bodies, preparing them for the worst.

Chapter 5

It was early evening when Angelique decided to make her house move. She and Anton gathered up any essential clothes and blankets plus whatever remained of the food. She knew there was sufficient food in the other house but she was unwilling to leave anything behind. Angelique had matured rapidly in the last week or so and had become very adult in her thinking about her new caring responsibilities.

But at night once she knew her brother was asleep, she would cry a lot. The young girl was afraid her quiet sobbing and prayers would wake him. Nevertheless, it was a release for her and gave her strength to go on. Anton was excited about moving, he didn't like being in the cellar but as he still didn't speak, it was difficult for Angelique to comprehend his fear of the place.

She guessed that he was happier by the way his demeanour changed when she told him about moving to a different house; he smiled and jumped about in an animated fashion, collecting clothes and items to take with them. For Anton, the cellar meant loud frightening noises and it led to the house above where, for him, bad things happened, things he did not want to remember.

Angelique held her brother's hand and the parcel of their belongings in the other whilst she edged her way to the very unstable staircase. It had become shakier each time it was used. Plaster dust fell from the supporting joists as the stairs wobbled whenever Angelique went to fetch water or take a look outside the house. About halfway up the staircase, there was a loud creaking noise that Angelique had not heard before; the staircase started to sway.

'Hurry Anton, hurry, we must get to the top quickly.' She shouted.

Anton was bewildered by the sudden panic in his sister's voice. He hesitated. Angelique needed to pull him along; it was as if he was rooted to the spot. But now the staircase was starting to lean sharply to one side as the children were almost at the top. Angelique reached the top step as a loud crack pierced the air and the staircase started to crumple under its own weight.

Anton was behind his sister, so he had not reached the top tread when the stairs disappeared beneath him. Angelique gripped his hand tightly as her brother dangled some twenty feet from the stone cellar floor. She threw the parcel she had been carrying away from her and lay flat on the top step, so that she could use her other hand to pull Anton up.

Fear was etched on the little boy's face and tears streamed from his eyes; his mouth was open in a silent scream. Angelique got hold of him with both hands and with a mighty heave, hauled him to her. She wrapped her arms around him and held him close to her body.

'It's alright now Anton, everything is okay, you're safe.' She stroked his face gently and brushed his dust-covered dark hair away from his eyes and the little boy sobbed and shuddered, sucking in great gulps of air as he held on tightly to his sister.

They lay together for some time before Anton quietened and Angelique was able to recover slightly from her herculean effort. It was astonishing for such a young girl to have found the strength to save her brother from what would have been at the very least, serious injury. But with each day of their ordeal, Angelique appeared to become stronger, physically and emotionally.

'Come now Anton, we must move to our new home.' Angelique got up from the floor. Anton looked down into the gaping hole that led to the cellar which they once lived in. The mangled wooden staircase lay in a heap on the stone floor. He started to shiver again but Angelique led him away towards the road outside their destroyed home.

Angelique glanced sideways at the room where her father was now buried and a tear formed in the corner of her eye. Not wishing to let Anton see her sadness, she discreetly wiped it away.

Angelique deliberately chose to walk to the other house just before dark so that she could see if any other townspeople were there. If any remained, they didn't show themselves. She was also mindful of the German patrols and hurried from one derelict building to another, keeping out of sight as much as she could. It was starting to get dark as they reached their destination.

The house had been damaged but was habitable. Some distance away, she could see the occasional flickering light and wondered whether that part of the town had not been so badly damaged by the bombing. She was excited by the thought that there may be people there that could help her and Anton to get to their grandparents in Givet. She promised herself that she would find out as soon as she could. The most important task now was to create a decent living space for her and her brother.

The children entered the semi-derelict house cautiously at first and then when Anton realised it was safe, he scampered from room to room exploring every nook and cranny. Angelique busied herself searching cupboards and drawers for anything that had been left there by the previous occupants. There was cutlery and saucepans, cups and plates, she found candles and matches, so now they could have some light and there was a small paraffin stove that would enable her to make something warm to eat.

It was getting dark, so she decided to light some candles in the kitchen in order to see what she was doing whilst preparing a meal for them both. In her excitement at finding this house and everything that came with it, she was unaware of the risk of putting lights on in the room. The German soldiers who remained in the town knew of the houses that were occupied, so they would naturally be suspicious if they saw lights on in a house not previously lit.

Angelique started to collect the ingredients for their meal; she had a good idea how to make a bean stew, she had watched her mother make it many times. Anton came running into the kitchen and threw his arms around Angelique's waist tightly. Angelique had her back to him and said, 'Whatever has gotten into you, young man?' Her squeezed her as hard as he could, which made her turn around. To her horror, a German soldier stood in the doorway. He was a big man and almost filled the doorway.

'Where are your parents?' he barked in German. He looked stern, an angry man, Angelique thought. He repeated his question in his limited French.

Angelique pretended not to understand although along with English, she was almost fluent in German. Anton clung on to her fearfully. Angelique spoke in French.

'I don't know where my mother is, she was taken away by the soldiers. My father is not here, I don't know where he is.'

The soldier understood enough French to work out what Angelique had said. He looked dishevelled, unshaven and didn't have a helmet on or carry a weapon, although he was certainly wearing a soldier's uniform.

Angelique didn't like the way he was looking at her-he made her feel uncomfortable.

'There's just me and my brother sir, we are resting here until we go to our grandparents in Givet.'

'So, you are alone then?' he again spoke in German.

Angelique shrugged her shoulders and pretended she didn't understand.

'We just want to rest before we go to our grandparents.'

'They look Jewish; their parents are probably Jews, so that's why they've been taken.' He was talking to himself, believing that the children couldn't understand German. 'Come here,' he commanded as he sat down on a chair in the corner of the room. He was smiling but the smile did not convey kindness or generosity to Angelique. She didn't move and Anton clung on even tighter.

'Come here at once,' he shouted, his face clouded over with anger. Anton shuddered and was burying his head into Angelique's body.

Angelique started to move slowly towards the soldier but Anton limited her steps as he was being dragged along.

The soldier stood up, in three large strides reached out and picked up Anton by his jacket collar lifting him off his feet.

'I will find a place for you, so that you are not a nuisance while I spend some time with your sister, okay?' He started to walk out of the room with Anton dangling off the floor. Angelique screamed out in perfect German.

'Please don't hurt him, put him down please.'

'Ah, you speak German then and all this time you have been deceiving me into believing you didn't understand. That was a very foolish thing to do, fräulein.' He let Anton drop to the floor who promptly scrambled back to Angelique.

'I am sorry sir; I was frightened to speak in German because my brother would not have understood and it would have confused him. He hasn't spoken since our mother was taken away. You are not wearing a helmet and have no rifle, so I didn't know what to do.'

'Well fräulein, I have decided to leave the German Army, so I don't need those things anymore. So, before I move on, you must quieten your brother down and find somewhere where he can sit quietly whilst you and I get to know each other a little better.' He again displayed that sickly smile that so unnerved Angelique earlier. She had no idea what his intentions were but she was intelligent enough to know that he did not mean her well.

Angelique silently prayed for her mother's return whilst the German soldier took hold of Anton and led him from the room. The boy was too frightened to resist but his little face was drained of colour with the sheer terror of what was happening. Angelique could hear the soldier tramping around the rooms looking for a place to leave Anton.

'Now sit there and don't make a sound or I will kill your sister. Do you understand me, boy?' Anton just shook with fear, tears streamed down his face.

This time he spoke in French albeit poorly.

'Do you understand me, you are to stay here and not make a noise.'

Anton nodded his head furiously.

Angelique shivered as she listened to the threats being made and contemplated getting a knife from the kitchen drawer but decided he was far too big and strong for her.

'If I failed to kill him, then Anton would be alone. I cannot take that risk,' she said to herself in a whisper. 'I must stay strong; I must stay strong,' she repeated over and over.

****

Andy and Rick approached the illuminated house they had spotted from a distance earlier and could now see that there were no military vehicles in the vicinity. They crouched down low and kept to the shadows. As they got closer, Andy suggested that they should get around the back of the house and make sure that they only had civilian occupants to contend with.

'You take the right hand side and I'll work my way around the left. Assuming we don't run into any Germans, we should meet up at the rear. We'll see where go from there, okay?' Andy kept his voice down to a whisper.

'Okay with me, let's get to it.' Rick was eager because he assumed that they would meet up with some friendly French folk and then perhaps the Resistance.

After a short time, they converged from each side of the building. Rick arrived first at the rear of what was the kitchen. He could hear the German talking, then shouting. Andy quickly met up with Rick, who held his finger over his lips in a "keep quiet and listen" motion.

Neither could understand what the conversation was about as it was either French or German but whatever was being said it didn't seem to be pleasant. Rick edged forward and could see into the kitchen through a small gap in the door. He motioned Andy over.

'It's one Kraut who looks like crap and he doesn't look as if he is armed. There are two young kids in there with him and he's frightening the shit out of them. What the hell is this guy about?'

Andy thought for a moment and in a hushed voice said, 'I'm not sure Rick but he's alone, no vehicle, no standard issue weapon, half of his uniform is missing and he looks like he might be on the run; a deserter maybe.'

They listened to what was going on and watched as the big German strode across the room and grabbed Anton by his collar, lifting him off his feet. Rick started to make a move through the door but Andy held him back.

'Can you understand what is being said?' Andy asked. Rick shook his head. 'Then how do we know he's not related; he may be their father or uncle. Let's wait a while and see what happens next.'

'Yeah, okay but if he doesn't cool it with those kids, I'm going in there and I'll rip his freaking kraut head off.'

They watched Angelique sink to her knees and hold her hands over her ears as the German shouted at Anton. She started to say her prayer.

'Maman, please help us, please come back.' It wasn't loud but sufficiently so for Rick and Andy to hear. They looked at each other bemused by what they were witnessing.

'He's no goddamn relation, he's going to hurt those kids, I feel it Andy. We've got to do something.'

'Okay, let's get in there before he comes back. We'll tackle him as he comes through the doorway but no gunshots, we can't afford to stir up a hornets' nest. We'll have to take him out the hard way; you go left, I'll take the other side. Let's hope the girl doesn't flip when she sees us. You ready?'

Rick nodded and they both entered the room. Angelique stood up and turned around on hearing the door open. She gasped as she saw the two men move quickly across the room to the doorway. Andy said very quietly and holding his finger to his lips.

'We're not here to harm you, we're going to help you. Don't give us away when he returns, do you understand me?' Andy spoke in English so doubted whether the girl knew a damned word of what he said but he hoped that their body language and demeanour gave enough clues.

'You're English!' Angelique said in a whisper clasping her hands over her mouth.

Andy was relieved that she spoke English.

'Yes and we will explain later, now keep quiet okay.' He smiled at her; a warm friendly smile that made her feel more comfortable than she had felt previously. Angelique's eyes filled with tears of joy as she realised her prayer for help was answered. The heavy clunking footsteps of the big German came back towards the kitchen.

Rick had armed himself with a large cast iron pan that Angelique had obtained when she was preparing to make something to eat. Andy silently signalled to Rick that he would attract the soldier's attention, so that Rick could do the necessary.

The German bellowed from the hallway as he approached the kitchen door.

'Now fräulein, you and I should have some fun now that your little brother is—' He stepped into the kitchen and was startled on seeing Andy, who had positioned himself directly in front of Angelique. 'What the hell! Who are you and what are you doing here?' He strode forward aggressively towards Andy as Rick stepped out from the alcove at the side of the door.

He gave a mighty swipe to the back of the German's head, which knocked him to the ground. He tried to get up but Rick hit him again, this time rendering him unconscious.

'Wow, he's a big guy and I hope he doesn't come around too soon.' He was about to suggest despatching the German permanently, when he realised Angelique was still there rooted to the spot. Angelique ran out of the room to find her brother.

'I need to see that he is okay,' she said as she hurried out.

'Andy, we can't let this animal live, we have to dispose of him. Anyway, if he comes to, it is maybe us he disposes of.'

'I know,' Andy replied, 'but I just can't kill someone in cold blood.'

For the first time, Rick displayed his annoyance.

'Are you kidding me man; you drop bombs from a great height and you don't think you're killing people in cold blood. What the hell do you think you're doing then? Just remember when they're dropping bombs on you and yours, they won't stop to ask any questions whether it's right or not. So, let's just get rid of the kraut before he wakes up.'

Andy went purple with rage and grabbed Rick by his shirt.

'Don't you dare talk to me about bombing people, yank. I know what it's like and believe me, I know the consequences. I lost my whole bloody family through German bombs, so don't even think that you can tell me about killing.' Andy pushed Rick away from him.

Rick was stunned and now understood why he got the response from Andy the last time he broached the subject of Andy's family.

'Hey man, I'm sorry, I had no idea, your whole family! Holy shit, that's a tough deal.'

There were several moments of silence before Andy had calmed down.

'It's okay, you weren't to know. It happened over four years ago in the London blitz and I just haven't got over it. I'm sorry for losing my temper Rick.' He looked down at the inert body of the German soldier, 'Let's get rid of this piece of dirt. There'll be no prizes for guessing what I think he was about to get up to.'

The two men dragged the lifeless body of the German out of the kitchen and into the rear garden. They got him to the edge of a ditch when Rick said, 'I'll deal with this, you go back to the kids.' He waited until Andy had gone back to the house, then picked up a large stone and smashed it into the German's head several times, making sure he was dead before rolling his body into the ditch. Andy had waited by the kitchen entrance for Rick to return and as they met, Andy held out his hand and took Rick's in his. They shook hands warmly and realised from that moment, a real friendship had been forged.

Angelique and her brother had been standing at the doorway for some time when Andy and Rick returned. Rick asked, 'Are you both okay?'

'Yes, we are and thank you and your friend for helping us. I think that soldier was a bad man. How did you manage to come here, are there other British soldiers here also?' She asked.

'Hey young lady, I'm American, so we're in this war as well, it's not just the Brits.' Rick was touchy about his country coming late into the war.

Andy interrupted, 'No, there are no other British or Americans here yet. We are the only ones. We had both been captured by the Germans and escaped from a prisoner of war camp where we were held in Germany. We are trying to get to the coast so that we can re-join our comrades. How about we introduce ourselves and then we may be able to get some food and then rest for the night. My name is Andy,' Rick stepped in.

'And I'm his buddy Rick, what are your names, how about the little fellow, what's your name, son?'

The girl responded, 'I'm Angelique and this is my brother, Anton. He cannot speak. I am eleven years old, he is six.'

Andy was looking closely at the children and suddenly felt the need to get out of the room and get some fresh air. The children were almost the same age as his when they were killed and the very presence of Angelique and her brother unsettled him.

'If you don't mind Rick, I need to go outside for a little while.'

'No problem Andy, me and what are your names, Angelique and Anton? We are going to mosey around this place and find some food. With what we have in our backpack, we should be able to make ourselves a nice pastrami on rye.' Rick smiled in his incomparable way; Angelique had a puzzled frown on her face.

Andy went out and sat on the stone step, reliving the agony of losing the people he loved most in the world. The two children stood in front of him were a terrible reminder of his loss.

Angelique resumed the gathering of the necessary elements to cook a bean stew whilst Rick and Anton took a walk around the house. Anton was quick to trust Rick and although still not speaking, led him by the hand from one room to another.

Andy came back into the kitchen and asked, 'Do you need any help?'

'No thank you, although,' she put on her adult face, 'you might like to get some cutlery and plates.' Andy was impressed with her maturity and her stoicism.

'Where are your parents, Angelique?'

Angelique stopped what she was doing and sat down, her face full of sadness. She described everything that had happened to them, occasionally wiping a tear away.

'That is why we must get to our grandparents in Givet. They will look after us and find a doctor for Anton.'

Andy was horrified by what the two children had had to endure. He had his own tragedy to live with but for children so young to watch their family destroyed in front of them didn't bear thinking about. The most heart wrenching of all was how Angelique had been forced to move her dead father's body.

He had no concept of how a child of that age could cope with that. Andy had studied the area from the maps taken from the German General and knew that Givet was forty miles to the north through the dense Ardennes Forest and in some areas was quite mountainous. He, therefore, could not understand how these children expected to get there.

Angelique continued preparing the meal and had quickly put her sadness to one side. Rick and Anton returned and Angelique was relieved and pleased to see a relaxed look on her brother's face.

The smell of a hearty stew started to permeate the air and everyone was soon able to sit down and eat a hot meal for the first time in many days. Andy was amazed at an eleven year old's culinary skill. After the meal, the men and children gathered as many blankets and coats that they could find and made up makeshift beds.

The children were exhausted and so fell asleep very quickly but Andy and Rick stayed awake for a short time whilst Andy recounted what Angelique had told him. Rick was sickened by what he heard.

'Let's decide what we do next in the morning, okay?' Andy yawned the last couple of words but it didn't matter, Rick was snoring.

Chapter 6

Angelique had woken up at first light and had started to brew some German coffee, courtesy of Andy and Rick's brush with the German General. The smell of the coffee aroused the two men but Anton remained fast asleep. Andy went over to the sink and swilled his face in the cool water. He badly needed a shave, bath and a change of clothes, none of which were very practical at this time.

When Andy had finished, Rick filled the sink and promptly dunked his head into it, he lifted his head and let the cool refreshing water drip from his soaked thick black hair to make a pool on the kitchen floor. Angelique rushed over with a large cloth and started to mop up the puddle around Rick's feet. Wagging her finger in a very adult fashion, she admonished him in French.

'Would you mind not being so messy and also respect this house, it is not ours.'

'English please,' Rick requested.

Angelique just turned away with a flourish of her long dark hair. Rick shrugged his shoulders and looked for a cloth or towel he could use to dry off. He eventually walked over to the kitchen table where Angelique was preparing the coffee and asked if he could have a cup.

'How about a cup of that coffee you're making, Angel—' he suddenly stopped 'that's it, that's what I shall call you, Angel because anyone that can make coffee smell that good has to be an angel.'

A smile broke the stern look on Angelique's face, which she tried desperately to contain but Rick had such a captivating way about him that she found it impossible.

'Are we friends again, Angel?' Rick asked.

'Yes of course but only if you keep this house tidy,' she said with a mischievous glint in her eye.

Anton had woken up but instead of going into the kitchen for breakfast, he decided to explore the house and after a short time suddenly came running into the kitchen to Angelique. He frantically tugged at her skirt and shook his head.

He was desperately trying to speak but words would not come. He just pointed at the front door of the house. Andy was quick to realise that the boy had seen something outside that frightened him, so he dashed to the front of the house.

'Everybody get down and stay out of sight, it's a German patrol. They're moving very slowly down the street towards us. Rick, get the pistols out; we may need to use them. Children, I want you to find somewhere in the house where you will be out of the way until we have dealt with this if we have to.'

Angelique led Anton to the small cupboard under the stairs that she had found on an earlier visit. Anton refused to go in, shaking his head, his lip trembling. For him, it was history repeating itself and it was history he did not want to visit again. Angelique pleaded with her brother.

'Anton, we must hide until the soldiers have gone, please now come in here with me.' He would not move in the direction of the hideout. Rick came over to the children and put his arm around Anton.

'Do you know what little fella, I think you and your sister are the bravest children I have ever met, now the only reason I would like you to go into the little hideout is so that Andy and I can deal with those bad men who may come in here. And I would like you to take care of your sister while we do that, is that okay?'

Angelique translated what Rick had said. Rick was a calming influence on Anton and in the short time the boy had known Rick, he already trusted him implicitly. Anton nodded his head and quickly shuffled into the cupboard with his sister. Rick closed the door and joined Andy, who was watching the German patrol.

'I think there are only three of them including the driver and they don't look terribly interested in what they are doing. What do you reckon, Rick? Are they going to come in here or not?'

'I don't know Andy but if they do, we'll be ready for them.' He patted the butt of his pistol.

'I agree, we should be able to take these three out as soon as they approach the front of the house but the problem might be whether we alert the rest of their pals, who may not be too far away. Our two pistols will be no match for what they might have in their armoury. So, if we do engage this patrol, we will have to move out quickly. Can you drive one of those things?' Andy asked pointing to the German jeep.

'No problem man, let me get to the wheel. What do we do about the kids, they won't be able to come with us, it would too dangerous?'

Andy had already decided he couldn't leave them behind to suffer anymore, they'd been through enough.

'We have to take them with us, Rick. I can't leave them here alone. I am already responsible for the death of my children. I'm not going to risk that again.'

'What do you mean man, you weren't responsible for your kid's deaths, it was the krauts that killed your kids.'

'I should have been there, Rick; I should have made sure they were evacuated away from London as they were supposed to have been. If I had done that then they would be alive today. Shush, the patrol is getting close.' Both men stayed low and out of sight with just enough view of the outside to watch the approaching German patrol.

To the relief of them both, the patrol passed slowly by and continued down the road and eventually out of sight. The two friends sat with their backs to the wall on either side of the front door and breathed in deeply, releasing the nervous tension that had built up since the patrol was spotted.

'I understand what you're saying Andy but I still don't think you can blame yourself. Someone else was supposed to have evacuated your kids and didn't do it, so you couldn't do anything about that. But as for Angel and Anton, I think I'll call him Tony, a good Italian name, eh? I think they'll want to go to their grandparents in Givet, so we've got one hell of a trek and it aint going to be easy.'

Andy was relieved that Rick would help him get the children back to what remained of their family.

'Thanks pal, I'm sure we can do this together. I don't think we should tell Angel what the plan is just yet, that is until we have a plan.' They both laughed and went together to release the children out of their hideaway.

Andy opened the door whilst Rick stooped in a mock bow, as a flunky would do when greeting royalty. The children emerged and Angelique curtsied whilst Anton mimicked Rick to the latter's great delight. The relief of not experiencing a confrontation with the German patrol was palpable and there was light heartedness in the children.

They congregated in the kitchen and discussed food and what they would do for the rest of the day. Angelique was insistent that she would prepare meals but was deeply concerned by the fact that she and Anton had no clean clothes, those that they wore had been worn continuously since their mother had been taken away. Angelique also wanted a brush and ribbons for her hair. These things together with their clothes were amongst the rubble of their parental home.

Anton started to get excited and signalled to Angelique that he wanted to play Marelle Ronde. He tugged and pulled on her skirt and drew the shape of the round hopscotch on the floor with his foot and then started to skip on one leg.

'He wants to play round hopscotch, do you know this?' Angelique asked.

The colour drained from Andy at the thought that they wanted to play the same game as his children used to play. He really didn't know how to handle it.

'What's the matter, buddy?' Rick asked.

Andy quietly explained the situation he was in.

'Help me out here pal, it's tearing me apart just thinking about it.'

'You know something Andy, I've grown to really like these kids and I know you have also. Perhaps if you get involved in what they want to do, it may help heal the pain I know you must be feeling. Give it a try, buddy and if it doesn't work out, then leave it to me; I'll take care of things. To start with, why you don't help Angel with the food and I'll go to another room with Tony and he can teach me this Marelle Ronde, whatever that is.'

Andy agreed to give it a try but first went into the kitchen where Angelique was gathering various components for a meal.

'I would like to help you, if that's okay, Angelique.'

'Do you not want to play the game with Anton and Rick?'

'No, my feet are far too big and I step on all of the lines. Perhaps another time.'

'You seem very sad Andy, I'm sure you must miss your family.'

'Yes I do, very much.' Andy was starting to feel uncomfortable but remembered the tragedy that Angelique and Anton had endured and knew they must feel unbearable pain from what was a much more recent set of events. He at least had four years of grieving.

'Tell me about them, please I would love to know,' Angelique was wandering about the kitchen collecting this herb, that dish, a pot from a shelf but listening intently while she skipped from one shelf or cupboard to another.

Before Andy could answer her, which he clearly did not want to do, she extracted a piece of paper from one of the pockets in the German backpack that she was emptying and gasped as she read it.

'What is it, Angelique?' Andy strode over to her and tried to read the paper which was of course, in German. 'Can you translate it?' he asked.

She was smiling.

'Yes of course,' she said indignantly. 'It is a communication from the Commander of the German forces to all field Commanders giving orders to move troops to defend the northern coast of France because the Americans and British have landed an invasion force that has broken through the German lines. I can't translate it all because there are words that I don't understand but this is good news, is it not?' She asked.

Andy picked Angelique up off her feet and swung her around.

'Yes it is Angel and it is fantastic news, what date does it have?'

Angelique scanned the letter carefully.

'It's dated the 7th of June.'

'Calendar, do we have a calendar anywhere in the house?' Andy visually searched the walls in the kitchen but couldn't see one. He started opening drawers and cupboards but his search revealed nothing.

Rick came into the room.

'What's all the excitement about?'

Andy stopped what he was doing and grabbed Rick in a huge bear hug.

'It's started,' he shouted, 'its bloody well started, Rick.'

'What the hell are you taking about man, what's started?'

'The invasion, the Allies have landed in northern France sometime before the 7th of June. They've broken through the German lines. The letter was being carried by the General we,' he lowered his voice, 'despatched. He must have been heading back to Germany for some high level briefing. That's why we need a calendar; it will tell us how long our soldiers have been on French soil.'

The two men danced around the kitchen much to the amusement of the children. Fortunately for Andy, Angelique had forgotten her earlier request to hear about his family. Things soon settled down and after they had eaten, the men decided to take a walk into the woods behind the house to discuss their next steps.

Andy scanned the front road to make sure there were no patrols in the vicinity and as it was clear, they walked quickly up through the garden and into the cover of the trees. Then each of them sat against a tree, quietly contemplating the events that had unfolded.

Rick had his hands behind his head and was deep in thought. He suddenly spoke.

'Do you really think that we're finally going to kick some ass?'

'Yes, I think so but who knows. If our boys have broken through the German lines, then it must have been a serious onslaught. The Germans have been in France since 1940 and have had plenty of time to build decent defences, so to break through into France would have been a major offensive. This could be the beginning of the end.'

'So, what do we do next? Wait here until the cavalry arrive or move west to meet up with them?'

'Rick, we're forgetting two things; one, we move west and we'll land up in the middle of a retreating Army being hotly pursued by our boys fighting their way into France from the north and east. Two, we have a commitment to fulfil to two children.

I've already made my mind up; I'm not going to abandon them here and I know you have said you would support me in that. But that was before we learned the news. So, I will understand completely if you want to make your own way west to our lines. I'm going to get the kids to their grandparents in Givet, somehow.'

'Hey man, we've got this far together, I don't intend to break away now. And anyway, I've come to be very fond of those kids; they deserve a break. So, let's head north to Givet.'

Andy was really pleased that his newfound friend would join in what was now a different objective for them both.

'Before we set out, we need rations, the kids need clothes and decent shoes for walking. I suggest we go out tonight and do a little scavenging. You okay with that?'

'That's fine by me. We should split up though to cover more ground.'

'I agree, let's get back inside.'

The children were sat at the table and Angelique held up what looked like a calendar.

'I found it upstairs,' she said. She looked rather glum rather than excited as might be expected and Andy was puzzled by her sudden change of mood.

Andy took the calendar from Angelique but decided not to look at it, instead he asked, 'Whatever is the matter, Angel? Are you not glad that France may soon be getting rid of the Germans?'

'I am worried that now that your soldiers are coming that you will rush off to join them and leave us here,' Angelique said dolefully.

Andy looked at Rick.

'Do you want to tell her?'

Rick winked and smiled his big Italian smile.

'Well Angel, Andy and I have made a decision,' he deliberately paused 'we're going to try our very best to get you and Tony to your grandparents in Givet but—'

Angelique squealed and leapt into Rick's arms. She was shouting in French, telling Anton what Rick had said.

'Whoa there, young lady, I haven't finished. But,' he started again, 'it will be very hard and will be dangerous. Andy, do you want to lay the cards out on the table?'

'Yes Angel, what Rick is saying is very true, it will be hard, it will be dangerous and it's forty miles, that's about sixty-five kilometres. We will be travelling off the roads through the forests and there will be some steep climbs, would you and more importantly Anton be able to make such a difficult journey?'

'We must do this, Andy. Our grandparents are our only family and if our mother returns, the place she will go to is their house in Givet. As for my little brother, he will be strong enough, I know.'

Andy looked at Rick with raised eyebrows.

'We good to go?'

'We sure are partner.'

Andy started to examine the calendar.

'Look, whoever lived here marked off each day from the 6th of June. The markings stopped on the 26th of June, that's nearly three weeks. So, I assume the landings started on the 6th and they have been fighting ever since. As we don't know what today's date is, we can't tell how long it has been after the calendar marks stopped.'

Andy thought quietly, *They will have stopped because the occupants fled from here when the Allied bombing wrecked this place. So that's it.* Andy turned to Angelique. 'Angel, can you remember how many days ago your home was hit by the bombs?'

'I think it was about one week ago.'

'Good, that will put us into the beginning of July. That means the invasion has been going on for at least a month and all being well, they could be making their way well into France by now. I think that is why we have seen very few Germans here. They've probably been sent out to reinforce their defences.'

Rick was getting impatient.

'Hold on buddy, where's all this getting us? I don't have a clue what you're talking about.'

'It gives us an idea of how much opposition we're likely to meet up with and if they're busy defending their western and northern flanks, then we could have a clear run up to Givet. You follow me?'

'Oh right,' Rick said in mock puzzlement 'I'm with you all the way, boss.' He stood up and saluted. Rick's pearly white teeth flashed in their unique way.

Andy grabbed Rick around the neck and playfully rubbed his fist in his chin.

'Are you ever going to take things seriously?' Andy didn't expect an answer. 'It's getting dark, so I guess we should make a move. Angel, Rick and I are going to search some of the ruined houses for more supplies. We have a long way to go, so we will need much more than we have. You and Tony should stay here and if there are any signs of a German patrol, then get into your hideout until we return. It will be best if you don't use any lights.' Angelique agreed.

Andy and Rick stuffed their pistols into the waistbands of their trousers and picked up anything they could find that could make up a rucksack. Angelique and Anton laughed when they saw Rick wrap the dark coloured tablecloth around his shoulders like an old ladies shawl. He played along putting the cloth over his head and started to walk with an exaggerated stoop until he got to the front door. His clowning stopped as he entered the road outside; he was, once again, a highly trained soldier.

'You go to the left and I'll take the right side, Rick and we'll meet again in one hour. Good luck.'

The pair skipped through the debris and stayed close to any shadow they could find for cover. They shook hands and headed for their allotted area of search. Angelique had pointed out where her previous home was to Andy earlier, so he decided to make his way straight there, knowing that there was going to be clothing for the children still amongst the rubble.

There wasn't much left of the house; two walls were intact, a third was partly still assembled and the other completely collapsed. Making sure that there were no German patrols in the area, he used his German made torch to grope around in the rubble. He thought he saw something other than bricks in the centre of the room and quickly shone the torch in that vicinity.

He realised what it was and quickly scrambled over the loose bricks and mortar to get a closer look. Angelique's father's face was now partly exposed and Andy knew it was him from the description he'd been given of where he had been buried by the fallen masonry. He had little time left, so he covered the body as best he could with bricks and rubble and whispered, 'I will look after your children, I promise. Rest in peace.'

Andy made his way up the now exposed staircase that led to the family bedrooms. He gathered that one of the rooms would be the children's and wondered whether the contents would still be there. As he opened the door of one of the rooms, he almost fell into the rubble and debris on the ground floor, there was virtually nothing left of the floor or most of the walls.

Turning to the other room, it was clear that the children had occupied this one; there were story books and the odd toy scattered about the floor. He focussed on the wardrobe and drawers and was able to accumulate a number of items that would be useful. Importantly, he found some heavy coats and sturdy footwear and thought Angelique, as a young lady, would be appreciative of changes of clothes, particularly underwear.

There was a hairbrush on the dresser, which he put in his pocket and picked up a small model motor car, which he also pocketed. He made sure that the children had sufficient changes of clothes but was mindful of the limits of how much they could carry.

So, apart from the heavy clothing and footwear, he kept the spare clothing down to a minimum. Andy had not found any food and knew the hour was almost up, so he made his way back to the house to meet up with Rick, who would hopefully be well stocked with supplies.

Rick was already waiting at the house and looked rather pleased with himself. He had found some dried beef and smoked fish, a couple of bottles of wine and a large round of cheese.

'There was plenty more in the cellar I found but I couldn't carry anymore. How did you do?'

'No food I'm afraid but I think the children will be pleased with these.' He spread the clothes out on the table. Angelique squealed with delight when she saw some of her favourite clothes and blushed slightly when she saw her underwear on full display.

Andy reached into his pocket, retrieved the hairbrush and held it out for Angelique to take. She took it from him gratefully. Anton looked on expectantly as Andy reached into his other pocket to reveal the model car. Anton clapped his hands joyfully and snatched the toy from Andy. Angelique admonished her brother very severely in French.

'Have you no manners Anton, have you not been taught to appreciate it when someone does something very special for you. Now say thank you this instant.' She had forgotten that her brother had not spoken since their parents had been taken from them.

He opened his mouth and looked pleadingly to Angelique; there was no sound but he mimed the word, "Merci".

Andy knelt down and put his arm around Anton.

'It is my pleasure Tony, I'm glad I was able to find it for you. We should eat now and then sleep. In the morning, we will pack everything we need and plan for our journey.'

Andy knew that this journey would probably be the most dangerous and difficult he had ever encountered. He feared for the children and what hardships they would have to face.

Chapter 7

Angelique could see her reflection in the kitchen window, one of the few windows left intact after the bombing raid, and slowly brushed her hair. Anton and the men were still asleep, but she could not contain her excitement at the thought of seeing her grandparents. More importantly, she was convinced that her mother would be there waiting for them. She had washed her hair and put on clean clothes and now all she needed was a pretty ribbon to tie her hair back.

I must look my best for Maman when I see her, she thought as she gently passed the brush through her long dark hair. Angelique stopped brushing her hair and suddenly became overcome with sadness by the last memory of her father; she remembered that she would never see him again, also to her horror, was the realisation that she may never see her mother again either.

She shut her eyes tightly in an attempt to drive those thoughts away and stop herself from letting despair consume her but it was too late; the suddenly grown up Angelique became a child again. Tears flowed and she let them fall freely, allowing her a release from her enforced adulthood. Andy came into the room and saw that the young girl was sobbing her heart out.

'Whatever is the matter, Angel?' He asked, putting his arm around her shoulder. Angelique spoke through her sobs and at the same time, wiped the tears away with the back of her hand.

'My father is dead and I will never see him again, my mother has been taken away and I don't know that I will ever see her again either, my brother cannot speak and I don't know what to do about it and I am so frightened.' The words came out falteringly, almost staccato and between each word, Angelique would gulp down air as the emotion overcame her again.

Andy allowed her to snuggle into the crook of his arm.

'I could never understand exactly how you feel, Angel. I also have lost people dear to me but my losses, although deeply painful, cannot begin to compare with what you have witnessed and experienced for someone so young, you are a very, very brave young lady.' He stroked her hair gently and she started to quieten. She looked up at him through her tear stained eyes and asked, 'You have lost some of your family too, Andy?'

'Yes I did, Angel; in fact, all of my family were killed four years ago in a German bombing raid over London.' Talking about it was still very painful but he realised it might help Angelique to cope.

'So that is why you looked so sad yesterday morning, you were remembering your family, no?'

'Yes, my children played hopscotch just like you and Tony and when he wanted to play, it brought back memories; memories that are very painful to me because I still feel it was my fault. They should not have been in London at that time and I didn't make sure they had moved to a safe place as they were supposed to.'

Angelique was about to speak when Rick stepped forward, he had been listening at the doorway.

'It was not your fault Andy; you had no control over what happened and deep down, you know it. As for you Angel, we cannot bring back your Pop or find out where your Mom is but we are going to get you both to your Grandparents or die trying. So, honey, we need you and Tony to be strong because that's exactly what Andy and I must be to get you where you want to be safely. Do we have a deal?'

Angelique stood up, straightened her back and held her head up high as Anton ran to her and took her hand.

'Yes, we will be strong Rick, we promise.' She looked down at Anton who nodded his head affirming the promise his sister had made on his behalf. Andy stood up, smiled at Rick and said, 'Well, let's get this show on the road then.'

Both men froze as they heard shouting from the street; Andy recognised the word "schnell", he'd heard it many times in the POW camp and knew that it was German soldiers.

'Angel, you and Tony must go to the hideout right now and stay there until you hear from us that it's okay to come out. Now go, quickly.' The two children hurried away; this time there was no hesitation from Anton. Andy and Rick collected their weapons and ran towards the windows at the front of the house.

Keeping low, they both slid along the polished wooden floor to a vantage point where they could see the outside. A man in civilian clothes was being pushed and shoved violently by three soldiers. They kept shouting at him.

'Schnell, schnell,' as they approached the front of the house. The man kept falling over and was kicked and hit with rifle butts until he got up and staggered on. Andy looked at Rick.

'Should we?'

'You're damn right we should.'

'Let's wait until they are opposite the front door and as soon as we open the door, we have to be on to them quickly; they'll be surprised, so we'll have a head start. You ready?'

'You bet your life I am but hold on a minute, what about the kids?'

Andy knew Rick was right to ask the question. Andy had vowed to help them; yet if they got shot up, the children would be left in grave danger.

'You're right, we can't risk not winning this fight, a fight for some poor wretch we don't even know.'

Angelique had come out of hiding and slid along the floor towards Andy.

'I'm sorry Andy and Rick for disobeying you but I heard what you said and I think you should help this man. I believe you will win and come back for us, so please, don't let him suffer any more.'

Andy and Rick looked at each other and saw the answer in each of their faces.

'Get back under cover Angel and look after Tony.' Rick saw that the soldiers and their captive were almost adjacent to their front door and Angelique had returned to the hideout. Andy reached for the door handle, nodded to Rick and flung the door open.

Rick got out first and fired two shots in quick succession, two soldiers fell to the ground, whilst the third with shock written all over face raised his rifle and aimed at Rick but Andy had already loosed off his weapon and shot him in the chest, lifting him off the ground.

One of the German soldiers was writhing, holding his stomach, crying for help; Rick fired one shot and he was still. The man they had been escorting was badly hurt from the beatings he had been receiving. Andy raised the man's head.

'Do you speak English? Who are you and why were they taking you away?'

The man coughed and struggled to speak but said falteringly.

'My name is unimportant; I am part of the Resistance and there isn't much time.' He coughed again and this time a trickle of blood seeped from the corner of his mouth. 'Are you English?'

'Yes, we have escaped from a POW camp in Germany and want to get back to our lines. But first we have two French children with us who we have promised to help get to Givet where their grandparents live. First of all, we must get you away from here before their friends come looking for them.' Andy nodded his head towards the three dead soldiers.

'No, mon ami there will not be time, you must go now, make your way to Charleville Mezieres and seek out Jean Claude Comte. If you are successful, say that you have been sent by Didier from Sedan, you will be helped, go now, quickly.'

'How will we know Jean Claude, what does he look like?'

'He doesn't look like any—it is the—' He coughed several times and held Andy very tightly before slowly loosening his grip. His arms fell to his side as he exhaled his last breath.

Rick had removed a backpack from one of the dead soldiers and passed it to Andy to place under the French Resistance fighter's head. Andy gently lowered Didier's head to the ground.

'Come on Rick, we have to get us and the children out of here right now.'

Both men moved rapidly back to the house and Andy shouted to Angelique.

'Pack as many things as you can carry Angel, we are leaving.'

Angelique dashed out of the hideaway with Anton in tow.

'Come Anton, let us get our things, we must move quickly.'

Andy was busy looking at the map while Rick organised the children.

'Just a few clothes to change into and a heavy coat because the nights may be cold. We need rations that we can carry and they must not be too perishable; stick to the beans and rice and the smoked meat and fish. Andy, what about the guns and ammunition outside, do you think we should take them?'

'We need to let them think it's the French resistance that's nobbled their men, so their weapons and ammo would have been taken. Take one rifle and ammunition Rick and put the rest in the house out of sight. But let's get moving, I believe it won't be too long before they send out a search party.'

Rick ran quickly outside and gathered the weapons and ammunition from the dead soldiers and stopped briefly by the side of the resistance fighter, remembering his catholic upbringing, he made the sign of the cross and gently touched the dead man's face. Running inside, he stashed the weapons and gathered the children and their possessions together.

Andy worked on a route out of the town, which had to be directly into the forest and out of sight of the town as quickly as possible. Rolling up his map, he collected the full backpack.

'Come on guys, let's get out of here.' The children looked excited and quickly followed the two men out of the back door into the garden and up the hill into the woods. The forest was made dark by the canopy of the trees but occasionally, the sun's rays would break through casting shafts of light on the lush green grass. Anton played a game as he walked behind his sister, jumping from one light patch to another.

He would stand in the sunshine, which would quickly change to dark as clouds or the wind changed the angle at which the rays of light could penetrate and so he would quickly move to the next shaft of light, hopping from one to another like a chess piece. He was enjoying himself and felt safe in the company of Andy and Rick.

Angelique quickly admonished her brother as he was falling behind and she continually had to wait for him as he played his game. Reluctantly, he took hold of Angelique's outstretched hand and walked as quickly as his small legs would carry him in order that they could catch up with the men in front. Andy's pace was purposeful and wanted to make as much ground as possible in the daylight, knowing that he could not expect the children to travel through the night.

'Let's carry on as far as we can Rick while the daylight holds. As we get towards dusk, keep an eye out for any good spot where we can rest, I'm sure Tony won't be able to keep up for long and we may need to give him a lift.'

At that moment, Rick looked back and said, 'I think that problem's already arrived.' Angelique had lifted Anton onto her back, piggyback style and was struggling to stand up. Rick ran back to her and picked the boy up onto his shoulders.

'Now, you make sure young man that you don't bump into any tree branches.' Angelique was relieved but exhausted from her effort whilst Anton cheerfully clung on to Rick's head as the group made their way through the forest.

They walked for several hours stopping periodically to allow Angelique to rest. Anton had been carried on Rick's shoulders most of the way but on the few occasions he was put down to walk but the distance he travelled became shorter as the boy became wearier. Andy and Rick took turns to carry him but with the weight of the supplies and the rough terrain, it became more and more difficult.

It was also noticed that Angelique was displaying visible signs of exhaustion; she was falling further behind and the men were continually having to wait for her. Andy believed they had only covered about 3 miles and Charleville-Mezieres was about another 3 miles further on.

In order to avoid exposure, Andy had kept to the wooded areas rather than taking a direct line across open plains and farmland, which meant that the route was much longer and more arduous. He decided that that they must now rest for the night even though there was still some daylight.

They found a sheltered clearing and set about preparing food and sleeping arrangements. Their first priority was to get some rest as tomorrow it was hoped that that they could complete the first leg of their journey. It was particularly important that Angelique got some sleep as she looked desperately tired and Andy was certain that the stress of her ordeal was beginning to take its toll.

Rick was tempted to gather some kindling and start a fire but he knew he couldn't risk attracting attention from the smoke that would rise above the tree canopy, so he made up portions of cold food and passed them around. Andy looked at Rick and motioned his head towards Angelique who was now fast asleep, so the napkin of food that Rick was about to give Angelique was wrapped up and put to one side for when she awoke.

Meanwhile, Anton had munched heartily into his cheese and salted biscuits, then lay down beside his sister and quickly fell asleep. Andy walked over to the sleeping children and covered them with whatever clothes he could find and tucked them in and as he did so, they snuggled up to each other, taking comfort from the warmth and security of their deep sleep.

He stayed for a while and looked at their innocent faces, they were at peace, for the moment. Andy joined Rick at the other side of the clearing and sat at an adjacent tree, he rested his head wearily on the tree trunk supporting his back.

'Out of forty miles Rick, we've covered three and it will get harder when we hit the really rugged terrain on the way to Givet. I'm really worried about whether the children haven't already suffered enough and whether taking them on this journey may be just too much.'

Rick was deep in thought.

'Yes, I think you may be right but I don't know what options we have. We can't abandon them and if we get to Charleville, we can't just leave them with this Jean Claude Comte who we don't know and we don't even know whether we can find him. These kids are made of strong stuff Andy and although it will take us a lot longer than we thought, they may surprise us.'

Andy reflected on Rick's words for a while.

'Yes, I think I should take a leaf out of Angelique's book, she is one tough young lady. We'll get them there, won't we Rick?'

'You can bet your goddamned cotton picking socks we will.'

'There's just something that's bothering me about this Jean Claude Comte; the French guy who died in Sedan, Didier was about to tell us something about this guy. When I asked him what he looked like, he said something that puzzled me and I haven't really thought about it until now, he said, "He doesn't look like any—it is the—" and then he died. He was trying to answer my question—"What does he look like?" I believe he was saying Jean Claude Comte was not a person but something else, perhaps the name of a restaurant, a street or a building.'

'Now that you mention it, what he said does seem a bit strange and perhaps we need to think about how we find Jean Claude Comte, whatever it or he is.' Rick was happy to let Andy wrestle with that one.

'Hey, there's a bottle of wine we need to get rid of, it will lighten the load we have to carry. How about we have a glass or two before we bed down?'

'Why not, we've got quite a few hours to kill before daybreak including whatever shuteye we can get, get the bottle out.'

The two men drained the contents of a very nice Burgundy, although it had to be said that neither of them paid much attention to the bouquet or the other niceties of a good French wine. Nevertheless, they were able to while away a couple of hours and for that time were able to put to one side the thoughts of the daunting task ahead of them.

'What you going to do after the war Andy, that's if we get through it, you have any plans?'

'Not really thought about it, I have nothing to go back to, so I guess I have to think about starting a new life from scratch.'

'Why don't you come to the good old U S of A? You could make a new life there and I know my family would welcome you with open arms; they're the friendliest people you would ever want to meet.'

'That's a nice thought Rick but there's a lot to do before I get around to making that sort of decision. I really do appreciate the thought, thanks.'

'Okay but just say the word buddy and well, you know the offer will be there if you want it.'

The two friends sat in silence for some time before slipping into a deep sleep, partly due to weariness and mostly due to a very nice French Burgundy.

Chapter 8

An eerie mist started to rise as the morning sun broke though the canopy of trees and warmed the lush ground at their base. Anton, feeling the warmth of the sun's rays on his face, stirred and sat up, rubbed his eyes and shook Angelique who was still in a deep sleep. He panicked, thinking there was something wrong with her when she didn't respond and shook her vigorously until she eventually moved, initially shrugging her shoulder in attempt to ward off whatever it was trying to disturb her.

Angelique could smell the morning air and sweetness of the forest floor on which she lay and suddenly sat bolt upright, startled by Anton's insistent shaking and prodding. She was still rubbing the sleep out of her eyes as her brother threw his arms around her neck in a warm brotherly embrace, glad that his sister was all right.

'Stop it, stop it this instant, Anton, I'm hardly awake.' She realised she may disturb Andy and Rick and so lowered her voice as she could see they were still sleeping. 'We must let Andy and Rick sleep a little longer, Anton, as they have been carrying you and all of the supplies, so they will be very tired. We still have a long way to go, so they will need a lot of rest; so come help me prepare some breakfast but we must be very quiet.'

Anton nodded his head and eagerly grabbed his sister's hand in a futile attempt to help her to her feet.

'Don't worry, little brother, I'm getting up.' Angelique stretched and yawned and for a moment was lost in the tranquillity of her surroundings as birds gave out their morning songs and calls and the fresh smell of the pine trees and grassy undergrowth made the difficult journey she knew they had ahead of them become unimportant, for just a moment anyway.

Eventually, she got up and gently took her brother's hand in hers and walked quietly to the bag containing their food supplies. Rummaging through the stores carrier bag, Angelique was able to find a few salted biscuits and some dried beef, which she cut up into four portions and laid them out very neatly on a cloth.

She wondered what they could do about water as there was none left, they were not able to carry much in the way of fluids anyway, so sooner or later it was going to be a problem and it was sooner than expected, the water bottle was empty.

'Whilst Andy and Rick are sleeping, shall we go for a short walk and see if we can find a stream, so that we can get some water. We mustn't go too far though, otherwise we might not find our way back.' Anton nodded his head, appeared excited about the idea and quickly fell into step beside his sister who, armed with a large empty bottle, had little idea where she should start looking.

However, she followed her instinct and they were quickly out of view of the rest area. Angelique guessed it would be a good idea to walk down the hill to lower ground where she thought there might be a stream.

'Water always runs downhill, so it has to stop somewhere,' she said to Anton, not really expecting an answer.

They had wondered downhill for some time not realising how far they had gone from their rest area but Angelique had other things on her mind as she could see a small stream beyond the trees and directly ahead and started to run.

'Come on, Anton, keep up,' she taunted as she raced towards the invitingly fresh running water. Now breathless, she lay down by the water's edge and paused whilst her brother caught up with her who slotted in beside her. They both lay on their backs, looking up at and azure blue sky and listened to the water wending its way to wherever, they knew not where but for a moment they could relax and enjoy the peace of their surroundings.

Angelique turned over and scooped up some water into her cupped hands, it was cool and had a slightly sweet taste of earthiness but nevertheless, it was fresh, enjoyable and more importantly, thirst quenching. She gathered another handful and drank heartily before dipping the empty bottle into the stream to fill.

Anton was soon copying his sister but was struggling to form a reasonably watertight cup with his hands and so had to get his head closer to the water and sort of splashed the water into his mouth, which worked fine until he leaned too far and fell in. The stream was fortunately shallow, so he wasn't in any danger but now extremely wet and also angry at Angelique for laughing at him as he sat with his bottom in the water. Her laughter was suddenly cut short as a French voice spoke from behind them.

'What are you doing here at this time of day and where are you from?' Angelique spun around and quickly retrieved her brother from the water.

'We are from Sedan and our house was destroyed in the bombing, so we are going to our grandparents in Givet.'

'Givet! My God, child, that's fifty kilometres away, how on earth do you expect to get there? Where are your parents?' The man was tall and carried a rifle but didn't seem threatening and then he motioned to the edge of the trees from where two other armed men emerged. 'These are my friends and if you are stopped by the Germans, you must not tell them that you have seen us or anybody carrying rifles, do you understand?'

'Yes, of course sir,' Angelique replied and was tempted to tell them about her friends when Andy and Rick approached with their hands raised high above their heads.

'Angel, please tell them who we are and that we are looking for John Claude Comte.'

The French men had trained their weapons on the two soldiers as Angelique started to explain who they were and why they were here but she was interrupted by the tall one who said with a great deal of surprise and directing his comment to Andy.

'You are English?'

'Yes sir,' Andy replied 'and this is my friend who is American. We escaped from a German prison of war camp and came upon the children in Sedan as we were trying to make our way through France back to our lines. They needed our help to get to Givet and we promised them that was what we would help them do. Now, I hope you will lower your weapons as we mean you no harm. All we want is to find Jean Claude Comte who we were told would help us.'

The men slowly lowered their rifles.

'Who told you about Jean Claude Comte?' the tall man asked.

'A man called Didier in Sedan who we tried to help,' Andy replied.

The tall one looked perplexed.

'What do mean "tried" to help, where is he now because we have not heard from him for nearly three days and our arrangement is for us all to be in contact every day.'

Rick stepped forward.

'If he was a friend of yours, then we're sorry to have to tell you he was killed by the Germans who beat him up pretty badly. We managed to give them a taste of their own medicine and took them down but not in time to save your friend. It was when we got rid of the krauts and told him what we wanted to do that he told us that he was with the French Resistance and we were to seek out Jean Claude Comte.'

'My name is Patrice, please let me explain to my friends what you have said,' the taller man turned to his friends to translate what he had been told as obviously they did not speak English. Andy could hear enough words to understand their shock and sadness of what they had been told.

Andy was conscious of the fact that the group was fairly exposed.

'Why don't we take cover in the forest where there will be less chance of us being spotted by the Germans, then you can tell us how we can contact Jean Claude Comte. By the way, my name is Andy and this is Rick, that young lady is Angelique and the little fella is Anton.' Patrice and his friends acknowledged each of them in turn and made their way into the thick forest tree line.

Earlier that morning, the two soldiers had woken up and quickly realised that the children were missing but seeing the food laid out assumed that they hadn't gone far. Nevertheless Andy was concerned that they should leave the safety of their temporary guardians without letting them know, they had no idea of the possible dangers they could face nor what to do if they were confronted by such an eventuality.

'I'm not happy that the kids have wandered off Rick, I think we should get the gear together, especially the weapons and go and find them.' Rick agreed but then had a thought.

'What happens if they come back and find we are not here? They will panic and think we've abandoned them.'

'I know it's a risk but they could be in danger and we can't just wait here.'

Rick had started to gather together the supplies and weapons when he suddenly exclaimed, 'Andy, the water bottle is missing; they've gone to find water and that explains why the food has been prepared and left out for us.'

'Rick, you're right and Angel would be bright enough to know that the bottom of the hill is the most likely place to find it. Let's go and find them, eh?'

'I'm right behind you,' Rick had shouldered the pack of supplies, stuffed a pistol down his trouser belt and slung a rifle over his shoulder. Andy carried the rest of the weaponry. They were approaching the edge of the tree line when they heard voices, French voices. They listened to Angelique replying in French.

Andy dropped to the ground and was joined by Rick who whispered, 'Who do you think they are?'

'Not sure Rick but I don't think they're Germans and they don't look like they're threatening the kids. Let's leave the supplies and gear here and go and introduce ourselves. I've got a good feeling about this.' They marched forward with their hands in air, although Rick made sure he kept the pistol in the rear of his trouser waistband.

After the French men, the children and the two Allied soldiers reached the cover of the trees, they all found a comfortable place to sit.

Patrice seems a nice guy, thought Andy and was convinced that the three of them were Resistance fighters.

'How come you guys are armed, are you not taking a big risk?'

Patrice ignored the question and said, 'You have said you want to meet Jean Claude Comte, yes?'

'Yes, we do, how can we find him or better still, can you take us to him?'

Patrice replied, 'we are armed because we are with the French Resistance and we have just returned from an attack on one of the German supply stores. Most of our group dispersed as soon as the attack was over and are now going about their daily lives that is assuming les Allemands allow them to.'

'What do you mean if les Allemandes' allow them to? I don't understand.' Rick asked.

Patrice explained, 'the Germans will look for retribution for the loss of their supply store last night and some of our men will be taken in for questioning, if they survive that then they will probably be shot anyway just as a demonstration of what happens to any would be resistance.'

Andy posed the question.

'So, what about Jean Claude Comte, is he in danger?

Patrice looked at his comrades for acknowledgement, they nodded an unspoken agreement.

'Jean Claude Comte is not a person, we are Jean Claude Comte. It is the code for the resistance in this area and Didier knew that if you or the young lady came into the town asking for Jean Claude, someone from our group would have contacted you. Those in the town who are not involved with the Resistance would not know the name and treat it as an innocent search for someone they did not know.

Each area in occupied France has a Resistance cell and they will have their own unique identification code. I am telling you this now because we believe that the liberation of our country is close and as you are embarking on a long and dangerous journey, you will need as much help as you can get.'

Andy paused for a moment, letting what he had been told sink in.

'Just how close are the Allies to freeing France and driving the Germans out? Are you able to get that sort of information?'

'Yes, we have some communication with London but it is sporadic. We know that the Allies landed in Normandy on the 6th of June and have made good ground. Most of the northern area is under Allied control and they continue to advance east from Caen and also north east towards Antwerp. We are expecting more information tomorrow.'

After many years of fighting against the German occupation, Patrice's face showed signs of weariness and exhaustion but as he spoke about the Allied landings, his face was brightened by a spark of hope.

'Do you have a map?' He asked.

'Yes I do, here it is,' Andy said as he extracted the map from inside his tunic.

'I see it's a German map and very detailed. How did you manage to get hold of it?' Patrice asked as he studied the map closely.

'It's a long story Patrice and perhaps if we get an opportunity, Rick and I will tell you about it. In fact, there is something else I need to talk to you about.' He was about to ask Rick to go and collect the supplies from where they had been left when Angelique approached.

'Excuse me Andy but I need to get some dry clothes for Anton, he is very wet and starting to shiver.'

Andy thought it an ideal opportunity to tell Patrice about the children but out of earshot of them and why it was important to get them to their grandparents. Rick interrupted, 'I'll take the kids over there Andy, it will save moving the supplies twice,' he gave a knowing wink to his comrade. 'Come on Angel and you young Tony, let's get some dry clothes on you.' He hoisted the very wet Anton up onto his shoulders and disregarding his own discomfort, marched off with Angelique at his side.

Andy took the opportunity to give Patrice and his friends a detailed account of what the children had endured, why Anton wasn't speaking, how brave Angelique had been and how devastating it would be if they did not complete their task and unite them with their grandparents in Givet. He told them of the children's belief that their mother would eventually be freed and would make her way to Givet.

'It is surely a very sad story, mon ami and I am sure there will be many more just like it before this war is over. As to their mother, I believe many Jewish women were taken to work in factories all over France, supporting the German occupation supply requirements such as making uniforms and bedding and the like; in fact, anywhere slave labour could be used. It is possible she may have escaped the fate of many of her compatriots who were transported east.' Patrice paused and then said, 'We will help you get beyond Charleville-Mezieres but we must get you some civilian clothes and proper supplies, if you're going to make it the rest of the way. I cannot help further than that because we have much work to do here and it is likely that we will be moving to Rheims to reinforce the fighters there. It is reported that the Germans are consolidating their forces in Rheims ready to help defend the Paris garrison.'

He then pointed to the map and showed Andy a position just north of Charleville-Mezieres.

'There is an old shepherds hut on the side of the hill overlooking the town. The Germans don't bother patrolling around there because they know it has only been used by the sheep farmers and if they wanted to check it out, they would have to go on foot, so you should be able to rest up there. You should go there today, it's about three kilometres. Can you get there with the children by tonight?'

'I guess so but it might be late, especially if we have to stick to the high ground.'

'Good, we will meet you there this evening and will bring with us clothing and supplies. You will find a paraffin stove in the hut and so you will be able to make some hot food. There is also a wood burner but I would advise against its use as the smoke from the chimney stack might attract unwanted attention. The stream runs down from the mountain past the hut and not too far away for you to get water. The hut will be a good resting point before you set off on what I think will be the most dangerous part of your journey. Bonne chance, mon ami.'

Andy warmly shook the hands of the three men and thanked them for their help as they left. Rick returned with the children and watched the Resistance fighters make their way down the hill towards the town but most likely their first port of call would be to a place where they could conceal their weapons and other fighting accoutrements.

Having outlined the route to the shepherds hut, the party made themselves ready. Rick asked Anton if he would walk a little of the way; Angelique translated and Anton immediately shook his head and with an impish grin pointed to Rick's shoulders.

'Okay little fella, you can hitch a ride for a short while but just remember that while I am carrying you, Andy will have to carry lots more of the supplies.' So, with Anton on Rick's shoulders and Andy loaded up, they were about to set off when Angelique insisted she should carry some of the equipment.

The journey was to take them through some thickly wooded forests and rugged ground that was regularly interspersed with rocky outcrops and therefore, decisions were needed either to go around them or over them. Either way, carrying Anton would be essential, so it was decided that on parts of the trek that were considered easy on the legs, Anton would have to walk.

After about an hour, the party rested with the exception of Anton who, the minute he was put down, just wanted to run around and explore, darting in and out of the trees and attempting to climb the more accessible ones.

Andy spoke to Angelique.

'You must tell Tony that he needs to rest Angel, he will need all of his energy when he has to walk, Rick nor I will be able to carry him all of the way.'

Angelique said, 'of course Andy,' and proceeded to tell Anton in French what Andy had said and added, 'I think you're being very silly and selfish Anton, so come and sit by me this very minute.' Sheepishly Anton approached his sister, sat down beside her, she put her arm around him and he snuggled up to her. Angelique swept the hair, which was damp with perspiration from his forehead, 'you seem to be very hot Anton, perhaps you have been running about too much, so I think it is right that you should rest now.'

Andy was about to get everyone on the move again when Rick held his finger to his lips and nodded in the direction of the two children who had fallen asleep where they lay. Andy whispered, 'Half an hour that's all we can spare; we must be at the hut by nightfall. I want us to be there when Patrice arrives rather than him wait for us.' Rick nodded his agreement and settled himself against a nearby tree trunk. After the thirty minutes was up, Andy found Rick had also dozed off and although he thought it would be nice to let them continue sleeping, he knew that they must move on if they were to make the rendezvous that evening.

'Come along, you sleepy heads, we have a long way to go,' he said clapping his hands. Rick stirred, got to his feet and started to load up the supply packs using the makeshift harness they had cobbled together. Angelique also woke up and shook Anton awake, who despite his apparent energy had fallen into a deep sleep.

'We must leave now, Anton and I believe it will be better if you walk a little of the way, is that okay?' Anton nodded his head but hadn't quite woken up and sort of staggered to his feet.

The party set out and soon found that Anton was lagging behind even with his sister holding his hand and urging him to walk faster.

'If you don't walk quicker Anton, then I will let go of your hand and let you walk by yourself.' Anton gripped his sister's hand tightly and tried to keep up with her. Andy, seeing the children struggling to keep up, decided to go back and do a stint with Anton on his shoulders.

'Come on young man, climb aboard.' He knelt down and helped the boy onto his shoulders, noticing that Anton was very hot. 'How long has your brother been hot, Angel?'

'I thought he was hot after he stopped playing when we rested but I think it was all the running and jumping about,' Angelique replied.

'I'm afraid it's even more important that we reach our destination quickly because I think your brother has a fever.' Andy stood up and let Anton slump forward resting his upper body on Andy's head. Rick had retraced his steps to see what was wrong and joined up alongside Andy, who was now striding out with Anton on his shoulders and Angelique just slightly behind. Rick reached up and put his hand on the young boy's forehead and confirmed Andy's fears, Anton was feverish and clearly unwell.

Andy was already striding out briskly whilst Angelique would fall behind then run fifty yards or so to catch up. Rick was watching her closely and feared she would run out of steam fairly soon.

'Andy, I think Angel is already struggling and I suggest that I drop the pack I'm carrying, so that I can give her some help. I'll stow the gear away out of sight and come and get it tomorrow, that way we can both move at a decent pace, you okay with that buddy?'

'Yes my friend, that's a good idea but do you think she'll let you carry her on your back?'

'I'm sure she'll be okay with it, especially when she realises she doesn't have a choice. Just step out and stretch your legs navigator, she'll soon realise she can't keep up and I'll go fetch her. When we get far enough ahead, I'll start looking for a safe spot to stash the gear.'

Andy was worried, he could feel the heat coming from Anton's body as the boy rested against Andy's head and he was burning up.

'We have to get to the hut as quick as we can Rick, we've got a very sick kid on our hands. Stow the gear somewhere and go and get Angel, we have to move as fast as we can.'

Rick put the supply pack and some of the weaponry in a thicket, marked the tree nearest to it with his knife and then moved to find Angelique, who was a considerable distance behind Andy.

'I'm sorry Rick but I cannot keep up, will you ask Andy to slow down?' Angelique was clearly exhausted.

'I'm really sorry princess but Andy must get to the hut really quickly because your little brother appears to be unwell; in fact, he has a very high temperature and we have to get him to bed and hopefully some medical attention from Patrice. So, I'm sure you will understand that I must carry you just like Tony is being carried, that is why I have hidden the supplies I was carrying. So, I'm going to carry you instead, okay?'

Rick stooped low and invited Angelique to climb onto his back, piggyback style. She thought for a few moments and logic told her that she didn't really have a choice and she was now really concerned about her brother, which overrode any embarrassment she might have fleetingly felt.

She clambered gingerly onto Rick's back and hung on precariously with her legs wrapped around his waist and her arms clasped around his neck. Rick stood up effortlessly and started to lope off in pursuit of Andy, thinking that at least Angel was a bit lighter than the pack he'd been carrying.

Chapter 9

'Look, look, just through the gap in the trees.' Angelique was first to spot the shepherd's hut and could see into the distance being as she was a little higher up than anybody else on Rick's back and in any event, Andy and Rick were fully focussed on their foot placement rather than looking up ahead. Rick lowered her to the ground, which he had done a couple of times along the way at Angelique's insistence.

'I want to walk now, Rick, do not be concerned, I will keep up,' she would say but after four or five hundred yards, she would lag behind and so Rick would pick her up again.

The hut was a small grey stone affair with a slate roof; it had a chimney stack at one end and a single small window with wooden shutters, facing west towards the town. It was only about five hundred yards ahead of them in a small clearing; Andy quickened his step and was relieved that he would soon be able to do something about Anton and his fever.

'I'll get down now Rick, thank you and walk the rest of the way.' Rick stooped and let Angelique down onto the ground. She bounded off in front of him, chasing after Andy who was now close to the edge of the clearing. He stopped whilst still in the line of trees.

'We don't know what we will find in there Rick or whether there is anybody already in there, so I suggest one of us should go take a look.'

Before Rick could respond, Angelique said, 'I should go because if there is someone there and they are French, I will be able to tell them about my brother.'

'I'm not sure Angel, it could be dangerous and what if there are German soldiers there?'

'Then I shall say that I'm looking for somewhere to rest after tending my uncle's sheep, it is getting late,' she said with a degree of bravado.

Rick put the palm of his hand on Anton's forehead who was now laid down on the grass.

'Jeez, the kid's burning up Andy, I don't think we can risk waiting too long. Look, the tree line is quite close to the back of the hut, so if I skirt around and stay in the trees, I can watch Angelique's approach and do something if there is a problem.'

'Angelique, are you sure you want to do this?'

'Yes I am certain, Andy; I am very worried about my brother.'

'Okay, let's do it. Angel, wait until Rick has taken up a position behind the hut and then go but act natural, you know, as though you really have been shepherding your uncle's sheep. At the first sign of danger, do not enter the hut but turn away slowly and return here. Is that okay?'

She nodded her acknowledgement and Rick set off through the trees to a spot behind the hut. After five minutes, Andy nodded to Angelique to go but caught her arm as she was about to step out into the clearing.

'You are a very brave young lady Angel and we are very proud of you.' Angelique smiled and blushed slightly, then walked out into the clearing towards the shepherds hut feeling very pleased with herself for taking on this responsible and adult task.

As she approached the front of the hut, she knew that she shouldn't hesitate because if she really were a shepherdess looking to rest in the hut then there would no hesitation. Rick could see her as she came within reach of the front door and panicked as he lost sight of her. She had entered the hut.

Angelique looked around and saw two cots each with a mattress and some rough blankets; there was a wood burner stove and the paraffin cooker, a wooden table and few rickety chairs. She realised that the others would start to worry if she spent too long in there and started to leave. She got to the entrance and opened the door only to find Rick just outside, poised ready to dash in with his pistol at the ready.

'Jeez, Angel, you gave me a fright, I thought you were inside just a little bit too long.' Rick turned and waved to Andy to join him and Angelique.

Andy picked up Anton in his arms and carried him the rest of the way to the hut. The boy was seriously feverish and was sleeping or more likely semi-conscious. Andy hurried to the hut and immediately lay Anton down on one of the cots.

'We must get water and plenty of it from the stream; Patrice said it was quite close. He needs to be given plenty of fluids but I don't know what else to do until Patrice arrives and hopefully he can get us some help.'

'I will go and get the water and then I must go back and pick up the supply pack I stashed away earlier, we will need some of those stores tonight and I don't like the idea of not having all of the weapons with us.'

'That's fine Rick but the priority must be to get plenty of water. As soon as we have that, I will swab Anton down to try and get his temperature under control.' Suddenly, Anton groaned and leaned over the edge of the bed and vomited violently.

'Quickly Rick, get the water, I'll see to Anton.' Angelique rushed over to her brother and gently lifted him back onto the bed whilst Andy had grabbed a cloth from the side of the wood burner and started to clean up the mess at the side of the bed but Angelique took the cloth off him and finished the cleaning up.

Within ten minutes, Rick had returned with some bottles of water together with a bucket that he had grabbed on his way out. He placed the full bucket of water by the side of Anton's bed and put the bottles on the table.

'I'll see you in short while, I'll go and collect the supplies, be back soon.' Rick leaned over Anton and gently brushed the boy's damp hair from his forehead, 'we'll get you right little fella, I promise.' There was a genuine look of sadness on Rick's face as he had grown very fond of the young chap.

Darkness had now fallen and a storm lantern had been lit inside the hut; a blanket had been tacked over the window to reduce the amount of light that might be seen from outside. Andy waited impatiently for Patrice to arrive, pacing the floor of the hut, constantly pulling the blanket back to look out of the small window and scanning the ground down the hill towards the town.

It was almost an hour later that Rick returned with the supplies and promptly started to select food items for the group to eat. They had snacked on salted biscuits on the way here but had had nothing substantial.

'Do you think we can make a hot broth from some of the salt beef we have left? I think Anton may need something warm inside him. What do you think Angel? You're the best chef in the house.'

Angelique walked over, examined the beef and said, 'Yes of course I can do that but will Anton be able to eat it?'

Andy responded, 'I don't know Angel but it's worth a try.'

Angelique busied herself gathering the utensils and other materials together to prepare the food. She got the paraffin stove going and mixed up the chopped up salt beef with some water in a pot and placed it on the small cooker, stirring the mixture frequently and as it warmed through, Angelique would take a spoon and taste it; she was quite pleased with the outcome, it was certainly edible.

She was about to say that the food was ready when the door opened. Andy had not seen the French men coming but it was exceptionally dark outside and the Resistance fighters were used to operating in the dark, it was their best form of defence.

'Good evening, mes amis,' Patrice said as he entered the hut with two of his compatriots. They were carrying several bags which they placed on the table and as Patrice was about to speak, Andy held up his hand.

'I'm afraid we have a problem Patrice, which will require your help if it is possible. The young boy has contracted a very high fever and we're at a loss as to how to deal with it. I do believe we need a doctor and some medicine.'

Patrice went over to the cot and could see at a glance that Anton was not well.

'Mon Dieu, this child is very sick indeed but Andy, there is no way I can get a doctor here before the morning. There is a doctor in the town that was trained in England and he is very helpful to us, so I cannot ask him to come here at night, it would be too dangerous.'

'I understand Patrice, so how early in the morning can you arrange for him to come here?'

'He will come as soon as it is light. I will get one of my men to go now to tell him that he is needed here urgently. In the meantime, you must give the boy plenty of water especially as he has been sick.' Patrice turned to one of his men and instructed him to go and warn the doctor of his required house call in the morning and before the man left, he added, 'and François, tell Doctor Duboise it is urgent.'

'Thank you Patrice, we are in your debt.'

'No, my friend it is we French who are in your debt and soon, we shall see the end of this war thanks to the Allies and the brave soldiers from both of your countries, our country will be free and we can start to rebuild. But that is for tomorrow, now we must deal with today.'

He went to the table and started to unpack the packages he had brought. There was fresh bread, beans, rice, pasta and some coffee. In another pack, there was a selection of clothes for the men which would make it easier for them to travel a little less conspicuously.

'Shall we leave Angelique to try and give her brother a little of her warm soup, so we can go outside and you can tell me how you came about the German map, I would be very interested to know.'

Andy nodded to Angelique and she acknowledged by picking up a bowl and spoon and went to sit by her brother's bedside.

Outside, it was a balmy evening with a clear sky which sparkled with bright stars, a scene that contradicted the mayhem that was going on some distance away in the skies and on the ground. The men sat down on the lush green grass in the clearing in front of the shepherds hut. Patrice asked, 'Do you smoke?' Pulling out a packet of Gauloises, he offered them around. Neither Andy nor Rick had smoked for some time but gladly accepted the offer. Patrice reached across with a lighted match and let the two soldiers draw in the smoke. Rick was not used to the strong French tobacco and coughed and spluttered after first inhaling but then settled down, drawing in not so deeply. Andy was equally unused to the cigarettes and suddenly changed his mind about starting to smoke again.

'I think I'll give it a miss Patrice, thank you.' He passed the cigarette to Patrice's man called Herve who gratefully received the extra smoke, carefully stubbing it out to save it for another time.

Patrice started the discussion that had brought them outside.

'So gentlemen, you were going to tell me all about the map.'

Rick answered, 'it was no big deal, we bumped off a German General and his driver, did a heist on his car and everything in it and drove it through Luxembourg and then into France when we had to dump it.'

Patrice smiled, 'so you are the two POW escapees that the Germans were so upset about a few weeks ago. Had it not been for the Allied invasion, the whole of the German Army would have been after you.'

'How do you know that?' Andy asked.

'We have ways of finding things out about what they are doing, we listen in to their communications, we eavesdrop, we even get some intelligence from London from time to time. Believe me, you are quite famous but I'm afraid quite dead, if ever the Germans caught you again.'

'Well, they aint going to catch us, not now, we've come too far and still have two kids to get to Givet,' Rick said in a very determined tone. At that moment, Angelique came rushing out of the hut.

'Andy, Rick, quickly, Anton has been sick again and I can't stop him shaking, hurry.' The men led by Andy rushed into the cabin to find Anton shaking violently and had brought up the soup Angelique had fed him.

'Get me some wet towels quickly, we need to try and keep him cool,' Andy commanded.

Patrice was concerned and had made a decision.

'Herve, come with me, we are going to get Doctor Duboise up here tonight, he may need a little persuasion. We will be back as soon as possible.' He and Herve left and disappeared into the darkness.

The cool towels were continually being replaced, Anton's shaking had subsided and Rick had to go out and replenish the water supply frequently. So, while Andy bathed Anton with the cool wet towels, Angelique made coffee, mixed some beans into the soup that was simmering on the stove and cut chunks of bread.

When the stew was ready, she filled three bowls, put a slice of bread with each and passed them to, who she looked on now as her two guardians. It was many hours before any of them had eaten anything let alone a hot meal, so they delved into the warming stew and munched on the bread with gusto. Anton had fallen into a deep sleep but was still feverish.

It was almost two hours later when Patrice returned with Herve, François and the Doctor, who looked extremely nervous.

'Doctor Duboise is taking a very big risk coming here at night because the Germans often call on him after dark to treat various invariably minor injuries. We have a man in his office in the event that they do call on him to explain that he has been called out on an emergency at a farm outside the town.' Patrice explained whilst the Doctor was busy examining Anton.

The Doctor took off his stethoscope and looked at Andy and Rick who had a comforting arm around Angelique. He spoke in almost perfect English.

'I was of course nervous about coming here tonight because it is important that I maintain a reasonable relationship with the Germans and that relationship allows me to support our Resistance fighters. But I'm glad you called me because I think the boy may have meningitis. I'm not absolutely sure but he has the symptoms.

It may turn out to be the mild form and in which case, it should clear in a week or two provided he has plenty of fluids and is kept rested and cool. If in the next forty-eight hours, a rash appears then he must be brought immediately to the hospital in the town. If that happens, you must not delay. I will leave some medicine to help calm his fever and I will visit again tomorrow.'

Andy asked, 'just how serious is this ailment, Doctor?'

'In the mild form, not so serious if you do as I have directed but if a rash appears, then that will indicate a much more dangerous type of infection and can be fatal if not treated early enough.'

Angelique started to cry even though she did not fully understand what the Doctor had said but could see the look of shock on Andy and Rick's faces. Andy consoled her saying.

'We will look after Anton, don't you worry young lady, whatever it takes.'

Patrice said, 'I will leave one of my men with you and they will help you with the boy if it is needed, especially if you have to get him to a hospital. You or Rick will not escape capture if you attempt to go anywhere near the hospital as there are many German soldiers there and some German staff. Herve will carry the boy and accompany his sister if it is needed and I suggest you stay here until he has recovered. It is likely of course that it will be unnecessary, it is in God's hands.'

The Doctor, Patrice and Françoise bade their farewells leaving Herve in the hut. Herve spoke no English but was able to communicate with Angelique.

'I am sorry your brother is unwell Angelique but the Doctor is very good and I'm sure he and your friends will make him better soon.'

For the next twelve hours, the group sat nervously watching Anton for any signs of the rash the Doctor had spoken of. Andy and Rick regularly replenished the bottles and bucket with water from the stream, taking turns to travel to the water supply. Angelique busied herself preparing food whilst repeatedly replacing the cool wet towel on Anton's forehead with fresh cooler material.

This activity went on through the night with Rick and Andy taking turns to catch an hour or two of sleep. Angelique stayed by her brother's side most of the night despite constant pleas from Andy for her to go to bed.

'No, I want to stay with Anton please, I cannot leave him.'

It was about two o'clock in the morning when Rick took over from Andy.

'Get your head down for a couple of hour's partner, I'll take over.'

Andy nodded towards Angelique who was fast asleep at the side of her brother's bed with her head resting by Anton's shoulder.

'Let her sleep there, she will wake if she gets uncomfortable,' Andy whispered.

Rick nodded and winked. He dipped a fresh towel into the bucket of cool water, wrung it out and quietly leaning over Angelique, gently replaced the one that was resting on Anton's forehead. The boy was still feverish but was quieter and sleeping, not restless and groaning as he had been earlier.

The rest of the night passed peacefully and as predicted Angelique stirred slowly, stood upright or at least tried to, straining to straighten out her stiff legs.

'How long have I been asleep?' She asked, 'and how is my brother? Is there a rash?' The questions came briskly, with urgency.

'Whoa there Angel,' Rick said quietly, 'everything is fine, there's no rash and he seems to be a little quieter.'

Andy had been awake for some time and had started to prepare food for breakfast, he was impatient for the return of Doctor Duboise.

'I'm hoping the Doctor will be here this morning Angel and he will know better on how Tony is. I'm going over to the stream to freshen up, so can I ask you to make some of your wonderful coffee?'

Angelique curtseyed mockingly.

'Of course Sir, it will be ready for your return.'

Andy bowed and walked to the door backwards, bowing frequently as he went. Angelique laughed and the two men had not heard her laugh for some time and it pleased them.

Shortly after Andy returned, Patrice arrived unaccompanied by either his comrades or the Doctor. Breathlessly, he gave an account of what had happened the previous evening on their return to the town.

'We accompanied the Doctor to his office, which in fact is also his home and saw soldiers and a German Staff car outside his front door. Fortunately, we didn't get so close that we would be spotted, so we let the Doctor continue the rest of the way by himself. I knew Françoise was waiting there, so we stayed under cover and observed.

After about half an hour the German Officer, who I think was an SS Colonel and his guards escorted the Doctor and Francoise to the waiting vehicle.' Andy and Rick listened intently. 'Françoise broke free from his guard as they were getting the Doctor into the car. The guards shouted for him to stop and then shot him as he ran away,' there was long pause as Patrice gathered his composure, 'so I fear that the Doctor was being taken for interrogation.'

Andy was enraged.

'Why? He was supposed to be a respected citizen in the town. Why would they want to interrogate him?'

'We believe he may have been under observation for some time, it is possible that some of my men who have been captured in the past may have said something about his activities for the Resistance and last night there was an assault on the railway in which some of my men were killed or wounded. Perhaps the Germans decided that they would round up anyone who might have been helpful to those that had been hurt in that attack. I don't know, there could be dozens of reasons.'

Rick then said, 'so I suppose you think the Doc will spill the beans about us being here?'

'If I know the Doctor as I think I know him, he is a very brave man and will not give you away but of course that cannot be guaranteed, we know how ruthless the SS can be. You will need to watch the approaches to the hut carefully for the next twenty-four hours and be ready to move quickly further into the forest at the first sight of troop movement in this direction.'

'But what about our sick boy, I don't think we should move him,' Andy said.

'No, I think you would not be able to do so without making his condition worse. So, I think the only option you have is to leave the children here. I would ensure that they were cared for and hopefully, Anton will recover. If the Germans came here, then at least just having a young shepherd girl here with her sick brother would be plausible. In the meantime, you must watch the approach, do not take your eyes off it. I will call again when I have more news. By the way, how is the boy, is he any worse?'

'No, thankfully he appears to have stabilised but is still very sick. Is there any way you can get another Doctor to us?' Andy asked.

'Let us wait twenty-four hours and see how things develop. If he gets worse, then we will carry him to the nearest hospital. Herve will come here later to help if that is required.'

Rick interrupted, 'if the Germans don't come for us, then I want to join you on some of your missions. I'm a trained soldier and I am wasting that experience here; I know I can help. Andy and Angelique can look after Anton and I would be doing something to help you guys. How about it?'

Patrice looked at Andy and Angelique.

'How do you feel about Rick joining me for a week or two while Anton recovers?'

Angelique was shaking her head furiously but Andy said, 'I guess you will do what you want to do Rick and you're right, we can look after Anton but you would be taking a big risk of getting hurt or even killed.'

'I knew that buddy when I signed up to this war and I have to do something.'

Angelique had started crying and Rick put his arm around her shoulder.

'Don't worry about me Angel, you've got to focus on getting your young brother fit and well and I promise I will be alright, trust me.'

Patrice then said, 'we should wait twenty-four hours and make a decision then. I must leave now, my friends, I will return later today or tomorrow when I should have some news.' He turned and walked briskly down the hill to the town, leaving Andy and Rick balancing the pros and cons of the next twenty-four hours.

Chapter 10

The next twenty-four hours seemed like a week to the group sheltered in the shepherds hut and Rick and Andy had spent the whole time visually scouring the countryside in front of them for movement of any kind. Angelique, in the meantime, worked tirelessly cooling Anton, feeding him with small amounts of broth and constantly badgering him to drink water.

Anton was mostly asleep but when awake he was barely so but the medicine left by the Doctor seemed to be having a positive effect on his fever and there had been no sign of a rash.

Patrice arrived later that day with a young woman who turned out to be a nurse.

'I could not find another doctor, well not one that we could trust anyway but I would like to introduce you to Mademoiselle Bresette, who is a nurse in our local hospital. She must go back to her work this evening but is happy to examine Anton and is experienced enough to make a diagnosis on his condition.' As the lady spoke no English, Patrice translated everything that was said for the benefit of Rick and Andy.

Andy held out his hand and introduced himself. Rick followed saying:

'Howdy ma'am,' in his broad American accent whilst Angelique momentarily stopped what she was doing for Anton and introduced herself saying:

'Thank you nurse for coming to help my brother.'

'Please, I would rather you call me Celine. I will look at the child now if I may.' She strode over to the cot on which Anton lay and sat by his side gently stroking his hand. She removed a thermometer from her bag and placed it under his arm and after a moment removed it, 'this young man is still running a temperature but it is not as high as I was led to believe, so I can only assume that the fever is subsiding.

I believe it is safe to say that if it is meningitis, then it is the milder form. He must still be watched very closely for any signs of a rash and he must be given plenty of fluids. Continue to give the medicine that Doctor Duboise left for him.'

Celine suddenly became saddened by the mention of the Doctor's name knowing the predicament he was in. She and the Doctor had worked together for most of the war years and some said there was more to it than just a working relationship.

Angelique was so happy.

'Thank you Celine, thank you,' she said grasping the nurse's hand. Andy and Rick waited patiently for what was said to be translated.

'What, Patrice, what did she say?' Andy asked impatiently.

Patrice eventually told the men what the nurse had said and they were relieved and delighted, particularly by the look of sheer joy on Angelique's face.

'It is not over yet,' Patrice reminded them 'the Doctor said Anton must be allowed to recover for at least a week or two. What could happen in that time is difficult to say with our doctor being in the hands of the Germans. You must stay on your guard, my friends and be ready to move quickly at all times.' He looked at Rick, 'are you still sure you want join with us until you are ready to move on?'

'You can bet your darned life I am. When do I start?'

Andy nodded his approval to Rick and Angelique had accepted that Rick had to do what he felt was necessary.

'You have some weapons and ammunition here I believe and I have no doubt you know how to use them but our fighting here is very different to what you have been trained for Rick, so I suggest you observe one of our operations tonight but I do not believe it would be right for you to take part just yet. I would like you to leave the weaponry here for the moment, it is too risky to be seen during the day carrying a weapon. After tonight, we will return here to collect whatever you need and I will find secure accommodation for you in the town.'

'I'll buy that Patrice; I just want a chance to do what I came across the pond to do and this is an opportunity I shouldn't let go.'

'Come then Rick my friend, get whatever you need together and you'll need this,' he tossed a French beret to Rick, who caught it, studied it and then realised what it was. Rick placed the beret on his head in a jaunty slant and said, 'Do I look the part?' Everyone smiled politely but made no comment.

Angelique then said, 'You look very handsome, Rick, and very French.'

'Merci, Angel,' Rick replied. Angelique giggled not at what he said but the way he pronounced "thank you" in French but at least he was trying, she thought.

Rick said goodbye to Andy, shaking his hand and then said, 'What the hell,' hugging his friend in a warm embrace. He then approached Angelique, who was looking tearful. He held out his arms and she ran towards him clasping her arms around his neck tightly.

'Don't leave us Rick please, I don't want you to get hurt.'

'I have to do this Angel, I have to try and get some payback for my brother, for Andy's family, for your family. You're probably too young to understand that princess but just trust me, I will keep my promise and help Andy get you and Tony to your grandparents, so don't worry about me, just focus on getting Tony well enough to travel. As soon as he is fit, we can all make our way to Givet, okay?'

Angelique nodded her head in reluctant agreement, stifled a desire to cry and kissed Rick on the cheek.

'Please come back soon.' She then slowly walked over to Andy who put his arm around her shoulder and she felt safe and comfortable as she nuzzled into his tall frame. She somehow knew that Andy would not leave her and Anton, although she understood Rick's desire to help the Resistance.

Patrice said, 'we must hurry Rick, Celine must get back to the hospital before nightfall and we have to meet with our comrades for a briefing on tonight's operation.'

'Yes, of course,' Rick said, 'let's go,' picking up his backpack and making his way to the door. He turned, smiled his inimitable smile and waved his hand in a flourish as he left. Andy and Angelique watched the trio walk down the hill and disappear from view. Andy was fully aware of the risks Rick would face and silently prayed for his safe return whilst Angelique believed utterly that Rick would return unharmed despite her initial qualms.

The two returned to the cabin and checked on Anton's condition, he was still sleeping and not restless, which was comforting. Andy suggested that he should get some more water while Angelique prepared some food for the evening.

It was a longish walk to the stream and Andy strolled slowly, taking in the evening air. He thought about the journey they had made to get this far and wondered whether any of them would fulfil what they set out to do. He had learned to banish thoughts of his own family because of the pain those thoughts inflicted on him but he thought frequently about Angelique and Anton.

Whilst there was much heartache and sadness in their young lives, there was hope and that gave him the drive, the impetus to achieve the goal of getting the children to their grandparents. He estimated that there was still about thirty-five miles to go and the terrain would get more difficult as they travelled deeper into the Ardennes Forest. He decided he would need to find a way to simplify the journey, somehow.

Meanwhile, Rick had been taken to a barn on the outskirts of town and was being introduced to the Resistance and realised that his major problem was communication. The only person who spoke English was Patrice and there was every possibility that he may not always be with him, so he concluded that sticking closely to Patrice was essential. Tonight, the target was to be a railway siding where the Germans had recently been loading supplies. Patrice said, 'This is an important target Rick; it seems that the Germans are worried by the pace of the Allied advance and are starting to load equipment onto the trains ready for a quick withdrawal. It is also possible that they have to move forward to strengthen the defences in Paris which, we are told, is about to be liberated. Whatever the case, their minds will be on other things and we can take advantage.'

'So, how are you going to play this then?' Rick asked.

'Four of my men will engage any guards that are there while two others will attach explosives to the supply carriages. I believe there are six of them hooked up, so they are going for the front and rear of the line. I'm hoping that the explosions will do serious damage to all of the wagons. You and I will cover the explosives men, although on this occasion you will observe only.

As soon as the operation is over, assuming we are successful, we will disperse to our predetermined weapons storage areas and then to our homes. The Germans will retaliate swiftly I assure you Rick, so you must stay hidden for several hours. They will undoubtedly arrest some of the townspeople and in the event I am arrested by them, you must make your way back to Andy, do not stay here and do not come back to the town. Am I clear on that?'

'That's okay with me Patrice but do you really think they might pick you up?'

'They have done so before and I was lucky to be let go after a severe beating. The next time I doubt that my luck will hold,' He paused, thinking for a moment about what he knew was likely to be his limited future. He regained his composure. 'We move out in one hour.' Patrice then reverted to speaking in

French and finalised his instructions to his group of men, 'let us go my friends and may God be with you.'

All of the lamps in the barn were extinguished before any door was opened, so that their meeting place would not be exposed. The sentry outside acknowledged Patrice and his men as they emerged from the barn into the darkness. He then joined in with the group. Rick stayed at the side of Patrice as they edged their way towards their target and every muscle and reflex tightened as the railway sidings came into view.

The area was well lit which facilitated the loading of supplies but this activity had ceased for the evening and all that remained were the two guards. Patrice watched the two armed guards sauntering rather than marching up and down the line of wagons. Rick knew that the group would have to get much closer to take care of the guards and allow enough time for the explosive team to do their job.

As it happened, one of the Resistance fighters opened fire prematurely, killing one guard and allowing the other to return fire. One of the French fighters standing next to Rick was hit in the chest and was dead before he hit the ground. Rick picked up the dead man's rifle and took careful aim at the lone guard who was sheltering between two of the wagons, which offered some protection from the volley of gunfire that was aimed in his direction.

'Tell the men to hold their fire Patrice.' Rick shouted.

Patrice signalled to his men to stop. Rick watched the movement of the man for a moment or two and knew exactly where to place the target in his sights. The soldier was leaning firstly to his left and then would roll over and look to his right, he repeated this action several times probably to try and draw the French fire.

It was during his next roll over that Rick let loose one shot and as he predicted, hit the target and killed the guard instantly. Patrice then said, 'We must move quickly men, cover the explosives team, German reinforcements will be here very shortly, now move out.' He then turned to Rick 'I did say that you should not participate tonight but I am thankful to you for doing what you did. We could have been delayed even more than we have been but even so I suspect that the Germans will be here very soon. They will have heard the gunfire, so you may be invited to join in whether you like it or not my friend.'

The explosives men worked quickly and had wired up the mines to the first and last truck. Rick had moved down to the sidings with Patrice and picked up the sub machine gun from the side of the dead German, checked the magazine was loaded and slung it across his shoulder. The group were about to leave when they were confronted by a German patrol of about twelve men who quickly dismounted from their truck and started to take up positions around the sidings.

They were firing at anything that moved and Patrice's men were certainly moving as rapidly as they could away from their attackers. As they retreated, the explosives were detonated causing a massive fireball and debris, showering the whole area, which kept the attackers heads down. Smoke and flames provided cover for the escaping French fighters but despite the cover, some of Patrice's men were either killed or wounded and had to be left where they lay.

Rick decided he was not going to leave anyone behind if they were alive and so he ran back through the smoke. Patrice shouted after him to stop but Rick took no heed. The first body he found was definitely dead but he carried on whilst hearing the zing of bullets passing by and pinging off the ground.

Unhooking the submachine gun from his shoulder, he knew he had to be prepared to defend himself once the smoke cleared and as he did, he came across a wounded fighter who had been badly hit in the shoulder, most of his upper arm had been blown away. The man was young, perhaps no more than 17 or 18 years of age and was writhing in agony with his shoulder shattered and bleeding profusely.

Rick said, 'don't worry buddy, I'll get you out of here but we have to move quickly before the smoke clears.' He helped him up off the ground and with one arm holding the Frenchman up and the other grasping the submachine gun, he moved as quickly as he could towards the route Patrice was heading in.

The Germans were firing indiscriminately being blinded by the smoke and flames of the exploded rail wagons but it was clearing and the German troops had started to advance. Patrice had followed Rick and almost bumped into him as Rick carried the wounded fighter from the scene. Patrice helped share the load as the young fighter was falling into unconsciousness.

'What the hell are you doing? I told you not to get involved until you learned how we operate.' Patrice was furious.

Rick replied, 'leaving our wounded behind may be how you operate but it's not the way we operate, so you can take it or leave it, that's the way it is and that's the way it's going to stay buddy.'

'So, where do you think this young man is going to get his wounds seen to, are you going to walk him into the hospital, which is full of Germans? How about you just take him to the Nazi headquarters because that is where he will end up if he survives his wounds.

We don't have military hospitals or medics following us around that's why we have to leave our wounded behind, they may as well be dead anyway. So, I thank you for your help but you must allow us to fight the only way we can.'

Rick stopped and rested, lowering the wounded man, who was now unconscious, to the ground. He realised he had been foolhardy and thought for a moment that he was back on the battlefield but it was not the battlefield he had become accustomed to and Patrice was right he thought.

'There are no medics, no field hospital, what the hell do I do now with this wounded kid?' He realised to his horror that the boy would probably bleed to death.

Patrice said, 'please leave me here with Bernard for a moment, just walk down that path, I will join you in short while.'

Rick reluctantly walked on, not aware that Patrice was about to end the life of his young comrade in arms to prevent the Nazi's getting hold of him, which would only prolong his inevitable and painful death. Patrice placed his hands over the young man's mouth and nose preventing him from breathing. The boy shuddered and made weak attempts to breath but quite quickly became still. Patrice closed the dead man's eyes, made the sign of the cross and said a silent prayer, before getting up to follow Rick.

'You've left him back there then?' Rick asked as Patrice caught up with him.

'Yes I did and just pray that he dies before the Nazi's get to him,' Patrice replied, lying. Rick did not respond but knew Patrice wasn't being completely honest.

They eventually reached the place where Rick was to be hidden, it was a cow shed on a remote farm, which was unlikely to be visited by the Germans. Arrangements were made for Patrice to collect him prior to the next operation but that would depend on whether Patrice and his men survived whatever retribution the Germans dealt out following the raid on their supply train.

Ten men from the town were arrested that day and for the next twenty four hours, Patrice waited to see if there would be any executions. Only two of the arrestees were involved in the attack on the railway sidings, so there was a risk that they would talk under pressure.

As it was, he was relieved when most of them were released. Just two men were held and ironically, they were not involved with the Resistance. The following day, Patrice came to the hiding place as planned.

'Did you have sufficient rations for your stay here?' He asked.

'Yes I did thanks and very cosy it has been too, just like home,' Rick replied acerbically. 'Is there another operation that I can get involved in tonight?' Rick asked with a note of impatience.

'There may be but we have some concerns about what is happening in the German camp. Shortly after our attack on the railway sidings, the Germans were unusually moderate in their retaliation and we wondered why. We were able to establish that they are being redeployed to the western sector to shore up the defence of Paris. The Commandant here is leaving a section of men primarily to guard the prisoners that are held in the town jail.' Rick listened intently. 'Unfortunately, I have lost many of my men, so a direct assault on the jail would be difficult, if not suicidal.'

'Surely there must be a way to get the Doctor out and of course anyone else that is being held there?' Rick was excited by the concept that he could help to get the Doctor out of the Nazi's hands.

'I'm sure there may be Rick but we don't know what condition the Doctor or any of the prisoners are in and we must find out exactly where they are held in the building before we do anything.'

'So, what do we do to locate them?'

'I have a plan but I need to speak to Nurse Bresette and get her to agree.'

'What!' Rick was shocked 'you're going to send Celine into that snake pit, you can't ask her to take that sort of risk. No way. She's a nurse, man, not a soldier or a Resistance fighter.'

'Celine has a special relationship with Doctor Duboise and I'm sure she will be only too glad to assist in his release.'

Rick was angry.

'You ruthless bastard, first you leave your wounded men to die or be captured and now you want to use a young nurse, why don't we just go in there and blast the hell out of the krauts that are there?'

'Yes you are right my friend, I am ruthless—this war is ruthless. Do you think I haven't seen mothers ripped from their children and fathers shot in cold blood just like Angelique and Anton's? Can you believe that I have seen young men hung from trees, young men no older than fifteen? These youngsters actually were fighters in the Resistance and captured and they were left to rot on the end of those ropes for the townspeople to see as a lesson. Well, let me tell you my American comrade, they are not the only memories I live with every day.

I have seen horrors that will live with me forever and if I have to be ruthless to try and stop what is happening in my country, then believe me I will be ruthless. There is no place here for a soft heart, so if you do not like my ruthlessness, then you are free to return to the shepherds hut whenever you like.'

Rick was subdued and quickly realised this really was a different war.

'I'm sorry buddy, I have no right telling you how to fight this fight, just let me know what you want me to do.'

'Okay, it is important that you are to stay here for another two days while we get the information we need. I will speak to Celine tonight and hopefully, we will be prepared the day after tomorrow. I will come to you here, are you okay with that?'

'Yes of course but as I'm not going to be of any use until the day after tomorrow, I shall go back to the shepherds hut and see how Andy and the children are, if that's alright with you?'

'Yes Rick but travel at night only, I can't afford to lose any more good men.'

Rick and Patrice shook hands and the Frenchman walked out into the night. Rick sat for a short while contemplating everything that was happening. Yes, he wanted to fight the Germans but in a way that he had been trained to do. What he was experiencing now was alien to what he had been taught. He kept thinking back to the words "there are no medics, no field hospitals" and concluded that as a Resistance fighter, you ensured you were not captured or wounded and there was only ever one other outcome-to succeed and escape unscathed.

Hell, this war is crap, he thought to himself and then quickly corrected his thought, *no, it worse than crap.* He got up, started on his journey back to the shepherds hut and suddenly realised that he had absolutely no idea what direction he should take and it was dark. He knew he would have to walk away from the town and uphill into the forest.

So he kept the limited lights of the town behind him. He decided that he would make his way into the forest and if necessary, stop and rest until daylight when hopefully he would recognise where he was. As he entered the tree line, he stopped for a moment and could just make out the babble of water as it coursed its way down the hill, so he knew that if he followed the river uphill, he would eventually reach the spot where Andy and Angelique would collect their water.

The sound of the stream gradually disappeared, so he was aware that he was walking away from it and after walking for some time and fearing that he could get hopelessly lost, he settled down at the base of a tree and eventually fell into a deep sleep.

Chapter 11

Angelique sat outside in the sunshine while Andy was tending to Anton. The boy was improving with each passing day and it had been two days since Rick had left to fight with the Resistance. She was sad and had a look of despair about her, which had been so since Rick's departure.

It was not so much Rick leaving but the memory of losing her father and mother, which was triggered by his going. Those losses together with her brother's illness were weighing heavy on her young shoulders. Andy came outside and sat down beside her.

'Whatever is troubling you, Angel, you can talk to me about it.'

'I am very unhappy, Andy,' she said and leaned her head onto his shoulder. Andy put a comforting arm around her.

'Do you want to tell me what it is that's making you feel bad?' He asked.

'Well, you know about my maman and papa already and of course, I am very sad about them but also, I have no friends and my brother is not well and I do not want to lose anyone else I care about. I just want this silly war to end and people to stop being killed. I hate it, I hate it,' she shouted and started to sob uncontrollably.

Andy held her small frame close to him and could feel the depth of her despair as she shuddered and sobbed. He cursed the war and what it did to innocent people and what it was doing to Angelique and her brother. He encouraged her to cry and hoped it would be some sort of release for her.

'There, there now princess, you cry all you want to,' Andy said as he gently stroked her hair, 'you have every right to feel the way you do, I know how horrible this war has been for you and Anton.' He continued to stroke her hair gently and remembered how he would comfort his own children when they were distressed. 'As to friends Angel,' he continued 'you will always have Rick and me as friends and that is a promise.'

Angelique stood up abruptly, pushing herself away from Andy.

'You cannot promise, no one can,' she was shouting angrily 'you can get killed, Rick can get killed and then Anton and me will have no one except our grand-mère and grand-père, who are very old. So, how can you promise?' She stormed off and went back into the cabin.

Andy struggled to know how he could make it right for this child, a child who had been through so much. Most adults let alone an eleven year girl would have buckled with wretchedness and misery having witnessed all that she had.

'For God sake,' he thought, 'I struggled to hold myself together with my grief, so how this young girl has been able to cope is beyond my comprehension. Damn this war!' He got up and followed Angelique into the cabin. She sat by the side of Anton's bed quietly crying. He walked over and sat by her side and he was about to start speaking when Angelique looked up and spoke.

'I am very sorry Andy, for getting angry; that was wrong of me. You and Rick have been so kind to us and I know we would not have got this far without you. Please forgive me.'

'There is nothing to forgive Angel, you were right. I was not in a position to make that promise because the road ahead is very dangerous and many things can happen. I guess what I meant was that it is our promise to you that we will do everything we can to get you to your grandparents and we will not take any unnecessary risks if we can avoid them.

I will speak to Rick when he returns and ask him to stay with us, although I cannot promise he will do as I ask.' He stoked her hair and she cuddled up to him. 'I want you to promise me that you will stay brave Angel because we will need you to be strong for your brother and to help Rick and me get you both to Givet.'

She wiped the tears from her eyes, looked up at Andy and nodded whilst nestling her head into his chest. She took comfort from the perceived safety of his strong arms and for a moment, she felt the same safety that she remembered getting from her father's arms.

Anton stirred and it was noticeable that he was not sweating as much; his hair was no longer matted with perspiration and some colour had returned to his cheeks.

'Hello, my little brother, how are you this morning?' she said moving his fringe of hair away from his eyes.

He mouthed the words "water please", in French of course and Andy waited for a translation but Angelique appeared stunned and sat open mouthed.

Angelique suddenly became very excited.

'He said he would like some water but Andy, I am sure I heard the words; only a whisper but I think he spoke. Will you get him a drink please Andy?' She turned back to her brother, 'say something Anton, please try.' She waited as Anton mouthed words but there was no actual sound. Anton was asking for his mother but only mouthing the word "maman". Angelique initial elation quickly subsided but as Andy passed her the water for Anton, he said, 'I am certain you heard something Angel, so keep hoping. It's a start and like you, he's a fighter and I know he will make it.'

Anton having drunk the water, quickly fell asleep again and it was clear to Andy that the boy was still some way off full recovery but if Angelique was right, then there was much to be hopeful about.

****

Just as the sun's rays broke through the tree canopy, Rick woke up with a severe crick in his neck from the position he had fallen asleep in.

'Jeez,' he said as he rotated his neck to free up the stiffness, 'anyone would think I'd been sleeping rough in the woods,' he said joking to himself. He looked around the area but didn't recognise it; all he could see were trees. Having stood up and stretched his legs, he could see that he was still climbing uphill but the shepherds hut could be anywhere to his left or his right.

There was a danger that he could get hopelessly lost and not get back in time to meet with Patrice, so he decided to make his way back down the hill towards the town. As soon as he could get near the edge of the tree line with the town in view, he knew he would be able to spot the route back to the cowshed and his hiding place but he may have to wait until nightfall before he attempted the final part of the journey across open ground.

The cover of darkness will provide me with some protection if I wait until nightfall to walk across the fields in the open but there is a risk that I could be stopped by a patrol. Then there's the possibility that there's a curfew which would make it even more probable, he thought as he weighed up his options.

In daylight, I could attempt to mingle with the locals as they moved about their business. Less risky perhaps. He started to walk down the hill and eventually reached the edge of the trees. *Damn, I've come way too far north,* as he surveyed the town that was now in full view, *I'm about a mile away from where I should be and hell, just look at the amount of military hardware that's on the roads. They're sure in a hurry to get somewhere.*

The road that ran alongside the river Meuse was jam-packed with military vehicles, artillery pieces and tanks, which convinced Rick that he would have to move at nightfall, so he settled down just on the edge of the tree line and watched the activity down below him. Rick remembered the knife he had taken from one of the German soldiers he had killed in Sedan and removed it from the inside of his boot.

To keep himself occupied, he found a large stone and started to sharpen the knife, firmly drawing the edge of the blade across the stone; backwards and forwards, backwards and forwards until the sharp edge glistened and glinted in the sunlight. He decided that he would have a wander about but keeping to the tree line edge and under cover, his aim was to go back further south to where he should be adjacent to the route he wanted to take.

Being in no particular hurry, he sauntered in and out of the trees stopping every now and then to look around and make sure he wasn't wandering too far off his intended line. Suddenly out of nowhere, a wild boar came charging towards him and he stooped down to retrieve the knife from inside his boot as the animal crashed into him, leaving a deep gash in the side of his thigh.

He rolled over with the boar on top of him. It was squealing and shrieking as it tried to get back to its feet and run off but Rick had already decided that attack was the best form of defence, thrusting the sharp knife into the animal's throat.

The boar screeched and howled as it rolled off Rick onto its side but was still alive, kicking its legs in a desperate attempt to get on its feet. Rick thought that it probably wanted to get away but he couldn't have taken the risk that it would attack him again, so he plunged the knife into the animal's heart, putting it out of its misery. It lay still as the last of its blood seeped into the forest floor.

Rick stood up gingerly and assessed the damage that had been inflicted on him. He had a large gash in his left upper thigh caused by the animal's tusks in its initial onslaught and he needed to stop the bleeding soon. He also had numerous scratches on his face, neck and chest where the boar was frantically trying to get off Rick and on to its feet. One of the sleeves of his shirt was badly ripped so he tore off a strip to use as a makeshift bandage.

So long as I can stop the bleeding, he thought, *the rest of the repairs will have to wait till later.* Rick sank down onto the lush forest floor, exhausted not just from the tussle with wild boar but also from the shock of the sudden attack. He concluded that he must have frightened the animal and taken it unawares for it to have attacked him as it did. It looked like there was only one route out for the boar and that was directly through Rick.

'I shall wait here for an hour or two to let the wound settle, can't risk walking and starting it bleeding,' he mumbled to himself as he fell into a sleep.

It was dusk when Rick eventually woke up and he was thankful that the wound in his thigh had not bled during the time he had been asleep. He very carefully got up off the ground and started walking to what he thought would be his jump off point.

Rick thought. *'I need to be quick otherwise it will be too dark and I won't be able to see any landmarks.'* He worked his way to where he thought he should be and edged closer to the tree line where he could see the route he needed to take. There was relief on two counts; he could see the farm building and outhouses, one of which was his temporary home and the other was that the German traffic movement had quietened significantly.

'Let's go then Rick my boy, move your big Italian American ass out of here,' he said out loud as he made his way down the hill. He approached the road and made sure there was little or no traffic as he scampered across to the other side but now he needed to cross the small bridge that led to the farm buildings.

It wasn't big enough to carry military vehicles, so he thought it unlikely that it would be manned by German guards. He waited behind a cluster of shrubs, keeping the bridge in view to see if it were clear. After a short time, he edged slowly forward towards the bridge, his heart pounded with the adrenaline coursing through his body.

He was at his most exposed once he got onto the bridge, which was well illuminated and to make matters worse, he was limping because his wounded leg had started to stiffen. He hurried on at as fast a pace as his legs would allow until he reached the other side. Rick was relieved when he was able to fade into the darkened unlit area beyond the bridge. All he needed to do now was find the cowshed.

'You finally made it back, my friend,' the voice said from somewhere in the dark.

It seriously startled him.

'Is that you, Patrice?' Rick asked.

Patrice appeared out of the darkness.

'Yes it is I, Rick and I'm glad you made it back but what has happened, you're limping and you look as if you've been in scrap with a wildcat.'

'You're not far wrong buddy, I was attacked by a wild boar and got a bit messed up in the tangle with him. I will need some help with some field dressings and antiseptic, if you can get hold of some for me.'

'Let's go inside and let me look at your wounds,' Patrice said.

Once inside the hideout, Patrice lit some oil lamps and asked Rick to lay down whilst he examined the wounds.

'You were lucky, the wound has missed any major artery but it is deep enough to be of concern and will need cleaning up with some antiseptic lotion. Any wild animal bite can quickly get infected, so I will get Celine to bring with her some medical supplies when she comes here later tonight. In the meantime, you should rest. By the way, how was the young boy, is he still recovering?'

'I didn't see him or Andy and Angel, I lost my way in the forest and decided to turn back, which was when I met Mr Pig.'

Patrice looked puzzled.

'Mr Pig!' He exclaimed and then realised, 'oh yes. I see what you mean, the wild boar. So, you must have not eaten for over a day in the forest, have you had anything at all in that time?'

'Not really what you might call eaten, just a few mushrooms and some berries but hey man, I'll survive,' Rick replied.

'Wait here and rest, I will be back shortly.' Patrice left through a rear door of the shed and returned about fifteen minutes later with some hot coffee, bread and slices of smoked ham, which Rick gratefully vanquished in short time. Rick having filled his empty stomach suddenly realised that Patrice had mentioned Celine coming to the shed tonight.

'Why is the nurse coming here tonight? It must have been arranged before you knew of my injuries, so she must be coming here for another reason.' Rick was concerned for her safety and that she was being involved in things that were dangerous. Patrice had already mentioned that he intended to use her for a future operation.

'You may as well know Rick, Celine is an active member of our cell and has been for at least four years, she has been in action several times but she has mostly supported us with her medical knowledge and her ability to obtain medical supplies. Tonight, we intend to attack the remaining Germans that have been left here and especially those who are holding our people in prison.

We are particularly concerned with the state of health of Doctor Duboise, who we are told through our sources that the Gestapo have been interrogating him almost continuously since he was arrested. No one knows what condition he is in, only that he is injured.'

'So, where does Celine fit in this?' Rick asked.

'Celine is sometimes asked to go to the German Headquarters to treat minor injuries; when I say Celine, I mean a nurse is requested. Celine always makes sure that it is she that goes. She has been able in the past to keep us fully informed of the number of soldiers there and more importantly, she has a detailed knowledge of the layout, especially where prisoners are held.'

'I see,' said Rick, not wishing to protest too much and perhaps show his growing affection for the nurse. Patrice, nevertheless, sensed that Rick was attracted to her and quickly added, 'Nurse Celine and our Doctor are, as you might say, connected and have been so for about three years and it is because of their relationship that Celine is desperate to help tonight.'

'Of course,' Rick replied, successfully hiding any disappointment in his voice, 'I understand. So, how can I help tonight?'

'You must first get that wound and those scratches seen to, you look terrible. We will discuss the operation when everyone is here later.'

At that moment, the door opened and two men entered. Patrice greeted them and introduced Rick, neither spoke English but their smiles and handshakes were welcoming. They were quickly followed by others and then Celine entered. Patrice spoke briefly to her, obviously to explain Rick's injuries whereupon she promptly knelt by Rick's side to examine his wounds.

Rick was surprised when she spoke to him in English, having been told when they first met that she didn't speak the language. She had specifically asked Patrice to say that because she was lacking confidence and wasn't as fluent as Patrice was. She had a strong French accent but made herself understood. She tore open the already ripped trouser leg to expose the wound more fully.

'So, you were attacked by a wild boar, you were very lucky not to have been more seriously injured.'

'Yeah, I guess,' Rick said, rather nonchalantly.

Celine rummaged through her medical bag and extracted a bandage, various antiseptic creams and lotions together with a small flask of French brandy.

'You will need a stitch or two in this wound, so I suggest you drink some of this while I close it up.' She was so matter of fact that Rick was convinced that there would little or no pain involved. That was until she pinched the two sides of the open wound together with her fingers and proceeded to apply the stitches.

Rick winced, gritted his teeth and tried to withdraw his leg in a reflex action.

'Keep still,' Celine commanded, 'it will take only a minute more.' Rick took another large swig of the brandy. 'There, it's finished. I will put antiseptic cream on and then bandage it up nice and tightly, so that you walk or run without fear of bleeding to death.' She smiled at Rick as he was about to take another drink of brandy.

'I think you've had quite enough,' as she removed the flask from his hand. 'Here's some disinfectant lotion, you should swab the scratches on your face and hands to prevent any infection and keep them clean.' She said, emphasising the last few words, convincing Rick that the last bit was an instruction rather than advice. Nurse Celine bandaged Rick's leg very expertly and said, 'there, that should keep it tidy, just try not to knock the wound area and break the stitches apart.'

Patrice had been talking to his men whilst Celine mended Rick's leg but then came over and joined the nurse as she packed her medical supplies away.

'How's the patient then Celine, behaving himself I hope?' He spoke in French.

'Yes Patrice, he has behaved and he'll be fine. Now what is the plan for tonight? I feel we must get to Henri and free him soon as I don't think he will survive much longer; we know what those Gestapo animals are capable of.' The anguish in Celine's face was plain to see and no one could doubt the strength of her feelings for the Doctor, apart from Rick of course who didn't speak the language but he did sense the concern in her voice.

'I understand your impatience Celine but there was no way we could have taken on what we will do tonight against the numbers of Germans that were here up until yesterday. Now that they appear to have moved out, we can tackle the sections that have been left behind.' He turned to Rick and spoke in English, 'I will brief everybody in French then after that Rick, I will tell you what we are doing.'

The dozen or so men sat on upturned boxes or wooden crates in a small semi-circle and were quietly chatting amongst themselves as Patrice called his meeting to order.

'We have intelligence from London and gentlemen, it will not be too long now before we will rid our town of the occupying German forces. The main bulk of them have been redeployed to meet advancing Allies, who are on the outskirts of Paris. Those that are left here are but a handful but nevertheless well-equipped and I am told, instructed to guard the Headquarters where the prisoners are held.

Small sections are also deployed at the main bridge river crossing to protect a possible German withdrawal. There are only a small number there because the Germans don't believe they will be retreating. The main group of about twenty guards are looking after the prisoners and manning the communications links. So tonight, our target is to release the prisoners and if necessary, eliminate those Germans that are still here. Any questions so far?'

No one spoke so Patrice continued and then translated for Rick's benefit.

'Celine has agreed to answer a call for a medical nurse to visit the German Headquarters tonight to continue some treatment that the current man in charge is receiving. He has been left in charge because his injury has rendered him unfit for frontline duty. A nurse from the hospital has visited each day to change dressings and administer medication, so tonight Celine will attend to the German Officer—'

Rick interrupted, 'and just what is she supposed to do once she has done what she was sent there for?'

Celine answered directly to Rick in English.

'It is simple, I will establish how many Germans there are to deal with and find out where Henri, I mean Doctor Duboise is and more importantly what his state of health is.'

Patrice took over.

'I, with most of the men including you Rick, will be under cover close by waiting for Celine to come out. Once we have the details from her, we will attack the target from the front and rear. We must get inside quickly to disable their communications link and then locate the Doctor and any others who are fit to walk unaided.

Two of our men Andre and Thomas, have been asked to cover the bridge and prevent that section of Germans from reinforcing those in the HQ. Are there any more questions?' No one responded. 'Okay, we meet in four hours' time.'

Patrice went on to describe exactly where they were to meet and what each of their responsibilities were. The group left the building in pairs leaving Patrice,

Rick and Celine to discuss her role in more detail before she left for the German Headquarters.

'Good luck Celine, I will see you later tonight, God willing.' Patrice kissed her on both cheeks and held her hand briefly as she turned towards the door.

'Don't do anything too risky Celine, if you sense any danger, please get out of there straight away. Oh and by the way, thanks for this,' Rick said, pointing to his heavily bandaged leg as she walked through the door. She turned, smiled and disappeared into the darkness.

Patrice sat down on one of the wooden crates and beckoned Rick to join him.

'Let's sit a while and have a cup of coffee and rest before we leave in a few hours' time. Perhaps you can tell me a little about yourself, Rick. Before you do though, I would like you to promise me that you will make every effort to get back to Andy and the children; that means that you take no unnecessary risks tonight. Your priority must be the children. Do you agree?'

'Of course Patrice, I never take unnecessary risks, only necessary ones,' Rick said with a wry smile.

Patrice took in a deep breath, closed his eyes and despairingly shook his head.

'When you do start on your way to Givet, you should stop at a farm a mile east of Montherme, it's about a day's walk from where you are and it may take longer with the children. The most dangerous part of the journey will be crossing the roads that run east west and there is a small river, which you will need to get over. How you do that will be your decision when you get there.

I will give you directions of how to get to the farm and I warn you, the terrain is rough, so be careful. Madame Givauche, who owns the farm and lives alone now, will help you; you will be able to rest and she will give you food for the rest of your journey.' Patrice looked sad as he spoke.

'You know this lady then, Patrice?' Rick was curious to know why the sudden look of sadness appeared on Patrice's face when he spoke of her.

'Estelle is very supportive of our cause and will help you in your journey. I will draw you a map of how to get there,' Patrice said, astutely avoiding Rick's question.

The two men settled down and were extremely relaxed, considering the bedlam that they were about to engage in.

Chapter 12

For most of the day, Anton had woken only to eat and drink but at least his temperature appeared to be getting back to normal. Andy was hopeful that they would be able to move very soon but of course that depended on the return of Rick. He had not been heard of for nearly four days and Patrice or any of his men had not called in to let them know what was happening, so Andy was starting to get a little anxious that something bad had happened.

Angelique was despondent that her brother had still not spoken despite her being convinced that she heard him say some words. So, all in all, the small group, hidden away in a shepherds hut in the Ardennes Forest were not in the brightest of moods. Andy desperately wanted to get to Givet and then get back to fighting the Nazi's.

He had grown very fond of Angelique and Anton and wanted to see them settled and happy with their grandparents.

Well, he thought wistfully, *as happy as they could be given what they've gone through. I wish there were some way I could change their lives, so they didn't have to experience the horrors of this bloody war.* It was at that moment that Andy realised that it wasn't getting back to fight the Nazi's that was driving him but another step on the road to the end of the war.

He wanted to see children with smiles on their faces and looks of excitement about tomorrow, not dreading each day in case they lost a parent or sibling or a friend. Andy despaired at the thought that most of the children touched by this conflict would probably remain physically and emotionally damaged for the rest of their lives.

Angelique joined Andy outside the front door of the hut and sat beside him. It was a pleasant, warm and quiet evening, apart from the occasional birdsong as the sun started to go down below the tree line. Angelique spoke first.

'We are running out of food Andy, we have enough for tomorrow then we will not be able to feed ourselves.'

'I know Angel,' Andy replied 'I've been keeping an eye on the supplies for a couple of days now. I will see if I can lay some traps tonight and see what I can get. Unfortunately, we may have to move out before Rick gets back if I don't catch anything, we can't stay here without food.'

'I could go down to the town and see if I can speak to some local shop keepers, they might want to help me if I tell them about Anton not being well,' Angelique suggested.

'Absolutely not young lady, it would be far too dangerous. I think you should stay here with your brother while I go and get some water and see what I can do about food.' Andy got up, made sure the pistol in his waistband was secure and collecting the empty water container, he said, 'I'll be back as quickly as I can, Angel.'

He strode off in the direction of the stream, knowing that he didn't have the materials to set a trap, let alone the knowledge of how to do it and the light was fading as the evening twilight started to merge with the night sky. Despite the evening darkness, the sky was bright with a full moon and he could at least see his way forward.

Andy could see the stream in front of him and he stepped purposefully towards it but then saw a deer lazily grazing near the riverbank. He stooped down very slowly and quietly, knowing the slightest movement would disturb the animal. Andy estimated he was about twenty yards away, hidden from view by the trees and low lying shrubs.

Being downwind from the animal would explain why the deer couldn't pick up his scent, so he stopped for a moment to think about the potential risk of a shot attracting unnecessary attention and he also knew that there would be only one chance.

He made his decision; drawing the pistol slowly from his trouser waistband, he quietly released the safety catch, raised the pistol into the aim position and whilst on one knee, he held the pistol with both hands to steady himself, fixing the sight firmly on the head of the animal. The single shot rang out and the deer dropped on to its side, still alive but thrashing about and struggling to get up.

By the time Andy had reached his prey, the animal had died and was completely motionless much to Andy's relief. After retrieving the water container which he filled, he considered how he would get the deer back to the hut. It was not a large beast, so he concluded that it was quite young and should be easy enough to sling across his shoulders. The bullet had pierced the area just below the ear and must have hit a main artery as its blood had formed quite a large pool.

Andy returned to the hut to get some rope, so that he could hang the animal and let it drain fully before taking it back. As he stepped into the hut, he saw that Angelique was cowering in the corner not understanding what the shot was that she heard and afraid that Andy had been attacked.

'What on earth is the matter, Angel?' Andy asked as he approached the young girl.

'I heard the gun shot and it was very close; I was afraid that something had happened to you Andy. It woke Anton up and he started to cry,' she said tearfully. Anton was upright on his bed rubbing his eyes, which were red from his crying.

Andy wrapped his arms around the two children.

'I am so sorry for leaving you alone like that and for scaring you, I really am but I had to get water and food. The food is waiting for us; that was the shot you heard, so we will have plenty to eat for some time. I have to go and collect the animal and bring it back here and in the meantime, I think we should light the wood burner stove, so that we can cook a big feast. I don't believe anyone heard the shot and I don't think anyone will see the smoke from the chimney, so long as we put the fire out before daylight. Do we have a deal?'

Anton was smiling and vigorously nodding his head whilst Angelique gave Andy a big hug before going over to the fire stove and started to prepare it. Andy was mightily relieved that the children's earlier distress had been quickly jettisoned.

Andy spent the next couple of hours preparing the deer carcass, he hung it on a tree whilst he gutted the animal and let it drain. Then he carved a large piece of flesh from the hind quarter and cut it into small pieces, which he then passed into Angelique.

Fortunately, she had seen deer that had been hunted in the surrounding area of her town, so was un-phased by the sight of the animal being butchered but she was careful to shield her young brother from the experience. Andy had removed the head and had skinned the beast, so its original form was reasonably disguised; thinking it best that the children didn't associate what they were eating with a deer but then he thought it was probably his Britishness that caused him to presume that they might have a problem with that.

It was getting late, Angelique had cooked a generous meal with the venison meat and Andy was about to say goodnight to the children when he could hear gunfire and small explosions in the distance coming from the direction of the town.

'Quickly Angelique, put the fire out; stay inside with Anton while I have a look outside and turn all the lights off.' Andy opened the door slowly; he could still hear the gunfire outside and was concerned that Rick might be caught up in a fire fight.

****

Two hours earlier, Celine Bresette, carrying her medical bag and dressed in her nurse's uniform walked casually into the town civic centre, which was now the German headquarters. She knew the German Officer she was to treat there and had done so on a number of occasions. Nurse Celine hid her immense distaste for him very well. There were few who were not aware of his cruelty and his ability to break the resistance of anyone unfortunate enough to be arrested by him.

Many of those picked up in the middle of the night never saw the light of day again and no one knew what became of them except a few like Celine who had access to the prison. She was certain that they were either executed or just died as a result of the treatment meted out by the Commandant and his henchmen; then quietly dumped well outside the town in pre-prepared graves.

The man who she was forced to treat made her skin crawl and her stomach churn each time she came into contact with him. He had been wounded in his back with shrapnel from an exploding shell and although he didn't have life threatening injuries, a nurse was tasked on a regular basis to clean, dress his wounds and remove any small pieces of shrapnel that tended to surface from time to time.

'One day, you will pay a heavy price for your crimes,' she would say to herself each time she entered the treatment room but then she would smile warmly at the Commandant.

'Ha fräulein Celine, I am glad it is you that is seeing to me tonight, it is nice to see you again,' the German officer said with a leer on his face that made Celine feel very uncomfortable. He sat astride a chair, resting his arms on the back with his upper torso exposed. A rather obese man in his mid-fifties and judging from his blotchy red complexion, he was obviously a very heavy drinker.

'Good evening Herr Commandant, I trust your wounds have not been too troublesome,' she lied 'I will take a look and see how we're getting on, shall I?' Celine slowly removed the dressing from his wounds, which were mainly clustered just below his shoulder blades in the fleshy part of his back. 'These wounds are healing very nicely Herr Commandant; it shouldn't be too long before you're able to re-join your fighting unit.' It was, of course, wishful thinking on her part rather than a medical fact.

'Do not wish that on me fräulein, I will be quite happy to stay here until the war is over, so I expect you to report your findings as none too favourable in that regard, if you get my meaning,' he said, raising one eyebrow and tilting his head to one side.

'Do you expect the war to finish soon then, Commandant?' Celine probed as she redressed the wounds on the officer's back.

'Sooner than you think young lady, you have noticed no doubt that most of our garrison here have moved out, they are going to defend Paris and drive the Allied Forces back into the sea.'

'What, the Allies are in Paris!' Celine feigned surprise.

The German officer started to extol the virtues of the glorious Third Reich and appeared to be reciting a well-rehearsed speech when he suddenly looked very old and had taken on an air of despondency.

'To tell you the truth fräulein, I am tired, our troops are tired and I do not think we will win this war. It doesn't matter if you know this, it will become evident in the weeks to come anyway. Nevertheless, I would be shot for telling you what I have but to be truthful mademoiselle, I really don't care.'

His shoulders had slumped and his demeanour had changed completely. Celine was unsure what had triggered this sudden change but she was certain of one thing, the Commandant had emotionally given up, knowing that his day of judgement was close.

What to do now, she thought. *I need to know where he is holding Henri.*

'There now, Commandant, you have all new dressings on and everything is healing nicely. Are there any other medical requirements before I leave, perhaps for any of your men?'

'No, there will no further need for your services, Fraulein. If you could find your own way out of the building, I have some unfinished business to attend to.'

'I hope it will not involve anything too strenuous Commandant; the stitches holding your wounds together shouldn't be put under any strain.' Again, Celine lied but she knew that his "unfinished business" almost certainly meant more interrogation of Henri. The German said nothing but waved her towards the door.

'Goodnight then Commandant, I or one of my colleagues will see you again in a couple of days.' Celine left the room and started to make her way out of the building but knowing that she couldn't go without finding out where the doctor was being held, she frantically searched for some way of hiding.

She stepped into one of the many alcoves that were part of the architecture of what was once the town's opulent civic hall. Some of the alcoves had a door leading from them into small meeting rooms or storage cupboards and Celine found herself entering one just as the Commandant, accompanied by an armed guard stepped into the hallway.

She watched the direction he took and decided to follow. He turned towards a staircase that led down below the building and Celine quietly went to the top of it, making sure she didn't expose herself. Whilst she waited for the sound of the footsteps on the stone steps to fade into the distance, she opened her medical bag and retrieved a large scalpel which she slipped blade first under the sleeve of her uniform.

Grasping the handle of the blade in the palm of her hand and her medical bag in the other, she started the decent of the stairs. Celine slowly reached the bottom of the stairway and could now hear the Commandant's voice, sometimes so quiet that she couldn't make out what he was saying but then he would shout and scream, clearly followed by a loud crack, like a slap or a punch.

Celine winced and tucked herself into the shadow of the wall, not knowing what to do next. She could see the guard posted outside the cell who fortunately had his back to her and was busily watching what was going on. She placed her medical bag on the ground and crept up to him silently.

Exposing the scalpel, she made one swift movement and with a cutting motion, sliced into the soldier's neck making a deep cut across his throat and completely severing his carotid. He grasped his neck but couldn't cry out and just made gurgling noises as he started to fall to the ground. Celine stopped the rifle from falling and caught the soldier, so that she could move him away from the Commandant's view.

The German officer was so engrossed in what he was doing, he didn't hear Celine creep behind him and plunge the scalpel into his back just beneath his shoulder blade. He screamed but only briefly because Celine, in a quick upwards motion, pushed the blade up and into his heart, then withdrew it as the officer fell forward onto the prisoner he had been interrogating.

She realised that it was Henri as he pushed the dead man off him and she could see he had been badly beaten and had little strength left. Celine threw her arms around him.

'Oh my poor Henri, what has this animal done to you? I will go and get my medical bag.'

'No Celine,' he could hardly speak, his lips were badly swollen and some of his teeth were missing, 'you must get out of here now mon cheri, they will soon discover what you have done.'

'I am not leaving without you Henri, come, let me help you get up.' Celine struggled but Henri could not stand. 'Well, then I will stay here with you, my darling,' she said, gently kissing his forward. Henri had slumped into unconsciousness as another German guard came down the stairs and discovered Celine's medical bag and the dead soldier.

He carefully approached the cell entrance and saw the dead Commandant laying in a pool of blood. He shouted some obscenities in German as he opened fire with his sub machine gun, killing Celine and Henri instantly. Her arms were still entwined with her lover's as they fell to the ground.

Patrice, on hearing the gunfire ordered his men to attack.

'Celine should have come out of the building, so we can assume something has happened to her; so we must make our move now. Are you fit enough to come with me, Rick?' Patrice asked.

'Yes I'm fine, let's hit the dancefloor but what about Celine, she could get caught in the crossfire.' Rick's leg was throbbing like crazy but he wouldn't have missed this for the world.

'If Celine is still alive, then she will have found somewhere to hide and if she hasn't then, my friend, she will be dead already.'

The fighters edged forward, firing at the windows and doors of the Civic Hall as fire was returned from one of the first floor windows.

'I can see him, second window on the left, give me one of the grenades and give me some cover.' Patrice passed him two grenades.

'Just in case you miss with the first.'

'I never miss, just make sure I'm covered,' he said with his usual smile. He then crawled forward, commando style, jumped to his feet sharply and ran for cover behind a car parked outside the building. The German defender was still holding the fighters back and now there was more of them firing from the adjacent window, so Rick knew he had to take him out.

He pulled the pin out and grasped the trigger whilst he waited to see if the enemy fire was being drawn away from his direction. He let go of the trigger, counted three seconds, stood and threw the grenade, half back style, right through the window. Within two seconds, the explosion ripped out both windows and disabled anybody that was there.

Rick had ducked down behind the car to shield himself from the debris. As the falling debris subsided, he removed the pin from the second grenade and this time threw it through the gap that was once a window. The explosion quickly followed and Rick knew he had hit his target.

The French fighters charged into the smoke-filled front entrance and quickly established that it was clear of enemy soldiers, then beckoned to Patrice to enter. Rick was still crouched behind his shelter, which was now covered in debris.

'Are you okay, Rick? That was a good throw, my friend.' Patrice asked.

'Yep, I'm fine but just a bit dusty and a bit rusty but I think I hit the spot.'

'Let's go in and find out what has happened to Celine. But before we do that,' Patrice turned to two of his men, 'go and join the others at the bridge and take out the guards there. Check whether the Germans have wired the bridge with explosives.'

He helped Rick to his feet and they both walked into the now shattered entrance. The two fighters that preceded them suddenly halted as they saw a German soldier emerge from the staircase, his hands were raised in the air and he was surrendering.

'Nicht shiessen, Nicht shiessen,' he shouted frantically as one of the French fighters who had his rifle trained on the staircase entrance, fired one shot killing him instantly. Patrice shouted at the same time.

'No,' but it was too late. They moved the body of the dead soldier to one side and descended the staircase. Rick was first to spot Celine's medical bag and could see the German soldier with his throat cut, laying alongside it.

'That's Celine's work, I'll bet,' Patrice said as he approached the cell door. 'Oh my God,' he cried out as he saw the carnage in front of him. The body of the Commandant lay on his face in a massive pool of blood, a long scalpel protruded from his back at an angle leading to his heart.

Then he turned his attention to Celine and Henri still in an embrace but with many bullet wounds, too many to have survived. Patrice sank to his knees.

'My God, my God, I sent her into this, it's my fault, I shouldn't have let her come here,' he cried, shaking his head in despair.

'There was nothing you could have done to stop her Patrice, nothing was going to keep them apart, even in death,' Rick said looking at the two bodies holding each other in a final loving embrace. He helped Patrice to his feet and put a consoling arm around his friend's shoulder.

Patrice quickly regained his composure, this wasn't the first dead compatriot for which he felt responsible and he needed to maintain control; there were other tasks to carry out, there would be time to grieve when the war was won.

'Herve, have four of the men collect Celine and Doctor Duboise's bodies and take them to their homes and Herve, have the men treat them with respect. The Germans can remain here for now.' Turning to Rick, he said, 'let's search the offices and see what intelligence we can glean.'

They spent the next hour or so rummaging through desks and examining wall charts and could see that the Allies were indeed close to Paris and that gave Patrice and his men heart.

'Gather together whatever you think is important, burn everything else that could be of use to them, should they return. Make sure all of their weapons and ammunition are collected and taken to the store.' Patrice was back in command of his emotions and marshalled his men as a good commander should.

After a time, Patrice said, 'Come my friend, you have done your work here for which I thank you and now I must get you back to your children. Don't forget what I told you about Madame Givauche, she will help you on your journey.'

Patrice, having instructed his men, went over to the bodies of his compatriots and gently made a sign of the cross on each of their forehead's and rested his hand on Celine's shoulder, a tear appeared in the corner of his eye, which he quickly wiped away but Rick didn't miss it.

He and Rick then made their way to the shepherds hut.

****

Andy waited patiently outside the shepherds hut for the gunfire and explosions to stop down in the town and hoped that Rick was okay. The silence that followed seemed like an eternity and was eerily quiet. Eventually, he went back inside the hut to see how the children were. Angelique was still awake but Anton had fallen into a sound sleep.

'Will Rick be okay Andy, what if he is hurt?' Angelique had been more and more distressed at each gunshot, each explosion; the sound of the gunfire which was not too far away frightened her even more.

'Rick knows how to survive, Angel, he's a trained soldier, so I'm sure he'll return soon. Get some sleep now princess and everything will be better tomorrow.'

Andy gave her a big hug and hoped he was right because soon he would have to make a decision about moving out of here. Moving the two children on his own was not going to be easy, especially with Anton still recovering. He didn't have any answers, yet.

Chapter 13

It was as the sun began to rise that the early morning dew started to evaporate under the warmth coming through the trees. The morning mist hung gracefully above the ground, swirling gently in the slight breeze. Andy enjoyed this time of day; he found it so fresh and peaceful. The beginning of a new day always gave him renewed hope that this day would be better than the last and his journey to eventual freedom would edge just that bit closer.

More importantly, each day got them nearer to the children's grandparents. Sometimes, however, he would question himself why he didn't suggest that the children perhaps could be left in a French town where the authorities could take care of them. Then he remembered that the children were of Jewish parentage and what had happened to their parents could also happen to them.

The horrors that those children had endured were surely enough. They should be looked after, protected and cared for by people who knew them rather than strangers. He scolded himself for even considering such a possibility and reasserted his promise that he would look after them and get them to Givet, no matter what. Just at that moment, Angelique emerged from the hut and sat down by the side of Andy. She hooked her arm through his and snuggled into his shoulder.

'How are you this morning Angel? You're up early,' Andy said.

'I couldn't sleep because I'm worried about Rick and about my brother and about my mama and about everything. Do you really think we will get to Givet, Andy? She pressed her head closer to Andy's shoulder, gaining some comfort from the warmth of his body.

He cupped his hand gently under her chin.

'Now you listen to me young lady, there will be nothing, I mean nothing that will stop me from getting you and Anton to your grandparents; not the Germans or their guns or tanks or bombs; I'll sweep them away with the back of my hand if they try to get in our way,' he said, making an exaggerated sweeping gesture with his hand.

Angelique laughed heartily and Andy realised that it was only the second time he had heard her laugh and was glad he had turned the moment of despair around. Having joked and lightened the conversation, he became serious.

'Promise me this princess that you will carry on believing, you must never give up hope, we will get there somehow and that's my promise to you.' Angelique hugged his arm tightly and looked up at him.

'I know you will Andy because you are a good man, thank you.'

Andy felt a pang of pain deep in his stomach when he remembered how he had not protected his own children and yet here he was making promises that could just as easily end in disaster. He vowed that he could not let that happen, again.

Where the hell is that goddamn yank anyway? he thought. A noise behind them caused him and Angelique to turn around sharply. Anton had tottered out of bed and found his way to the door. Rubbing the sleep from his eyes, he asked in French.

'Where's my breakfast, Angelique? I'm hungry.' This was the first time that Anton had been out of bed and outside of the hut and Angelique was overjoyed.

'Sit with Andy while I get you something to eat.' Then the shock of hearing her brother speak suddenly sank in, 'you spoke Anton, you spoke; Andy, my brother spoke,' she shouted excitedly, hardly believing what she had heard, picking her young brother up off his feet and swinging him around wildly, hugging and kissing him.

Anton screwed his face up showing the normal sign of disgust of a six year old boy being kissed by his sister. She put him gently down on the floor and said, 'I'm going to make you a very big breakfast, sit with Andy while I prepare it.' She skipped into the hut and was deliriously happy.

'Come here, young man,' Andy held out his arms and beckoned to the boy to join him and Anton didn't need another invitation; he quickly sat at Andy's side as he wrapped an arm around the small boy. 'Yes, today is going to be a good day, I'm sure,' he said to himself.

Angelique eventually came out of the hut, carrying two plates of food and was about to hand them to Andy and her brother when she stopped in her tracks, her mouth opened in shock and she almost dropped the food as she saw Rick and Patrice approach through the clearing to the hut.

'It's Rick,' she cried out. Andy stood up, smiled and waved towards the oncoming couple whilst Angelique put the food down on the step and started to run towards them. Anton, despite his earlier illness followed her shouting:

'Rick, Rick.' Angelique was the first to reach the pair and Rick had trouble keeping his balance as she leapt into his arms.

'I'm so glad you're back and haven't been hurt Rick; we've been very worried about you.'

Rick put her down and as she walked beside him, he said, 'I'm fine Angel and now we can get on our way to Givet like we promised, especially now that this young man is—wait a doggone minute, did I hear Tony shout my name?'

Anton had slowly caught up with the group and was swept up onto Rick's shoulders.

'Look at me Angelique; I'm taller than you are now.'

'Hey, he's speaking.' Rick was genuinely overcome. 'Now you can tell me how to play your hopscotch game properly, Tony.' Angelique translated what Rick had said and Anton shouted with a beaming smile on face.

'Yes, yes, I will tell you how to play Marelle.'

The party eventually reached the shepherds hut where Andy had patiently waited. He let Rick put Anton down before warmly greeting his friend with the sort of embrace reserved for very special friends.

'Boy, it's good to see you Rick; I have to say I was getting a bit worried. And you also Patrice, I'm glad you are well. We heard the gunfire and explosions last night and naturally we thought—well, you're both here now, that's the main thing. Come inside and tell us what has happened, I've seen a lot of German troop movement in the last twenty four hours.'

Patrice looked towards the children and was happy for them, Angelique's face was beaming and Anton, having found his voice was prattling away to his sister.

'I'm better now, so we can go and see grand mere and Maman who will be waiting for us.'

'We don't know whether she will be there yet Anton but I'm sure she's on her way,' Angelique said with little conviction. She did not know where they had taken their mother or whether she had been set free. She dared not think the unthinkable and was reluctant about building up their hopes.

Patrice whispered to Andy that he thought it best that the children didn't hear his recall of the previous evening's events.

'Perhaps the children would like to play outside while us men talk about planning the next part of their journey to Givet?'

'Yes that's a good idea, Patrice,' Andy turned to Angelique, 'Angel, Anton needs some exercise and fresh air after being in bed for so long, why don't you take the food you made and have a picnic by the river but don't go too far away, okay?'

Fortunately, Angelique was excited by the idea and having her little brother back again and had not considered the motive of the adults to have them go out of earshot. She quickly set about collecting the plates of food and some water and taking Anton's hand.

'Come little chatterbox, let's have a picnic,' She said teasing him. Andy didn't understand what she said to her brother but Patrice smiled warmly and as the men walked into the hut, Patrice gave a translation which warmed Andy's heart, although he was worried that Rick seemed strangely solemn.

Once inside, Patrice started to speak of the battle that occurred the previous evening.

'We are at last rid of most of the occupying forces from our town, although those that we killed last night are being replaced as we speak. Their main group may well come back and try to hold the Allied advance using the river that runs through the town as a line of defence. But we have good news that it will not be long before Paris is liberated.'

'That's wonderful news, Patrice.' Andy was genuinely pleased but was puzzled by Rick's sad look. 'Everything went okay, didn't it Rick? You don't look too pleased, what's happened?'

Patrice interrupted, 'I'm afraid our so called success came at a heavy price, Andy. I lost two very important friends and I know you will be saddened to know that Doctor Henri Duboise and Celine Bresette were both killed during the action last night.'

Rick cut in, 'they were both murdered Andy, they weren't casualties of war, just plain old fashioned murder. They were unarmed and gunned down in Henri's prison cell and I can tell you that the way the Doctor had been beaten by those bastards, you would not have recognised him, so it was unlikely he would have survived anyway.' Andy saw anger in Rick's face that he had not seen before.

'I am so very sorry Patrice; they were good people and we will be eternally grateful for the help they gave to us.' Andy looked to Rick 'and what about you,

you appear to have a wound to your leg.' Andy could see the tear in Rick's trousers and bandage on his upper leg, which was bloodstained.

'I'm fine, don't worry, it'll be okay, I had a bit of a punch-up with a wild pig and I'll tell you about it later. I might have to rest up for a day or two before we set out. Patrice reckons that the ground we're going to cover is pretty rugged if we are to avoid the roads.'

Patrice acknowledged what Rick had said and agreed.

'Yes, I have told Rick that it will be difficult and have given him directions to the farm of a friend of mine, she will look after you for a few days before you continue the journey. I must return to my men now and prepare them for the return of the Germans when they come. Good luck on your travels and give my best wishes to Estelle, tell her I hope she is well.'

Patrice stood and shook hands warmly with Andy and then grasping Rick's shoulders, he kissed him on both cheeks, French style.

'You are a very brave soldier and I thank you for the bravery you showed last night, we might have lost many more fighters had it not been for you.' Patrice turned, walked to the door, 'I will walk to the river and see the children before I go. Goodbye, my friends.'

He then made his way to the river where he knew the children would be enjoying their picnic. Surprisingly, they sat quietly having eaten their food and were enjoying the sunshine. Patrice said hello to them as he approached.

'I just thought I would say goodbye to you both before I leave because I may not see you again, unless of course you would like to visit me in Charleville-Mezieres when this war is over.'

'Yes, we would like to do that Monsieur Patrice, wouldn't we Anton?' Angelique replied. Anton nodded his head bashfully. 'Come now Anton, you can speak now; thank Monsieur Patrice for his kind offer.'

Anton looked up and mumbled a thank you. Patrice smiled.

'You both have a long and very difficult journey ahead of you but I know that you are both strong and will get to where you want to go, especially with the help of Andy and Rick. Good luck and may God be with you.' He stooped and kissed them gently on the top of their heads and said goodbye.

Rick recounted his adventure with the wild boar to Andy and whilst they both found the encounter mildly amusing, they were subdued by the sadness surrounding the events that followed, particularly the deaths of Celine and the doctor.

'Who is this friend of Patrice? I think he said her name was Estelle. Do you know anything about her?' Andy asked.

'No, I don't Andy but I guessed there was once something going on between them because when I asked how he knew her, he quickly changed the subject and for a moment, I detected that he was a very unhappy man in that moment but then he quickly became himself again.'

'We may find out a bit more when we get there. I suppose her hospitality and the rest at her farm will be welcome if the ground is as bad as Patrice has indicated. When do you think you're going to be able to start?' Andy was impatient to get going and knew that now that Anton had recovered, it would be wise to move out sooner rather than later.

'Let me rest today and tonight and I'll let you know how I feel in the morning. I don't think we can delay too long because if Patrice is right and the Allies liberate Paris, then this area will be swarming with the retreating German Army. That's why we will have to stick to the forest away from the roads.'

'Okay but let me look at your leg and put a clean dressing on it, you can't let it get infected. Celine left us with some bandages and medical supplies.'

The children burst into the hut, wildly excited by the idea that they would soon be on their way to their grandparents. They had chased each other all the way back from the river, playing hide and seek and generally having fun. Anton was exhausted having expended what little energy he could muster whilst Angelique, particularly, looked radiant which was brought on by the positive events of the day.

Andy had gathered the medical supplies and was taking the old dressing off Rick's leg when the children entered. Angelique stopped in her tracks as she spotted the gash in Rick's leg as it was exposed.

'What is wrong, Rick? I thought you had not been hurt.' She rushed over to his side. Anton peered over her shoulder.

Andy calmed her down.

'Don't worry Angel, it's only a scratch and so long as we keep it clean, Rick will be alright. Rick had a fight with a wild boar and I'm sure he will tell you all about it later.'

Rick said, 'we should be ready to start our trek through the forest tomorrow Angel and don't worry about me. Andy's right, it's just a scratch. So today we need to start packing everything we need for the journey, so that we can leave early tomorrow morning. Do we have any of that wonderful coffee you make, Angel? I could sure catch a cup.'

'Of course Rick, I shall make some for all of us.' Angelique took her brother's hand and led him away to where she would make the coffee. Andy said in as a discreet a voice as he could.

'Are you sure you can make that promise? You don't know what this wound is going to be like tomorrow.'

'I'll make sure we move out of here tomorrow morning even if you have to carry me buddy,' he said with his usual wide grin that showed off his brilliant white teeth.

'In the meantime,' Andy said seriously, 'you need to show me the route to Madame Givauche's farm. How far is it? What route should we take and how long is it likely to take, given that we may have to carry you!'

'Stop worrying, navigator and pass me the map.' Andy spread the map out on the floor, enabling Rick to explain the route that he had been given by Patrice.

'The farm is just there,' Rick said pointing to a small cluster of buildings about a mile or so to the east of the town of Montherme. Andy was quick to spot the terrain.

'It looks like we will have to do some serious climbing if we are to avoid the roads.'

'Yep and we'll need to cross some roads and a river to get to the farm. But hey man, we've come this far and we're doing okay.'

'I hope you're right Rick but it's not us I'm worried about, it's the kids and whether they can cope with the difficult ground we must cover.'

Rick said, 'okay, what about we wait until the allies break through, which doesn't sound as if it will be too far off. Then we could ride in style to Givet.'

'Yes, we could Rick but we don't know how long that will take or whether we will be overrun by the retreating Germans in the meantime. I don't think we can take that risk. And, we made a promise, remember.'

Rick agreed, 'you're right buddy, it would be risky.'

Angelique overheard the conversation and quickly interrupted, 'We will not be a burden to you, I promise. We will keep up and not complain. Isn't that right, Anton?' She quickly translated for Anton who nodded furiously in agreement. Angelique was afraid that Andy and Rick might consider the journey too difficult and not go on and going on to Givet was the one thing that had helped her face all that had happened. She started to cry and Anton, on seeing his sister's tears, also cried. Both men immediately leapt up to comfort the children.

'Angel, Tony, we're going to Givet, that's what we said we would do and that's what will happen. Isn't that right, Rick?' Andy said.

'You're goddamn right that's what is going to happen even if I have to hopscotch all the way. So, no more tears you two, okay?'

Angelique sniffled a little but was highly amused at the thought of Rick playing Marelle all the way to Givet. She translated to Anton what was said and he let out a squeal of laughter. Not surprisingly, Anton understood some of what Andy and Rick had said and was starting to understand more English with each passing day.

Since the children joined with the two soldiers, virtually all of the conversations were in English and as his sister was fluent in the language, Anton sometimes felt isolated. He was determined to learn and would soon shock his sister even more.

For the rest of the day, Andy and Rick worked on the route they would take to Madame Givauche's farm. Andy figured that it would take about a day, assuming plenty of stops for Anton and allowing for the fact Rick may need more time. The map they had was not detailed enough to show the terrain so they worked on Patrice's view that there would be lots climbing and some difficult ground to cover.

The children busied themselves gathering supplies, wrapping precooked venison, which was all there was to eat now and filling water bottles. They had enough supplies to last them until they reached the farm, Andy concluded but he was also aware that they would struggle if the trip took longer than planned.

As night fell, the group quietly ate their last meal, the last meal that they would eat in the shepherds hut. The subdued atmosphere was due entirely to their anticipation of the journey ahead; each of them, apart from Anton, anxious about what dangers there might be.

Andy thought about how Anton might cope with the rigours of the journey and then there was Rick, would his wound stand up to the climbing on rough ground? Some might think it odd but in Andy's mind, he was unconcerned about Angelique, she was made of stern stuff.

Rick was secretly concerned about the wound in his leg, it felt somehow not right and he thought there might be some infection but he was not going to say anything about it, not yet anyway. He hoped he could walk it off.

Angelique was worried about everything, her brother, Rick and Andy but significantly not about herself. She knew she could manage the journey; she had to for her brother and her mother for whom she prayed every night.

'Okay folks, I think it's time we got some shuteye; we have a long way to go tomorrow,' Rick announced.

'Shuteye? What is this shuteye?' Asked Angelique who was bemused by being confronted by an English word she had not heard before.

Andy interrupted before Rick could confuse the girl anymore.

'It's slang for sleep, Angel.'

'Of course,' she said 'shuteye, shut your eyes. Yes, I understand now.'

Angelique helped Anton into his bed and settled herself down. They were quickly asleep. Rick and Andy finished what was left of a half bottle of wine that had been left by Patrice and were grateful for the respite. They too were quick to the beds and did not stir until first light the next morning. Andy went outside to get the morning air into his lungs and could see that the roads that skirted the town were heavy with military traffic.

He wondered how Patrice and his men were dealing with what looked like a serious influx of German military. He could hear gunfire down in the town and the occasional explosion, so assumed that the Resistance were making the German retreat as difficult as possible.

Andy went back inside the hut.

'Come on guys, we had better make a move; things are hot down in the town.'

The children got up straight away and were munching on some cold meat before Rick got up. He felt a searing pain in his wounded leg and it was throbbing, confirming his fears of last night. Andy saw the look on Rick's face.

'Are you okay to go, Rick? You don't look right.'

'Yep, I'm fine partner, just a bit stiff, it'll work loose once I get moving.'

'I hope you're right, friend.' Andy was doubtful. 'How about we go for a quick walk outside just so you can loosen up a bit.'

'Yeah, let's do that.' Rick made his way towards the door, limping quite badly. Andy followed and watched Rick grit his teeth with each step he took. 'See, I'm fine, so let's get going.'

Andy wasn't convinced but agreed. The supplies were packed up with Andy electing to carry the heavy packs. Rick bent down to pick up one of the smaller packages when Anton beat him to it.

'I carry it, Rick,' he said in almost perfect English. Everyone's jaws dropped open and Rick said, 'Goddamn it, the little fella is speaking English, well done Tony.'

Angelique was flabbergasted.

'You can speak English Anton, how wonderful, we can practice together now.'

'Goddamn right, yep,' Anton replied, mimicking Rick's American accent, causing everyone to laugh heartily. It was to set them up well for the journey that they were about to embark upon.

Chapter 14

With the sound of gunfire in the distance, Andy, Rick and the children marched with conviction away from the shepherds' hut that had been their home for several weeks. Rick wasn't limping quite so badly but he was clearly in some discomfort. Andy, who led the way frequently, looked back to see how Rick was progressing.

The children were full of energy and skipped along happily with Rick. Anton was trying his best to speak in English but was tired of being continuously corrected by his sister and quickly reverted to chattering in French.

They passed by the river where they had previously gathered their water supplies and got to the other side via a narrow crossing point. Andy was heading in a northerly direction, attempting to stay under cover as much as possible. They had been walking for about an hour when Anton decided he wanted to rest, much to Rick's relief who was now toiling with every step. Andy joined Rick who had sat down by a tree.

'You need to tell me if you can't go on, Rick.'

'I'll be okay Andy, just needed to hole up for a short while. Don't worry, I won't slow you down. I promise I'll keep up with Tony,' Rick said jokingly.

Andy tapped him on the shoulder.

'Your decision friend, I know you won't hold us back if you can help it. But if it gets too bad, tell me, we'll rig up a base for you and go on ahead to the farm. Madame Givauche I'm sure will be able to get you some help.'

'No problem Andy, I'll let you know if I get that bad.'

'We'll rest here for another thirty minutes then move on. I'll go and see how the children are doing.' Andy walked over to where the children had settled themselves during the break. Anton was laying down, not sleeping but enjoying the warmth of the morning sun whilst Angelique was standing up with her arms folded staring out through the trees to some nondescript point in the distance. She turned as Andy approached.

'Rick is not well, is he Andy?'

'He's doing okay Angel; he just needed a rest. There's no need to worry, we will get to the farm and probably rest up for a while. That'll give Rick time to recover properly.' Andy himself wasn't entirely convinced. 'We will get going again in half an hour.'

Thirty minutes later, the party set out again and had walked for about one hour when they came to the edge of a clearing. There was a sharp rocky escarpment directly in front of them. To skirt around it to the left would take the party down to the main road and in full view of the military traffic. Andy considered the possibility of going around it to the east but had no idea how far to the east it would take them to bypass the obstacle in front.

'I think the only option is to go over the top,' Andy said, 'we have no idea what the ground would be like around the other side or how long it would add to the journey. Do you think you can handle this, Rick?'

Rick scanned the escarpment, which was high on the east side and sloped almost vertically on the western edge. It would involve a steep climb to go over it.

'It's probably a plateau at the top Andy, so going around to the east isn't going to eliminate the need to climb at some point. I think I'll be okay but what about the children?'

'I will carry Tony, are you going to be able to climb on your own, Angel?' Andy asked.

'Yes, I think so, I will do my best, Andy,' Angelique replied.

Anton suddenly shouted out, 'I can walk as well, goddamn it,' in his best English. Angelique immediately chastised him in French for copying Rick's cursing. The two men tried to discreetly hide their overwhelming desire to laugh and Andy said:

'No, it will be safer if you sit up top on my shoulders when we get to the difficult bits, Tony. Okay, let's go.'

There was some distance to get to the start of the climb and as they got closer, the scale of the obstacle in front of them got larger. Rick was hiding his discomfort well and the two children didn't appear phased by what lay ahead. Andy however, had noticed an ominous darkening in the sky and hoped they could get to the top before the weather turned. He had up until now kept the pace steady to prevent any undue pressure on Rick to keep up but now he needed to increase the pace.

I can't risk getting caught halfway up if a storm comes, he thought. They marched on and could feel the incline becoming steeper with each step and soon they were having to lean into the hill to make headway. Andy stopped.

'Come on young man, you can hitch a ride now.' He stooped down, putting the heavy backpack on the ground before lifting Anton onto his shoulders. Rick moved across quickly and reached for the backpack when Andy shouted, 'leave it Rick, I'll take it; you walk with Angel and make sure she's okay.

'You can't manage Tony and the load of supplies; come on man, I can take some of it.'

'Thanks Rick but I'll be okay. We've got to get over that lot up there,' he said, nodding towards the craggy rock face ahead. 'You just make sure that you keep up.' He set off and Rick along with Angelique fell in behind.

The clouds had gathered and were looking more threatening than earlier. The wind had also strengthened. The group were not only fighting against the steep incline but now the wind also. They threaded their way through the rocky outcrops and Andy knew that the rain would follow soon and he needed to find somewhere to shelter if the weather worsened. Stopping, he said, 'I'm going to put you down for a short time, Tony while I speak to Rick.' He gently lowered Anton to the ground, removed the backpack and waited for Rick and Angelique to catch up.

'What's up buddy, you need to give me some of that load?'

'No Rick, that's not the problem, look up at that sky, what's it telling us? I think we're in for a heavy storm and we don't want to be stuck out in the open when it happens, so we need to find some cover sooner rather than later. You agree?'

'I sure do partner; the wind is getting stronger and the sky looks real angry, so we're going to see some heavy rain soon. But look around Andy, what cover, I don't see any.'

'I know Rick and that's our problem. We can't have the children exposed out in the open like this, so I suggest we move on as quickly as we can and hopefully find some shelter on the way.'

'Okay buddy, let's get moving and by the way, I'm taking this.' Rick held his hand up to stop Andy protesting and quickly picked up the backpack. 'Carrying this'll take my mind off the leg,' he said, smiling in his inimitable way.

As soon as they started to move, the rain came down and was getting heavier by the minute and was being driven into their faces by a strengthening wind.

Anton perched upon Andy's shoulders, tucked his head down and tried to shelter but he was still very exposed. Angelique held on to Rick's hand and both of them struggled to maintain a forward momentum.

Andy scanned the ground ahead, searching for a possible refuge and could see nothing but the rock face to the left and scattered boulders dotted about the hillside. The ground beneath their feet was becoming extremely wet and finding stable footholds was now becoming difficult, so the climb up and between the jagged rocks and boulders was an added difficulty.

Andy was about to stop the party and just shelter as best they could in the lee of a large boulder until the storm passed when he spotted what looked like an opening in the rock face about sixty metres ahead and to the left.

Possibly the entrance to a cave, he thought. It was close to the escarpment wall before it fell away in a vertical drop. 'Follow me,' he shouted, straining to be heard above the howling wind. The group staggered on, their weariness starting to become evident with each step but they eventually reached the shelter.

It wasn't what one could call a large cave but more of a deep concave groove in the rock face, carved by nature over millions of years and appearing as though some giant hand had scooped out a piece of the crag. It was certainly big enough to provide the much needed respite for the wet, cold and bedraggled travellers.

They scuttled inside and were greatly relieved to escape the driving rain and wind. Angelique and Rick were the last to arrive and Andy was glad to see that Rick did not appear to have gotten any worse despite the difficult terrain and weather. Angelique was soaking wet, seemingly more than any of the others. Andy asked, 'Do you have any dry clothes in the packs, Angel?'

'Yes I do but I can't change here, not with everyone watching, can I?' she said indignantly.

'And you can't stay in those clothes either, both you and Anton must get dry clothes on or you will get a cold and we cannot let that happen when we still have a long way to go.'

Rick interrupted, 'here's what we do Angel, us men will stand facing out towards the opening and you can go to the back of, let's call it our cave and you can change. We promise we won't peek.' Once again, Rick's disarming smile was sufficiently persuasive.

'You promise you won't look; you absolutely promise?' pleaded Angelique.

'You have our word, princess,' Andy added.

'Okay then, when I have my clothes ready, I will tell you so that you can turn away.' After a few moments of rummaging through the supply pack, she said, 'Okay, I am ready to change now. Please face the other way.'

Andy and Rick stood with their arms folded near the edge of the entrance, watching the rain fall and were joined by Anton who, amusingly, copied their stance. After what seemed an interminable time, Angelique announced that she was ready.

'You may turn around now, thank you. And now it's your turn, Anton,' she said in French. She helped her brother get into dry clothes and Andy was now more relaxed but both he and Rick would have to put up with being a little damp for the time being.

During the next two hours, they watched the rain drive down past the opening to their shelter and they ate some cold meat, drank a little water and generally rested as the storm persisted. When one of the water containers had been emptied, Andy took it to the edge of the cave and held the bottle up to a rivulet of water that was falling from the roof top and filled it with fresh rainwater.

'Whilst this rain is on, we must make sure we capture as much in our containers as we can, I have no idea where the next water source is and we still have a long way to go.' Andy announced.

Rick admired Andy for his attention to detail, his determination and intelligence but had still not gotten used to the British seriousness he displayed; at least he assumed it was a British trait.

After several more hours of rain, the wind started to quieten, the rainfall reduced to a light shower, the sky brightened and the rivulets of rainwater that had cascaded from the rock face outside were now merely drips.

'The sun is starting to show through the clouds, which means we should be able to dry the clothes. I don't think it will be wise to move on just yet though because the ground will be very wet and dangerous. So, let's concentrate on drying everything out and getting as much rest as possible.

Once the sun comes out properly, the boulders that are dotted about outside will get quite warm and be ideal for laying the wet clothes on to dry. Rick, I'm going to have a mooch outside, see what the ground is like and now that the light is better, have a look at what's ahead of us. I'll be back shortly.'

Andy walked out into the sunshine and although it was warmer, the water on the ground was still draining away and it was quite slippery under foot. Andy took several tentative steps up the side of the escarpment towards the top and reckoned that they had managed about half of the climb. He concluded that it would be too dangerous to attempt the rest of the ascent before the ground had dried out much more.

After an arduous thirty minutes of climbing, Andy was able to see that it was a large plateau just as Rick had predicted, which confirmed that the original decision to climb to the top rather than go around was right. There was quite an expanse of open ground and he knew that at some point, they would need to descend to the valley floor, cross a river and then climb again to Madame Givauche's farm.

Slowly, he made his way back to the cave and glad that he had a clear view of the next part of the journey. As he approached where he had left the group, he could see clothes spread out on the boulders.

They've been busy already, he thought. 'Well children, I see that you've kept yourselves occupied while I've been away. I hope Rick has been resting and you haven't worked him too hard.'

Rick said, 'No, I've been quite lazy Andy; the kids did all the drying out of the clothes themselves. And they made me take off my socks and jacket to dry as well. What did you find out there?'

'Well, you were right, it is a plateau and there was no way we could have avoided climbing to the top at some point except by going down to the valley close to the road. There's a lot of open ground to cross but that shouldn't be a problem as it's well out of sight from below.

We will have to drop down to the valley floor at some point though before we'll have a climb again to the farm. The ground is far too soggy to go just yet but if we want to get to Madame Givauche before nightfall, we probably need to leave in the next two hours. How's the leg?'

'A lot better, thanks nurse; you did a good job cleaning it up and doing the dressing. You may have missed your true vocation!' Rick joked; Andy found it highly amusing.

The time soon passed and during that time, the clothes had dried in the early afternoon sun. They took the opportunity to pack everything away and so they set out as planned. Andy pointed out that the ground underfoot could still be dangerous. Whilst it took Andy thirty minutes or more to reach the plateau earlier, he had not taken into account carrying Anton.

Every step Andy took was meticulously placed for certainty because he was well aware that falling with Anton on his shoulders could cause the boy serious injury. Rick had taken the supplies pack and Angelique carried the sack containing the dried clothes. She was gripping Rick's hand tightly, petrified that she might slip and fall; Rick's strong arm steadied her.

After an hour of strength sapping climbing, the group finally made it to the plateau and was glad to rest. It was mid-afternoon and the sun was now strong after the storm. Rick and Andy's damp clothes were soon dry. The rest stop was short because Andy needed to push on. Anton could now be left to walk, so Andy stepped out.

Rick and the children followed close behind. By late afternoon, they had reached the point where they could descend to the valley floor and cross the river. Andy and Rick studied the ground below and the river crossings and could see that the bridge was not manned. The roads, however, were busy with heavy military vehicles moving in both directions.

'We need to figure a way of getting across the road without being seen; the river bridge doesn't seem to be a problem if we can get that far. What do you think, Rick?'

'Yep buddy, I agree but I think we may have to wait until sundown, catch a gap in the traffic and cross the road that way.'

'You're right; I think that's our only choice. Although it means we will have to find our way to the farm in the dark and I'm not sure the directions we have are detailed enough for that.' Andy paused 'Okay, let's wait here until dusk and just hope that the German convoys get to where they are going before we need to move.'

The sun started to set and the night closed in when the group edged their way down the hill towards the road that sat in the base of the valley. The road was quieter but not completely free of military traffic. Andy and Rick held on to the children closely, very aware of the danger they may place them in if they were caught in the company of escaped POW's. It was on this realisation that Andy stopped and took Rick to one side.

'I know this may sound like madness but the children would not be stopped if they walked along the road to the bridge. They would be just two kids holding hands on their way home. Why would the Germans want to stop them?'

'A bit risky buddy, they would have no protection. We can't just send them out there having come this far.'

'I know it sounds mad Rick but think about the risks we're putting them under by sneaking around in the dark. If we get involved in a fire fight, they will be in the thick of it.'

'But what about Angel and Tony? Do you think they're going to feel safe walking on their own? I do agree with you that they could possibly be in more danger trying to get to the bridge with us rather than on their own. I just don't like either idea.'

'They may feel safer with us Rick but once we hit that road and have to dive under cover on the riverbank; I'm not sure how safe they'll feel then.'

'Why don't we ask them?' Rick offered.

'Okay. Angel, Tony, we need to ask you something before we go any further.' Andy sat down on the grass and had the two children with him. 'Rick and I have been discussing what to do next because it is going to be very dangerous when we are out in the open, crossing the road and hiding in the riverbank to get to the bridge. We didn't see any German soldiers on the bridge earlier but we don't know whether there are any there now.

The alternative is that you both walk along the road to the bridge with you holding your brother's hand just as if you were going home. Both Rick and I are worried about that but I think it would be less of a risk. How do you feel about it? Do you want to stay with Rick and me or do you want to meet us at the bridge?'

'There is no question Andy, we should walk slowly to the bridge, I don't think we would be stopped. Wouldn't we also be able to warn you if soldiers were there?' Angelique responded in a matter of fact way.

'That's a very good point, Angel because we can't see from here if there are any there. Are we agreed then Rick, that Angel and Anton walk on ahead and meet us at the bridge?'

'Yep I guess so, provided Angel and Anton feel okay about it. What about you, young man?' Rick turned to Anton and picked him up off the ground, 'are you okay to escort your sister to the bridge?'

Angelique translated everything for Anton and he said, 'Yep, yep,' with a chirpy grin on his face. Rick put him down on the ground and tousled his hair.

'You're both very brave kids.'

Andy said, 'Okay. Let's get to it. Angel, when you get to the bridge if there are any guards stay on the right side, we'll be watching from quite close by. Keep on walking until you are out of sight of the bridge and we will find another way of crossing and will find you. You must stay on the road that leads from the bridge. If there are no guards, keep to the left side of the bridge and wait there. Do you understand?'

'Yes, right side if there are guards, left side if no guards.'

'One more thing; Rick and I will get you as close to the road as possible, then you must start walking as naturally as you can. Do not look back. When there is a gap in the traffic, Rick and I will get across the road and onto the riverbank where we will then make our way to the bridge.

We will get there before you and will be able to watch you most of the way but there will be times when we will not be able to see you on the road but do not worry, we will be at the bridge when you get there. Now, are you absolutely sure you and Anton can do what I ask, that you won't be too afraid?'

'Absolutely, we are sure and definitely not afraid, isn't that so, Anton?' She asked her brother in French. He nodded his agreement.

They made their way down the hill towards the road and on getting as close to the road as they could without being seen, Andy indicated to Angelique that she and Anton should make their way on to the roadside. Traffic levels had abated significantly and the two men watched the children walk towards the bridge. Angelique had crossed to the river side of the road and were still in view as a convoy of six German trucks came from the opposite direction.

'Jesus H Christ, she's waving to the krauts,' Rick said.

'Doesn't look like it's a problem, some of them are waving back, we did ask her to act natural.'

'Yeah, I guess so. Shall we join the party?'

Both men raced across the road and dived into the bushes that covered the bank leading down to the river. It was a good decision not to have the children with them as the slope down to the river was steep and the vegetation difficult to negotiate. Headlights flashed above them as another convoy passed by. They scrambled as fast as they could through the shrubbery, keeping as low as possible, pausing every minute or two to see where the children were.

Andy was pleased that they were approaching the bridge and could see it from where he was. Angelique walked confidently whilst holding Anton's hand; Andy's admiration for her grew daily. Rick had moved on a further fifty metres and was watching the children's every step. Angelique entered the bridge and Andy and Rick held their breath as they waited to see which side she would move to.

After a few paces, she moved to the left side and Rick pumped his fist. Both men moved as quickly as they could to catch up with the children. They ran the last few metres to the bridge and quickly joined with the children who were waiting on the other side as planned. Andy picked up Angelique and swung her around; Rick had hoisted Anton on to his shoulders.

'You did a great job and we're very proud of you both, now let's go find Madame Givauche.'

Chapter 15

A short way past the bridge, the group stopped. Andy took this time to tell the group:

'According to the directions Patrice provided, we must get off this road and make our way east along a track for about two hundred metres. When we reach a fork in the track, to the left there will be a statue of the Virgin Mary on the corner and that's the road we must take for another mile-uphill I'm afraid and into the forest. The farm should be visible when we get to the first clearing.'

Turning to Anton, he said, 'Climb aboard, young man.' He lifted the boy onto his shoulders while Rick collected the supply pack and they set off on what they hoped was the final leg of their journey before they could rest in a warm, dry environment and most importantly, get some hot food.

The bright moonlight shone down through a clear sky, which helped Andy see some distance ahead. Neither Andy nor Rick expected such a clear night given what the weather conditions were earlier. This helped Andy step out more positively. Had there been a cloudy, dark night he doubted that he would have found the farm.

The two men and Angelique walked on purposefully whilst Anton sat comfortably on Andy's shoulders. They quickly reached the holy statue at the fork in the track. The icon was shrouded in an elaborate niche that was perched up on a stone plinth and was surrounded by rose shrubs and posies of flower placed there by the locals.

Andy couldn't make out the colours but the scent was strong and beautiful in the night air. They paused at the statue for a short while, not just enjoying the perfumed setting but taking the opportunity to say a silent prayer. Rick blessed himself and addressed the serene, silent figure.

'If anyone can help us get through this, you can.' The group moved on, taking the left fork as directed and started the difficult climb up the hill into the forest. Rick was starting to limp again and he knew that his wound needed cleaning and a new dressing. Blood had seeped through the existing bandage and although it didn't feel infected, it had certainly opened during his scrambling through the bushes at the riverbank.

He didn't want to delay Andy and the children from getting to Madame Givauche and the respite her home could provide. So, he resolved not to say anything at this stage and wait until they reached the farm. The climb into the forest was more difficult than they imagined and they were all extremely tired, particularly Angelique who had never complained but both Rick and Andy could see the strain on the young girl's face. Eventually, she stopped and gasping for breath said, 'I can't go any further, please can we rest?'

'Of course, Angel, we will all have a break, take as much time as you need princess, we're not too far away now.' Andy felt that the summit was quite close and if so, the rest of the journey would be easier but he knew Angelique was almost at the limit of her endurance. Anton went over and sat with his sister, gently and lovingly stroking her hair. Andy and Rick sat together and Andy asked, 'Do you think we're pushing the kids too hard, Rick?'

'They're gutsy kids, Andy and I don't think we could stop what they want to do even if they wanted to crawl on their hands and knees to get there. So, no we're not pushing, they're driving.'

Andy got up to stretch his tired legs and as he did, he knocked Rick's leg slightly in the process. Rick let out a cry, which he tried unsuccessfully to disguise.

'Goddamn it man, if you're not careful, you'll be carrying me as well as Tony.'

'I'm sorry Rick; that was clumsy of me.' Andy was unsurprised. 'You're not as fit as you've been making out, are you!'

'I'm okay buddy, just a bit tender especially when some great hulk in size tens bumps into me,' Rick replied jokingly.

Andy smiled at Rick's stoicism despite his friend's obvious discomfort.

'The first thing we must do when we reach the farm is get that leg seen to. I'll go and see how Angelique is and hopefully, we should be good to go soon.' Andy sauntered over to where Angelique was resting. 'Hi princess, are you feeling any better?' She still looked very tired but had regained some colour to her cheeks.

'I'm better now, thank you and I don't want to hold us up any more; so if you want to carry on, I will be able to keep up.'

'Okay, if you're sure Angel, we'll move out now. Come on young man, you can climb aboard again but as soon we get to the top of the hill, you're on your own feet with your big sister, okay?' After Angelique's translation, Anton agreed and clambered onto Andy's shoulders. 'Rick, are you okay to carry on?' Andy asked, 'Yeah, sure am partner, just lead the way.'

They had been climbing for about twenty minutes when Angelique needed to stop again, she was thoroughly exhausted and sat on the ground crying.

'It's my fault, I'm sorry Rick but I can't go on, I need to rest again.'

Andy, who was totally focussed on the path in front, had continued his climb and hadn't heard Angelique. Rick stopped and put the supply pack down.

'Here's what we're going to do Angel, you're getting onto my shoulders just like your brother is with Andy,' quickly and forcefully he added, 'no arguments young lady, you want to get to Givet, then I guess you don't have a choice, okay?'

She reluctantly agreed and started to climb onto Rick's shoulders. Rick had stooped down to allow her to get on and he knew that the next big test was for him to stand up. Although she was older, thankfully she wasn't very heavy.

'While I am carrying you Angel, can you take the supplies?' Angelique took hold of the backpack, which was now much lighter than when they started out. Rick grimaced as his legs took the strain but he was a determined man and forced himself forward.

Andy reached the top of the hill and gently put Anton down. He looked back to see Rick carrying Angelique and saw that he was struggling.

'Stay here Tony, do you understand?'

'Yep Andy,' he said and sat down with his legs crossed. Andy ran down to help Rick.

'Why didn't you shout for me, are you crazy?'

'You had enough to do getting Tony to the top and anyway, we got this far,' Rick said breathlessly. Andy helped Angelique down off Rick's shoulders who had sank to the ground and asked, 'Can you make it the rest of the way Angel or do you want me to help you?'

'No thank you Andy, I think I can go the rest of the way on my own now.'

'What about you Rick, do you need any help and don't try and josh me.'

Rick struggled to an upright position whilst trying to bravely disguise his difficulty.

'I'll be just fine buddy, let's go.'

They eventually reached the clearing that Patrice had spoken of in his directions and could see the farm buildings ahead of them. There were several outbuildings, some of which were illuminated. Andy said, 'We should carefully approach Rick; we have no idea whether she has any visitors.' As they got to about one hundred metres from the nearest building, a dog barked which made them stop. They edged forward slowly; the dog continued to bark and then suddenly quietened.

'You can come in; the dog will not bite.' A woman's voice announced, 'I've been expecting you, so come quickly, you must be hungry.'

Andy approached and saw a very attractive woman, probably in her late thirties or early forties, who held out her hand in a welcome gesture. Andy grasped her hand, grateful that they had reached what would be sanctuary for the time being.

'My name is Andy and this is Rick. The children are Angelique and Anton,' and after Rick had greeted the woman, the children kissed her on both cheeks and said their greetings in French.

'My name is Madame Givauche, Estelle Givauche, please call me Estelle. I have heard all about you but no doubt you can tell me more; please come, come inside, you must be tired and hungry.'

A fire raged in the hearth, throwing out welcoming warmth throughout the room. The farm was sparsely furnished but clean, the kitchen was typically French with a stone floor and rack upon rack of pots and pans. A large thick wooden table was in the middle of the room, providing an area on which all the preparation took place. The smells of garlic, spices and herbs permeated the air.

'I think the first thing that should be done is for the children to have a nice hot bath, it certainly looks like it is well overdue,' Estelle said in a mildly scolding manner. 'I shall prepare some hot food while they are doing that.

Angelique was overjoyed that she was going to be able to soak in a hot tub whilst Anton displayed some disappointment, as he would rather just sit by the fire. The two children were ushered to the bathroom and were given towels.

'Do you have a change of clothes?' Madame Givauche asked. Angelique said that they did have some but that most of their clothes needed laundering.

'Well, leave that to me Angelique, enjoy your bath and when you are finished, there will some hot food for you.' She left the children and returned to the living room to find Andy removing the bloody dressing from Rick's leg. 'What on earth has happened here?' she exclaimed.

'Rick had a disagreement with a wild boar last week but thankfully the animal came off worse. I think the wound has just opened up and doesn't look like it's infected but it needs cleaning properly.'

'Here, let me look.' Estelle gently wiped away much of the dried blood from around the wound, 'no, it doesn't look infected but it does need some antiseptic and a clean bandage. I'll get some from the kitchen.' She returned after a short time carrying what looked like a doctor's bag. Sitting next to Rick, who was resting his wounded leg on a chair, she said, 'Now let me see what we have to do with this.' She rummaged through the open bag and said as she held up a small dark brown bottle, 'ah, this will do nicely.' Dabbing some of the orange liquid on to a piece of cotton bandage, she swabbed the wound. Rick cried out, 'Jesus H Christ, what the hell is that you've hit me with.'

'Do not blaspheme in my house, monsieur and it is just a little iodine, so stop crying like a baby!' Madame Givauche said sternly. Rick and Andy were in little doubt that Estelle was not to be messed with. She finished dressing Rick's wound, gathered the various medical supplies into the bag and left towards the kitchen. 'I will be preparing some food for you all.'

'Excuse me Estelle,' Andy said sheepishly 'would you have a razor about the house so that we can shave? We haven't shaved since we escaped from the camp nearly two months ago.' The men were indeed looking extremely unkempt.

'I would not advise that you do that; if you are clean shaven, you will attract unnecessary attention, better you leave the beards. There are some scissors that will help you to tidy them up a little.'

The smells coming from the cooking food in the kitchen were delicious, so when Estelle returned with scissors, towels and a bottle of cognac the men were ecstatic. They each were given a large glass of the brandy which they sipped slowly, savouring the warming liquid as it reached their unaccustomed palates.

'I have some room for the children to stay here but you must stay in the outbuilding. There is a room there in the roof space with two beds and washing facilities. It will be safer for you there in case we have a visit from the Germans. We can see them coming up the track, so we have time to hide you away.

There is a small attic that runs off the room and is well concealed, so in the event we are called upon, you must move all of your belongings into the attic and make sure there is no trace of you being there. I will take you over to the rooms after you have eaten. The children won't be a problem if we are visited as they are French and I can say they are just visiting.'

'We are extremely grateful for your help Estelle and we know what danger us being here puts you in, so we will stay only as long as it is necessary,' Andy said.

'I am not afraid Andy; I am past caring about what the Germans can do to me; you may stay as long as you wish. Anyway, from what I am told by the local Resistance, it will not be long before we are rid of the German army from our country for good.' She looked sad, weary and very much like someone who had suffered a great deal. One thing was clear in Rick's mind, something had happened between Estelle and Patrice and he was aching to know what it was.

The children returned from the bathroom, looking clean and refreshed as Estelle summonsed everyone to the kitchen. The table had been laid with Estelle's finest cutlery, dinnerware and there were wine glasses for the adults. A large pot of food sat in the centre of the table alongside a bowl of bread and two bottles of Burgundy.

Madame Givauche's guests were stunned by what appeared to them to be a banquet. She proceeded to ladle out the food, which turned out to be a classic chicken chasseur and each of them plunged into the serving with gusto. They had not eaten any hot food during the two days of their arduous journey and so, they were now more than ready to demolish anything that was put in front of them.

Much of the meal was eaten in silence with everyone focussed on the food. Estelle Givauche, however, watched on with sympathy, especially for the children, they had suffered much, some of which she was aware of. She also had a great admiration for the soldiers who had given up the opportunity to return to their own front lines in order to help the children. During that moment, she reflected on her own life particularly the time in 1940 when the Germans invaded France.

She ate slowly whilst watching her guests, who were totally immersed in the process of eating. She particularly noticed Andy and thought that despite his unkempt appearance, he was quite attractive. Lowering her eyes in embarrassment, she quickly dispelled the idea that she would find another man appealing.

The meal ended and Estelle could see that the children were exhausted and ready for bed.

'Come you two youngsters, it's time you were both in bed, come with me now.' She held out her hand and led the children from the room. Angelique paused at the door and turning to the two soldiers said, 'Thank you Andy, Rick, for everything you have done for us. Goodnight.'

Anton repeated what his sister had said but in French. Estelle guided them to the bedroom where the beds had been freshly made up with clean sheets and warm blankets. She opened a dresser drawer and removed some nightwear. Estelle paused momentarily, holding the garments close to her bosom and with her eyes closed, she gave a large sigh before turning to the children.

'Here is some nightwear for you both, now get changed and hop into bed so that I can tuck you in.' She gave a gown to Angelique and a smaller one to Anton. The children never questioned why the Madame was suddenly able to produce the night attire; they were too tired to bother with questions.

They quickly changed and were eager to get into their warm beds. Estelle settled Anton down first, who was quickly fast asleep. She then turned to Angelique, who was kneeling by her bedside quietly saying a prayer. She let the child finish and said, 'I hope your prayers will be answered, my pretty sweet thing.' Estelle stroked Angelique's hair 'Now you get yourself into bed and sleep well, we will talk in the morning.' It was not long before the young girl was asleep. Estelle stood looking at the sleeping children and said, under her breath, 'God has forsaken many of us in these last few years; I pray that he will not forsake you also.'

Estelle announced that the children were now sleeping and suggested that she show the men where they would be bedding down.

'I suspect that you both will need a good night's rest, so we can leave our conversation until the morning when I'm sure there will be much to discuss.' They walked a short distance from the main building to the outbuilding where Rick and Andy were to sleep. The room had two single beds and a washbasin in the corner, which was situated close to a small room that turned out to be the toilet. Madame Givauche explained, 'This room was available for two workers I used to employ on the farm but they are no longer here so, for the moment it is yours.' She then showed the men a very cleverly concealed door in the wall next to the toilet that led into another small room. There were no windows and it was dark, so they could make out little of what was there.

'You will be able to see it properly tomorrow, in the meantime, while you are here, you must regularly look down the track through that window,' said Estelle, pointing to one of the windows.

'How often have you had visits from the krauts then, Estelle?' Rick asked.

'More than any of us would like but recently not too often. It would seem that they are being kept busy by the Allies who I am told are not far from liberating Paris. I shall bid you goodnight and will get one of the children to call you in the morning if the coast is clear. Goodnight Messieurs.'

They both said, 'goodnight Estelle,' almost in unison as she closed the door behind her. Andy was first to grab the scissors and a towel and went to the washbasin. Rick lay on the bed with his hands behind his head.

'How long do you think we should stay here, Andy?'

'I'm not sure, Rick. We need to make sure that the children are fit to travel and you are too.'

'If the Allies are close to liberating Paris, then it won't be long before they're pushing through here. Why don't we just wait for them?'

'Firstly, we don't know how long that will be; second, we don't know how much resistance the Germans are putting up and therefore, whether the Allies will ever break through and lastly, if the Allies do drive the Nazis east back towards Germany, then you can bet that there will be all hell let loose in this area as the Germans retreat.

If it's the latter, then we need to get out of here before that happens and deliver the kids to their grandparents in Givet. We can then concentrate on getting back to our units. So, friend, can we leave this conversation until tomorrow? I want to clean up and get my head down.'

'No problem big man, I'll do my clean up in the morning.' Rick took off his boots, slipped under the blankets and was asleep in less than a minute. Andy was able to finish trimming his beard and decided that it looked quite smart; he finished with a good wash down and then got into his bed. Both men slept for a full ten hours before the voice of Anton pierced through their unconsciousness to make both men awaken with a start.

'You must come Andy, Rick, petit dejeuner.'

'Ah man, I just want to sleep some more, what is he saying?' Rick sat up and scratched his head. Andy also sat upright.

'I think he's telling us we have to go the farmhouse.'

'Oui, oui come now,' Anton said excitedly.

'Okay, okay, young fella, we're coming, we just need to clean up, so you go back now and tell Madame Givauche that we will be over soon.' Rick said, sort of shooing the boy out of the room. Anton had a vague understanding of what they said, so he left.

Andy remarked, 'you will have to be quick partner or you may miss breakfast.' Rick scrambled out of bed, took the scissors and started to trim the ragged growth that he had acquired since his departure from the German POW camp. Both men eventually felt that they were now presentable and after a good night's sleep, walked over to the farmhouse with renewed energy.

Earlier that morning, Angelique was more alert and thinking clearly after her good night's sleep. Questions formed in her mind about the nightwear she and Anton had been given. The nightgowns were a little small for her and too large for Anton but had clearly belonging to children of a similar age.

So, who did they belong to and why did the Madame have them here if the children were not here to use them? Most odd, she thought. At that moment, Estelle entered the room.

'Good morning, children, I hope you both slept well.'

'Yes, we did, thank you, Madame, I feel much better now,' Angelique said and decided to ask, 'this nightgown is very pretty Madame, who does it belong to?'

Estelle Givauche's face darkened and then quickly softened.

'Well Angelique, I don't really like to speak of it but it belonged to my daughter who unfortunately is no longer with us. She and her younger brother died shortly after the war started. They were very much like you but a bit younger.'

'I'm so sorry Madame, what happened to them?'

'I don't wish to talk about it, Angelique,' Estelle said sharply. 'Now get yourselves washed and dressed and come down for breakfast.'

Angelique was devastated by the thought that she had upset her host.

'I am very sorry if I have upset you Madame, I didn't mean to pry.'

Madam Givauche sat at Angelique's side and put an arm around her.

'You haven't upset me my child, I just find the memories very painful and I know that you too have been terribly hurt by this horrible war. Perhaps before you leave, I will tell you what happened to my children.'

'Really Madame Givauche, it is not necessary. I should not have asked.'

'We shall see my child, we shall see. In the meantime, you should both get yourselves ready for breakfast.' Madame Givauche got up and left the children to wash and dress. She had laid out the table with an array of breads and croissants, various jams and butter and a steaming jug of coffee.

The children were the first to arrive and the Madame asked Anton to go and tell the soldiers that breakfast was ready. She showed him which building he should go to and directed him out of the door saying:

'Hurry now, the coffee will be cold.'

'Good morning gentlemen, I trust you slept well,' Estelle said as the two men entered the farmhouse. The children were already feasting on the delicious homemade jam spread thickly on the fresh bread and only gave a cursory "good morning" to Andy and Rick. It was Estelle who commented first on the soldier's new and tidy appearance.

'My word that rest has done you both the world of good and I also see that the scissors were not wasted. Please come in and sit down.' Andy, she noted, was indeed even more attractive than she first thought and once again was quick to suppress the notion.

Following the breakfast, Estelle suggested that the children could help with some of the farm chores and they were delighted by the idea.

'Andy and Rick can also come with us and see what we do but I would suggest that you both keep one eye on the road leading up here in case there are visitors.'

For the rest of the day, the children fed chickens, milked the goat and generally had fun playing with the sheep and other farm animals. They were particularly amused when Madame Givauche insisted that Andy and Rick should bring in the two cows from the field for milking. Their amusement centred on the comical shenanigans by the men trying to get the cows to go in the direction required.

Of course Andy and Rick largely exaggerated their difficulties for the benefit of the children. Anton picked up a piece of charcoal and in the open space in the yard, he drew a hopscotch map on the ground. He shouted to Rick who was still recovering from chasing the cows.

'Rick, Rick, Marelle, you can play?'

Angelique interrupted, 'no Anton, Rick has a sore leg and you must let him rest. Play tomorrow perhaps.'

Rick had indeed expended more energy than he should have and was feeling it, so he was glad of Angelique's intervention.

As evening fell, Estelle retired to the kitchen to prepare an evening meal with the help of Angelique and Anton, while Andy and Rick decided to explore the safe room in the outbuilding. They also wanted to get a good look at the surrounding area before it became too dark in the event that they had to get away quickly.

Once again the evening meal was delicious, warming and gratefully received. Angelique and Anton were quick to be excused, so that they could go to bed, the fresh air and the activities around the farm had made them extremely tired. After the goodnights were exchanged, Andy and Rick settled down in front of the fire with a fresh bottle of Estelle's Burgundy and had almost finished it by the time Estelle had returned from seeing the children into their beds.

Andy stood up as Estelle entered the room.

'I hope you don't mind us drinking your wine Estelle, it's a long time since we were able to relax like this.' Whether it was the wine and relaxed atmosphere or not, he was finding his thoughts being frequently directed towards Estelle whom he found quite an appealing woman.

Rick nodded his agreement as he gulped down another mouthful and added, 'Why don't you sit and join us, Ma'am?'

'Yes I will join you, I don't have much company here nowadays, so it will be a welcome change and perhaps you can tell me all about your adventures since escaping from the Germans.'

The night passed quickly with the aid of several bottles of wine and Rick and Andy's detailed account of their journey from a German POW camp through Luxembourg and into France and the meeting with the children. Estelle was engrossed by the story and in particular, by their account of the children's horrendous experiences.

'My God,' she said, 'does this war not spare anyone, not even young children?' She got up wearily and said, 'Goodnight gentlemen, I will see you in the morning.'

Andy's eyes followed Estelle out of the room and he thought that if he were here for a longer period of time, he would like to get to know her better.

Chapter 16

Several days passed by with the children enjoying the relative freedom of the farm. Rick's leg wound had healed nicely and he was fit enough now to compete in a hopscotch marathon with Anton, who laughed heartily every time Rick lost his balance or stepped on a line. Andy looked on with sadness, remembering his own children's joy when he and they played. Estelle had noticed Andy's apparent discomfort around the children as they played the game. She decided to wait for an opportune moment to ask what it was that troubled him.

The war seemed a long way away from what was an idyllic setting in the beautiful Ardennes but occasionally, they could hear the rumble of artillery guns, the drone of aircraft high in the sky and could see the constant stream of military vehicles on the road below. The children, for the moment, seemed to ignore these reminders but for Andy, they were constant indicators of why he was here and why he needed to leave soon.

Andy wore a troubled frown, so Estelle suggested, 'Walk with me Andy and let us talk a little while Rick and the children play.' Andy hadn't registered that Estelle had spoken; his thoughts were distant and intense. 'Andy, are you okay?'

'Yes, I'm fine,' he said shaking his head apologetically. 'I'm sorry Estelle. I was thinking about other things, what was it you asked?'

She smiled sympathetically.

'Would you care to walk with me while the children are playing?'

'Yes, that would be nice, thank you.' The couple set off in the direction of a large clearing to the north of the farm. A slight hill led to a ridge that overlooked the valley and river below and the pair sat on the grassy hilltop in silence for quite some time as Andy marvelled at the view.

'This is truly remarkable Estelle, especially when we consider what is happening in the wider world. Apart from what we can hear in the distance, it is very peaceful. It's just extremely sad that children have to grow up in this environment and then have to rebuild what has been destroyed.'

'Yes it is sad, Andy but I cry out for the children who are no longer here and cannot enjoy a future peaceful world.' Andy was suddenly reminded of his own children and how right Estelle was that all this fighting would be in vain; for them at least. The pain he felt was etched in his face and Estelle could see that he was deeply disturbed.

'What is it Andy, have I said something to upset you?'

'No Estelle, please do not think that; it is another matter that our conversation reminds me of that saddens me.' Andy felt comfortable and at ease with Estelle and decided he would tell her what had happened. 'During a German bombing raid on London in 1940, my wife and two children were killed.' Andy swallowed hard and continued falteringly.

'It was my fault that they died,' he fumbled for his words and was now struggling to contain his emotions. 'I should have been there to make sure that they were evacuated out of London and I wasn't, it was my fault.'

Estelle suddenly looked very tearful and bowed her head to avoid exposing the sadness flowing from her eyes. Andy was taken aback.

'I'm so sorry Estelle, I didn't realise my story would distress you so much, I'm sorry; it was very selfish of me.' He put a comforting arm around her shoulder and she wept uncontrollably. Eventually, her sobs subsided and she looked up at Andy.

'It wasn't your story Andy, I have also lost those close to me and when you mentioned your children, I remembered burying my own.'

Andy couldn't take in what she was saying.

'I'm so sorry Estelle, here am I acting as though I'm the only one in the world who has to deal with a terrible tragedy. Tell me please, what happened?'

Estelle had regained her composure.

'My husband was killed fighting the Germans when they invaded in 1940 and then two years later, my children died in a terrible accident. For the last two years, I've tried very hard to shut it all out.'

Andy was distraught.

'And I have brought it all back, how could I have been so thoughtless?'

Estelle smiled at him reassuringly.

'You were not to know, Andy and anyway it may have done us both some good to talk about the catastrophe in our lives. I think we have both tried to shut it away.'

The pair sat in silence for quite some time until Estelle asked, 'How old were your children?'

'Kate was just eight years old and Charlie was six. They were lovely kids and loved playing hopscotch, which is why I find it difficult to watch Anton play the game. How about you, how old were they?'

'I had two children also, a boy, Eric who was seven and a girl, Anais who was four. They were beautiful and after my husband died, they were my life. Only Patrice kept me from falling into the depths of despair and has been magnificent in providing the support I needed.

'He encouraged me to keep the farm going even though I was alone. But even then, especially at night when I had time to think, I could feel the whole thing crushing the life out of me. That was when I started to get involved with the Resistance and that kept me very occupied after each day when I finished my farm work.'

Andy assumed that Estelle's children had been killed in some sort of farm accident and did not want to pursue it further, so decided not to ask. At that point, Rick approached.

'Hello folks, enjoying the scenery? It sure is beautiful up here, Ma'am.' He sat down beside Andy and hadn't noticed the reddening of Estelle's eyes that followed her crying. Nor did he notice the lines of sadness in Andy's face that were deeper, more intense than before. 'The children have decided to do a little exploring, so they've gone off towards that ridge on the other side of the hill. I've told them to be back before dark.'

Estelle jumped up sharply.

'Which ridge?' she shouted, 'which ridge and how long have they been gone?'

'Whoa there Ma'am, they have only gone for a walk, they need to exercise their legs and have a bit fun. It's no big deal.'

'Never mind no big deal Monsieur, which way did they go and how long have they been gone?' She shouted at him with an intense urgency in her voice.

Rick could see the seriousness in Estelle's eyes and knew it was best to do as he was told. Pointing in the direction of the ridge he said, 'They've been gone about an hour.'

The colour drained from Estelle's face.

'Oh my God, not again, please God not again, come, we must find them quickly and let us hope we're not too late.'

The three of them set off together. Andy asked, 'Just what is the trouble at that ridge Estelle, what do you know about it? We need to know if we have to do anything.'

'Yes, of course,' Estelle stopped and gathered her breath before she replied, 'there is a large cave there which is or at least should be boarded up. Inside the cave, there are a number of paths through and down into the cave floor. The danger is a huge sump hole that is always full of water and it cannot be seen unless the cavers have torches. If anyone falls into the sump, it is virtually impossible to get out without assistance.'

Andy interrupted, 'your children?'

Estelle just nodded her head, 'one of you must go to the farm and collect rope and torches. Quickly now.'

Rick was puzzled but could sense the urgency and volunteered, 'I'll go, I've seen rope and torches in the workshop next to the barn. I hope you find the kids and we don't need any of the stuff that I bring back.'

'So do I Rick, so do I. Now hurry, please.' Estelle was agitated.

Rick ran off to the farm whilst Andy and Estelle walked briskly in the direction that Rick had indicated, although it was clear that Estelle knew exactly where she was going.

'Is that what happened, Estelle? Did your children fall into the sump?' Andy asked.

'Yes. They had been missing for three days when Patrice found them. Since then, the entrance has been boarded up but in two years, it's possible that the boards have been disturbed. I cannot let this happen again, Andy.'

'The children may not be in there, Estelle and could just be wandering around in the woods. And if they have gone into the cave, then we will get them out faster than they went in, I promise.'

The pair walked on purposefully until they reached a large rock face that contained the cave entrance and as thought, it had been boarded up. However, one of the boards had been moved to one side which, disturbingly for Andy and Estelle, left a sufficient gap for a child to slip through. Rick approached, carrying Anton on his shoulders and the equipment he had collected. Breathlessly, he said, 'Any sign of Angelique? I found this little fella wandering around on the way up. He was saying something about his sister but I couldn't make what it was.'

Estelle asked Anton some questions in French and the boy responded excitedly. She translated, 'He says that they decided to play hide and seek and he hid behind the rocks but he got tired of waiting and came out from his hiding place but couldn't see Angelique anywhere. He says he looked all around and got frightened but he sat for a while waiting for her to come back and that was when Rick found him.'

'Is this the cave you spoke of?' Rick asked, pointing to the cave entrance.

'Yes, this is the cave entrance and we initially thought they may have crawled through the gap but now with Anton being here, I'm not sure,' Andy said with a sense of urgency in his voice. 'Maybe she came up here and thought Anton had gone in to hide and followed him to bring him out. Now, we can either spend more time looking around the area or we can go in.'

Estelle said, with anguish in her voice.

'If she has gone inside, there is a grave danger she has fallen into the sump. You cannot delay, it will be cold and very deep; she will not be able to survive there long. Please, please go in and find her, I will look after Anton.'

'You're right Estelle, we cannot delay; Rick and I will find her if she's in there. Okay buddy, you ready?' Rick had already started to tear at the remaining entrance boards and had prised off enough of them to allow the men to enter the cave. Andy stepped inside and shouted, 'Angel, are you in here?' He shouted out once more. The men paused and listened for a sound, any sound but there was none.

Estelle said, 'the cave is very deep with lots of different pathways, if she has gone too far, she will not hear you. Please hurry, find her before it is too late.'

'Don't worry Estelle, we will find her if she is in there. We'll be back soon.' The two men stepped into the cave, each carrying a length of rope and a torch. It wasn't long before any light from the entrance had diminished and the torches were necessary.

Rick took turns with Andy to shout out Angelique's name as they carefully made their way along the tunnels. They approached a point where the path split into two; they stopped, shouted again and waited for a response.

****

Two hours earlier.

Rick had had enough of the Marelle game as he had learned to call it and wanted a break.

'Okay, you guys,' he said, 'I'm going to rest awhile, what do you want to do now?'

'We're going to go for a walk, aren't we Anton?' Angelique said in French then repeated it in English.

'That's fine by me but don't go too far, okay.' Angelique agreed and the two children walked off holding hands. Rick noted the direction they were heading, which was up the hill towards the high ridge and decided he would stretch out and enjoy the afternoon sunshine. It was not long before he nodded off.

Anton decided that just walking was boring.

'Let's play hide and seek, Angelique.'

'No, we must stay together because you might get lost.'

'Oh please, let's play, I will hide first and you count, please, please, I won't go far away, I promise.' Angelique couldn't ignore her brother's persistence.

'Alright but you must not go too far away, so I am only going to count to ten.' She turned her back, 'off you go then, I'm going to start counting now; one, two, three, four,' She got to the count of ten and turned around. She figured that he couldn't have got far in ten seconds, so studied the potential hiding places within that range and fortunately there were not many. She looked behind a small thicket of shrubs that were close by and there he was huddled up in a ball, making himself as small as possible. She crept closer and shouted, 'found you.'

Anton squealed and giggled but then said, 'That wasn't fair, you didn't give me enough time to hide properly, let's do it again and this time you must count to twenty.'

Angelique paused to consider whether she should or not then reluctantly agreed, 'Alright, little brother but just this one more time. I shall turn away and start counting now, one, two, three,' She got to twenty and realised it was far longer than she anticipated, so was a little concerned that Anton may have gone too far.

Anton ran as fast as his little legs could carry him towards a rocky outcrop. Although Angelique had finished counting, Anton knew he was hidden from her view, so carried on further up the hill and concealed by the large cluster of rocks. He hid behind one of the boulders and waited. The warmth of the sun and the amount of energy he had expended through the day made him feel quite tired and as he waited for his sister to discover his hiding place, he fell asleep.

Angelique considered where he might have gone and took note of the ground around her. There were many places he could have got to in twenty seconds but now the range of options facing her was significantly greater.

She searched behind collections of shrubs, looked behind boulders and realised she was getting close to what she considered the limit of how far he could go in the time allowed. She didn't know that she had now travelled in the opposite direction to where he actually was and had no chance of discovering his hiding place.

'Alright, Anton, that's enough, you win, so come out now.' She shouted. There was no response. 'That's enough Anton, I shall get very angry if you do not come out immediately.' She was infuriated that he was being so disobedient and selfish. He must know he was worrying her, she thought. Looking around, she could see the rock face a short distance away and could see the boarded up entrance to the cave.

'Oh my God, I hope he hasn't gone in there.' She ran as fast as she could and hoped that the entrance was secure but alas, her heart sank when she saw that one of the boards had been loosened and that there was certainly enough room for Anton to clamber through. She pushed the loosened board to one side and shouted, 'Anton, come out of there this instant, I am very angry with you but I promise I will stop being angry if you come out straight away, I promise.' She waited for what seemed like an eternity for an answer or for Anton to show his face; he did neither and now she was extremely worried. Angelique stood up and visually searched the area as far as the eyes could see before she took her next steps.

Edging the loose board to one side once again, she stooped and slipped into the cave. It was very dark once she had proceeded inside for a few strides and it was eerily quiet. She shouted Anton's name again and again but to no avail. It was now pitch black and each step she took was taken with trepidation.

Using the walls for guidance and support, she edged forward continuing to shout out her brother's name. She was beginning to believe that Anton had not entered the cave after all and was thankful if that was the case but she still had to find him.

I should go back to the farm and tell Andy and Rick; they can help me find him, she thought. On taking another step to turn around, the wall that she was using for support disappeared from her grip suddenly and she lost her balance. Her feet went from underneath her and she found herself sliding on her back down a steep incline, to where she had no idea and not knowing how far she would fall was what frightened her most.

The air was now much colder as she made her involuntary descent and although it was only a matter of seconds that she was not in control, it felt that it was never ending. The splash of water was the first sensation she felt and then the cold and then being completely submerged. The water was deep and she struggled to get back to the surface, gasping for breath as she reached above the water for something to hold on to.

Angelique managed to swim to the wall edge but it was sheer with nothing to grip. The water was incredibly cold and breathing was difficult. She pushed off the wall and swam to the other side, although at this stage she didn't know whether there was another side. Nevertheless, she knew she had to get out of the cold water soon because moving her legs and arms was now becoming more difficult.

As her breathing became more laboured, she pushed herself harder to get to the other wall and after a great struggle, touched a solid wall. She reached for something to hold on to and could put her hands on what appeared to be a ledge. Angelique had no idea whether it was large enough for her to get on to and out of the water but, using both hands she used what strength she had left and tried to raise herself up.

At the first attempt, she slipped back into the water and now the coldness of the water was crushing her lungs; breathing was now painful; her strength was failing.

'I must do this for Anton,' she said to herself as she surfaced again. She grabbed the ledge and held on for a time, gathering her strength before making another attempt. Angelique breathed in deeply, overcoming the pain and tightness in her chest and she then, whilst holding the ledge, pushed herself under the water and using the momentum of upward motion through the water, she was able to reach the ledge and sit sideways on it.

The ledge was indeed big enough for her to get her legs completely out of the water but it was just a ledge and not a path to safety. For now, she could rest and recover her strength, although she was unaware that she was in great danger of hypothermia and she would need to get warm sooner rather than later.

Angelique was feeling very tired after her exertions and the extreme cold, consequently, could hardly keep her eyes open. Her senses were now blurred as hypothermia started to take hold.

****

The present.

Andy and Rick had reached the fork in the tunnel and were deciding whether to split up or try one tunnel at a time. Andy said, 'I think we should try the right side first; I don't think the sump will be too far away in either passageway. So, let's rope ourselves together, we don't want either of us to end up in the hole.' Rick agreed and they took one of the ropes and tied each end around their waists. They walked on tentatively with Andy leading the way and noted that the walkway became narrower as they proceeded. Andy stopped and saw the steep falling away of the footpath and could see the shiny rock face that acted as a slide directly into the sump.

'Angelique, Angelique, are you there, can you hear me? Let's use both torches, Rick to scan the waterhole.'

'Let's hope she's not in here Andy, it's bloody freezing and no one could survive long in it.'

Andy interrupted, 'look, Rick, over there, is that her?' The torchlight had picked up the motionless body of Angelique laying on the ledge.

'You're damned right it is Andy, it is. Angelique, Angelique,' he shouted as loud as he could. Both men were shouting and Angelique stirred.

'Don't move princess, I'm coming for you,' Rick said. 'I will go as far as I can using this narrow ledge that Angelique must have missed, it will get me closer to her.'

'When you get to her Rick, tie the rope around both of you and I will haul you out of the water as quick as I can. Go get her, buddy.'

Not wanting to be weighted down, Rick took off his boots then he removed his shirt and jacket before skirting the waterhole using the thin ledge but it could not get him close enough to the girl, so at some point he would have to go into the water. That time was now and he plunged into the icy water.

'Jesus H Christ, it's cold,' he shouted as he swam towards Angelique, who was desperately trying to sit upright. He reached the ledge, 'are you okay Angel, we're going to get out of here, so I want you to take this rope and tie it around your waist. Can you do that?'

She nodded weakly as she took the rope end from Rick and tied it around her waist. Rick now had to persuade Angelique to get back in the water. He shouted to Andy.

'It's damned cold Andy; as soon as she hits the water, pull like hell and get her out of here. I'll make my own way over, just leave a torch on, so that I can see the pathway that I took coming in here.'

'We agreed for the two of you to come across together.' Andy shouted back.

'It'll be too slow, we need to get her out of here fast, buddy, just do it man, I'll be okay.' Rick didn't get any argument so he continued. 'Right Angel, you're going to have to get back into the water, don't worry I will lower you down slowly, so that you don't go fully under but you must hold on to the rope with both hands because Andy is going to pull you over to him very quickly. You ready?'

Shivering violently, Angelique nodded her head. Rick lowered her gently into the water and shouted, 'Go Andy, go.'

Andy had already taken up the slack on the rope and hauled Angelique towards him through the water. The wave of water washed over his feet as Angelique was propelled through the waterhole. Andy saw her as she got to the edge and lifted her out. She was only semi-conscious at this stage and looked in a serious condition. He took the rope off her waist and lifted her into arms shouting back to his friend.

'Rick, are you okay?'

'I'm alright, just get her out of here into the warm sunshine, I'm right behind you.' Rick was almost halfway across but feeling the effects of the icy water.

Andy had taken his shirt and jacket off and wrapped them around Angelique as he carried her out of the cave.

'I've left your dry clothes for you when you get out of the water, don't stay in there too long, friend,' he shouted back as he hurried away.

Estelle had waited with severe foreboding and apprehension as Andy appeared with Angelique held limply in his arms.

'We must get the wet clothes off her, Estelle and get her into the warmth. I must go back and help Rick.'

'Oh, the poor child, quickly give her to me. I will see to her.' Estelle had already taken hold of Angelique and started to remove the saturated dress. 'Andy, you go back and help Rick; I and Anton will get her back to the farm.'

She then spoke in French. 'Anton, as I am carrying Angelique, you must rub your sister's legs to get her warm, can you do that?'

'Yes Madame,' Anton replied and immediately tried to do what he had been asked but Estelle had already started moving quickly down the hill and he was having difficulty keeping up. Estelle knew that time was of the essence.

Andy in the meantime had returned to the cave and was worried that Rick had not yet appeared. He shouted, 'Rick, you okay?' and then on reaching the waterhole, he found Rick sat on the edge, vigorously rubbing his legs.

'Can't feel my legs man, so can't stand; have to get the circulation back. How's Angel, she okay?' Rick was shivering severely and finding it difficult to speak coherently.

'Estelle has got her and taking her back to the farm, I think she is going to be fine. But now we have to get you out of here. Can you feel anything in your feet or legs yet?'

'I think so,' Rick said as he struggled to his knees and then tried to stand but failed.

'Put your arm around my neck Rick, I'll support your weight,' Andy said and stooped to help his friend. Rick eventually got to his feet and with Andy's help started to make a move.

'Let's get the hell out of here.' He said as he clung on to Andy.

In the meantime, Estelle had reached the farm, having stopped several times to rest. The sun was shining and it was a very warm afternoon, which helped Angelique but she needed a warm bed and warm clothes. Her first priority was to get the child a hot drink because she would need warming from the inside as well as the outside. She was so thankful that her own tragedy had not been repeated.

By the time the men returned, Angelique had been tucked up in a warm bed and was sleeping soundly. Colour had returned to her face and the shivering had stopped and so what she now needed most of all was plenty of rest.

Rick was now walking unaided and the wet clothes and boots were gathered up by Estelle, who thrust a hot cup of freshly made coffee in the men's hands. They were thankful that Angelique appeared to be recovering and so stretched out in front of a raging fire, relaxed in the knowledge that everything was now alright.

Chapter 17

The following three days passed by slowly for Andy as he watched Angelique slowly recover. After nearly two days of almost continuous sleep, disturbed only by the bowls of hot broth served up by Estelle, she brightened up and by the next day was almost back to her normal chirpy self. He was very relieved that she appeared to be fully recovered although initially they were all very worried about her condition.

Andy looked out beyond the farm and decided he would walk for a while to clear his thinking. For the first time, he did not have a clear plan in his head mainly because of the uncertainty around his assumptions about the direction the war was taking. He thought that the Allies were probably pushing on from the west and north and the Germans were being forced back to the east towards Germany.

If he was right, then his little group of travellers may well get caught up in the German withdrawal. His instinct told him that they should move out sooner rather than later. Looking back at the farm, he could see Estelle talking to Rick, so he stood for a while and watched. His eyes were especially focussed on Estelle, who he had grown fond of; although he had made every effort to disguise his admiration.

He realised that his feelings for her were getting stronger because each time he saw her, he felt a warm sensation inside. It was a strange feeling for him as this was the first time since he lost his wife that he felt any sort of emotion for another woman. Could it be that it was just this crazy war distorting everything; was the high risk of being killed causing a surge in emotion and a need to find someone to cling on to? He asked himself these questions before walking on.

Estelle's eyes strayed towards Andy who was walking up towards a viewing spot overlooking the valley and thought how odd it was that she should feel attracted to him. She immediately dismissed those thoughts and turned to ask Rick if he would ensure that the cave entrance was secure again.

She was petrified that another accident could happen. He agreed and couldn't help noticing how she almost forgot that she was talking to him. He noted the direction of her gaze and thought he might mention to his friend that he appears to have an admirer. For the moment, he would concentrate on the task he had been given and elected to take Anton with him and thought the boy might feel more involved, after all the attention that had been heaped on Angelique in the last few days.

'Would you like to come with me and help carry some tools, Tony?'

'Yes, yes,' he shouted excitedly in French. 'Now that my sister is better, I can leave her for a little while,' he said in a very grown up manner, ostensibly taking on the mantle of the grown up protective brother. Not understanding anything the boy had said, Rick assumed he said yes.

Rick gathered a couple of planks of wood, hammer, nails and a pair of pliers, some white paint and a brush. He passed the paintbrush and nails to Anton.

'Look after those nails for me Tony, they are very important for us to complete this job, okay?'

Anton nodded his acknowledgement and grasped the package of nails tightly, adopting a very serious and determined look that amused Rick who played along by also putting on a look of seriousness as they set off to the cave. It wasn't long before Rick needed to hoist young Anton onto his shoulders but then had to juggle the materials as well. Anton joyfully accepted the lift but continued to grasp his parcel of nails with passion; they were his responsibility.

They approached the cave entrance and Rick was able to assess quite quickly what would be required to seal it off securely.

'Okay big fella; let's get this show on the road.' Rick lowered Anton to the ground and placed the tools and equipment where he was to use them. In less than thirty minutes, Rick had hammered into place the existing wooden slats that were loose from recent visits and attached extra boards to the large wooden stanchions at each side of the entrance. Anton stood by his side, diligently holding the pack of nails, passing him one at a time and making ready with the next.

'Now, we must paint our sign on the wood to tell people it is dangerous, how do you say dangerous in French?' Anton adopted a puzzled look, having not understood a word of what Rick said. 'I guess you don't know what the heck I'm saying, eh young fella. Okay, I guess I'll have to improvise.' He dipped the paintbrush into the paint pot and started to sketch out a skull and crossbones. As soon as the picture became recognisable, Anton shouted excitedly.

'Dangereux, dangereux.' He drew the word with his finger in the dusty earth in front of the cave entrance. Rick looked closely at Anton's drawing and then pronounced the word exactly as it was spelt. Anton laughed at Rick's comical attempts at a French accent.

'Okay, okay I get the picture,' Rick said 'I'll paint the word right here,' he said pointing to a space below his skull and crossbones. Taking great care, he completed the task and then stood back to admire his artistry. Anton mimicked Rick and stood with his hands on his hips, nodding his head approvingly. 'You think it is okay then, Tony?' Rick held his thumbs up, waiting for Anton to respond.

'It good goddamn it,' Anton replied in his faltering English. Rick gave him an admonishing look.

'No more cussing from you young man, capishe?' Rick said wagging his finger. 'Come on, hop on and we'll head on back.' Rick lifted the boy who chuckled as he hoisted him onto his shoulders, picked up the tools and made his way down the hill to the farm.

Andy had found a spot to sit overlooking the valley and closed his eyes momentarily when Estelle approached.

'I hope I'm not disturbing you Andy; do you mind if I join you?'

'No, not at all Estelle, in fact I'm glad of some company. Perhaps you can help me get my thinking straight.'

'What is troubling you, Andy?'

Andy turned onto his side and facing his companion, leaned onto his elbow.

'I have a dilemma, Estelle between staying here and waiting for the Allies to come through or moving on to Givet. If I choose the stay here option, I have no idea how long it may take for the Allies to reach us nor whether we'll get caught up in the German withdrawal, which could be very nasty if they are having to fight for every inch of ground.

The other option would mean moving out almost immediately, so that we stay east of the fighting as we travel north. I don't know how long it will be before the Germans reach this part of the country or whether Angelique is fit enough to make the journey. So Estelle, basically, I just don't have an answer right now.'

'I understand,' Estelle replied, 'it cannot be easy when you have the children to consider. If I can offer my advice, Angelique may be fully recovered and sufficiently fit very soon now but I also think that the Germans are some weeks away. As far as I know, they are still fighting in Paris.

I think we'll still see some of the high ranking officer's running back to their rear lines, so there may be some activity in this location but I hope Patrice and his men will make it very difficult for them. So, my considered view is that as soon as Angelique is fit, then you should go north.'

'Thank you Estelle, I appreciate your advice and I think you're right; we should head out as soon as Angelique is well enough. What about you, are you going to be okay after we've gone?' There was genuine concern in Andy's voice.

'Yes, I'll be fine, I've spent the last four years more or less on my own; I've got used to it now. I will continue managing the farm and helping Patrice and his men when they need me. They sometimes have to come to me to hide or they need some medical attention.'

'If I may say so, I think you're a very brave lady.'

'I'm not brave Andy, its Patrice's men who are the heroes, I just do what I do to forget. But at least helping them gives me purpose.'

He wondered about the relationship between Patrice and Estelle.

'Have you known Patrice long?'

'All my life, he's my brother.'

'Oh, I see, it's just that we got the impression that Patrice wanted to avoid talking about you except to say that he wished you well and Rick thought he was very sad about that. I'm sorry I'm prying.'

'Patrice was the one that found my children and recovered them from the cave, so it pains him deeply to remember.'

Andy looked into Estelle's eyes and could see immense pain and sadness. He leaned over and kissed her on the cheek.

'I'm sorry,' he said, 'I shouldn't have done that.'

Estelle flushed slightly and touched the side of her face where he had planted the kiss. Holding her hand there momentarily she said, 'That's alright Andy, it was a pleasant surprise but why?'

'Apart from believing you to be an exceptional woman, I wanted to let you know that I admire you greatly and that was my ham fisted way of telling you— no; admire is the wrong word, although I really do admire you,' Andy was starting to get flustered and uncomfortable, 'what I'm trying to say is that ever since I first saw you, I felt something, something I hadn't felt for a long time. So there, it's out and I know I'm being overfamiliar and it's improper of me to assume that—'

Estelle put her fingers to Andy's lips to silence his awkwardness and kissed him fully on the mouth, a gentle yet eloquent kiss. Andy responded but neither of them expected passion because it wasn't about passion but about fulfilling a need for love and the gentle embrace that both had missed and almost forgotten during the horror of this war.

Andy and Estelle held on to each other in a warm embrace and were immersed in the moment that neither wanted to end. They eventually parted and sat side by side, each lost in their own thoughts. Estelle broke into the silence.

'As much as I would like this to be Andy, I'm sorry but this cannot possibly work? After you leave here, you will find a new life and forget about me.'

'I will not forget you, Estelle because I truly believe my feelings for you and I don't think it's just a passing moment or an opportunity to find some brief respite from the situation we're in. No, we can get to know each other a little better I know but there is time for that.'

'No Andy, there isn't time for that I'm afraid, you will leave here soon and then you will go back to your unit to carry on fighting the war and then back to England, where I'm sure you will find someone there to start your life again. And me, I don't want to leave this place, this is the place where my children are buried and I cannot leave them.'

'Perhaps I can come back when this war is over and we can start again where we leave off here. No commitment necessary, I'm sure you will find someone else in the meantime anyway and I would respect that. But just in case, I would like us to agree to meet again when the war is over, do we have a deal?' Andy had totally convinced himself that he could never find another like Estelle and was pleased to see the warm smile on Estelle's face.

'Okay, we have a deal,' she said with a disbelieving glint in her eye. They kissed and embraced each other once more before slowly making their way back to the farm. On the face of it, a love had blossomed in a twinkling of an eye and may have appeared, in normal circumstances, surprising, yet that was the nature of war; there was no normal; emotions were always running on the surface; fear, hope, sadness and love; all could manifest themselves in an instant-there was never time to dilly dally.

That evening at the dinner table, Rick noticed a distinct difference in Andy's demeanour. He couldn't quite put his finger on it but it was certainly different to yesterday but then he saw it; Andy glanced at Estelle and she looked straight at Andy; there was a warmth and glow in their eyes that he hadn't seen before. *Well, I'll be doggone*, Rick thought.

'What's the plan now, Andy?' Rick then asked mischievously.

Andy found it difficult to break his gaze away from Estelle.

'It's the same as it's always been Rick, as soon as Angel is fit, we will go. Why do you ask?'

'Oh, just wondering whether you might want to stay here a bit longer,' Rick replied with an amused, knowing tone to his voice.

Both Andy and Estelle reddened a little on the realisation that Rick had been very perceptive and had guessed their newfound relationship.

Andy replied uncomfortably, 'there's no change in plans Rick, we'll go as soon as we're ready. When we've finished eating, you and I should discuss the options we have regarding the route we should take.' Rick nodded his agreement and winked playfully.

Following dinner, Estelle and the children cleared the table whilst Andy nodded to Rick to follow him outside.

Rick was bursting to know what had happened between his friend and Estelle.

'Okay you old dog, what goes with you and Estelle?'

'She's a wonderful and brave woman Rick and I'm very fond of her and I think she thinks the same of me. When this goddamn war is over, I'm coming back here, I know it.'

'Wow, it's that serious man, are you sure?'

'Yes I'm sure Rick, never been surer of anything in my life.'

'Well, goddamn it buddy, I'm really pleased for you. But what about the plan to get to Givet? You can't leave here now surely?'

'No, Rick we will carry on as planned. Estelle and I have agreed that as soon as Angel is fit to go, then we go to. If what we have found between us is real, then it will last until I return.'

'Whoa there, just hold on friend, what about Patrice, I'm sure there was something going on there?'

Andy smiled and explained the situation with Patrice and Estelle.

'Shoot,' Rick whistled 'he's her brother. That must have been tough pulling those kids out of that cave. I can't imagine what they must have gone through. Shit man, as if this war isn't enough.'

The two men returned to the farmhouse where Estelle had just finished seeing the children to their beds.

'Would you like a glass of wine, gentlemen?' she asked.

Wine arrived and the three of them sat in silence enjoying the peacefulness of the evening even though the rumble of artillery fire could be heard in the distance. Rick broke the relative silence.

'Why don't you two take a walk in the warm evening air and let me finish off this bottle in front of the fire?' There was a glint in his eye but both Estelle and Andy were fully aware of Rick's motive but they gratefully grasped the opportunity.

Outside, the sky was clear and speckled with glistening stars; the smell of pine wafted the air and apart from the rumbling in the distance, one would never guess they were in the middle of a war. Andy and Estelle walked side by side and reached a wooden bench that overlooked the valley. They sat down Andy put his arm around her and she snuggled her head into his broad shoulder.

The warmth and security of each other was all that they wanted and they stayed quietly in the warmth of the night air for nearly an hour. The innocence of their relationship was beyond question. They had found solace away from the horrors they had both experienced and it enabled them both to realise that there was still beauty, warmth and kindness in this world where up until now, they had only experienced ugliness, terror and hostility.

Estelle broke into the peacefulness.

'Please let's not make any promises Andy, this war isn't over yet and neither of us can be sure of what could happen. Who knows where the next few weeks or months will take us? It's all too uncertain.'

Andy paused for a moment.

'I will only make a promise if it's in my power to keep it but I agree there is a war to finish and I have two children to get to their grandparents. So, yes, there is uncertainty but when I think of what Rick and I have come through so far, I believe nothing is going to stop me surviving this war and then coming back here.'

Estelle nestled into Andy's frame and for the first time in many years, she did not feel alone.

Back at the farm, Rick had emptied the bottle of wine and fallen asleep in the chair. Estelle and Andy entered the farmhouse very quietly and tried hard not to disturb Rick. They stood in the centre of the room, their arms wrapped around each other and occasionally glancing at Rick in the chair to make sure he was still asleep before kissing. Estelle whispered, 'We should say goodnight Andy, you will have a long journey in the morning.' Andy looked at her inquiringly. Estelle continued, 'Angelique will be fine to travel tomorrow, so you must make the most of the time you have before the fighting reaches us here.' Andy opened his mouth to protest but Estelle placed her finger over his lips and said quietly.

'Let's talk in the morning, for now, goodnight and sleep well.' She kissed him tenderly before turning away with a tear in her eye, knowing that it was probably the last time she would feel the warmth of his lips on hers. Andy was slightly stunned and stood rooted to the spot in the centre of the room. Rick had been awake for some time but had kept his eyes closed and occasionally had opened one eye to see the couple embracing and kissing each other.

He closed that eye quickly and successfully suppressed the smile that wanted to break out. Rick was happy for his friend and indeed for Estelle also, both had had more than enough unhappiness in their lives. Andy was still standing in the centre of the room, staring at the door that Estelle had used for her exit. Rick feigned his awakening but not very convincingly. He stretched and yawned.

'Wow man, I was really knocked out, what time did you two guys get back?'

Andy was aware that his friend had witnessed his goodnight kiss with Estelle because of the smug look on Rick's face that he couldn't disguise and anyway he had got to know Rick very well since they got together in Germany.

'Come on Rick, you saw what went on, so stop horsing around.'

'Yep, you're right buddy, you got me and I think it's great that you and Estelle have got together. I just didn't want to pour cold water on you both; that would have been unkind.' He laughed a bit too loudly and Andy was concerned that Estelle would hear him.

'I think Estelle wants us to leave tomorrow as she thinks Angelique is well enough to make the journey now. She's probably right but I don't want to go this soon, I would have liked a few more days here.'

'That I can understand my friend; if I had my girlfriend Frankie here, I wouldn't want to leave either. Man, I can just see her;' he closed his eyes 'she is drop dead gorgeous.' Then he let out a big sigh, 'not to be for now anyway. The important thing to remember is what we have promised the kids and delaying a start may be a risk.'

'Yes, I know, that's why we will have to leave in the morning, so let's go and get some sleep.' The two men went to their beds and Rick was asleep quite quickly. Andy lay awake for some time, thinking about Estelle and wondering whether their liaison was actually real or not. Could it be, he thought, that it was just the situation that two lonely, traumatised individuals had found some escape from their past? 'No, it is real and I will prove it when I return,' he said to himself as he fell asleep. Estelle was having similar thoughts and doubts and truly hoped it could turn out the way she now dreamed it would.

The following morning, Andy was awake very early and had gone outside to watch the sunrise. The morning mist was rising through the trees, the smell of freshness permeated the air and Andy contemplated the day ahead. Estelle stood at the kitchen entrance door and watched the man she thought she may have fallen in love with, sit with his back to her facing the sunrise. She thought should she go to him or leave him to his thoughts? She decided she couldn't risk missing one last opportunity for a moment alone with him and so approached him quietly.

'It's beautiful, isn't it?'

Andy wasn't startled, in fact he had hoped she would join him and was half expecting it.

'Yes it is Estelle, come and sit with me a while.'

'I cannot stay too long; I need to prepare breakfast.' She said as she sat down beside him. 'You will all need some good food inside you for the journey and I will also prepare some for your stores.'

'It looks like you have already decided that we're leaving. I thought we were going to talk about it this morning,' he said sadly.

'I think you have already decided Andy, it doesn't need a decision from me. You know it is right to go as soon as you can and we both know that is now.'

'I know you're right Estelle, it's just that I don't want to leave.'

'And I don't want you to leave but I know that if you stay, the danger will increase each day that you delay.' She kissed him on the cheek and said, 'let's go and get some breakfast together before anyone gets up.'

Rick was about to interrupt the couple when he overheard Estelle's words and decided to return to bed for half an hour to allow them some privacy.

Estelle had already baked some bread and had coffee simmering on the hob. The two of them enjoyed breakfast together and said very little but they did gaze into each other's eyes quite a lot. It was as though they were memorising every aspect of each other's faces.

Andy said, 'I will not forget you Estelle and I will return even if you cannot wait for me then I would still like to see you as a friend.'

'I will be here Andy, have no fear of that but I hope that if you find someone else in the meantime that you would both come and visit me here as friends.'

Andy took Estelle's hand in his and whispered, 'I'm absolutely certain I will not find anyone else.' His face suddenly brightened when he remembered to ask, 'give me the address of the farm, I shall write to you.' Estelle obliged and passed a piece of paper to him with her address on it, which he folded neatly and placed it in his pocket. At that moment, Rick emerged chirpily shouting.

'Good morning, I hope you both had a good night's sleep,' Estelle immediately thought that Rick assumed that they had slept together and blushed quite badly.

'I don't know about Andy but I slept very well, thank you,' she said haughtily.

'I took a little time to get off because you were snoring, my friend but I eventually slept like a log,' Andy said to Estelle's great relief.

Rick laughed loudly.

'Me! Snore, never.'

The children emerged from their bedroom; Angelique looked quite bright, so Andy knew there was now no excuse for them to stay here any longer.

'Angel, Tony, we are going to leave here today to start making our way to Givet, so after breakfast you must begin getting your things together for the journey.' There was an obvious sadness in Andy's voice, which he tried to disguise but neither Estelle nor Rick were fooled. He continued, 'I hope you will tidy your bedroom and help Madame Givauche put things back to the way they were. There will be time for you to say goodbye to the animals.'

Angelique translated what Andy had said for her brother who appeared to get very excited about the thought of leaving. For him, it was another adventure.

The rest of the morning was taken up preparing equipment and supplies during which time the two men discussed the route they would take. The road down in the valley that ran parallel to the river Meuse was heavy with military traffic and the rumble of artillery was getting closer and louder, so travel by road was out of the question.

The only other option was to stay on the high ground and preferably under the cover of trees. The journey would be as arduous as any they had undertaken so far, especially for the children. Although the Ardennes was considered an area of beauty, the ground ahead, nevertheless, was rough, craggy and harsh. So Andy and Rick both knew the going would be slow. They estimated that it may take another three days accounting for the many rest stops that would be needed.

The morning went quickly, too quickly for Andy but the time had come when they were ready to leave and Andy reluctantly asked the children to say their goodbyes to Madame Givauche. Angelique was the first to approach Estelle.

'I thank you so much for the way you have looked after me and my brother, Madame and I am so sorry for the trouble I caused in the cave. Andy has told me of the terrible accident there was there, so please forgive me for being so foolish in making you remember.'

'There is nothing to forgive my child, you were not to know. I'm just very glad that you survived and it has been a great pleasure in having you both here as my guests. I hope you will come and visit me here when the war is over.'

'Yes we will Madame, won't we Anton?'

The boy moved towards Estelle and cuddled his head into her skirts and said, 'Thank you Madame, you are a very lovely lady.'

Tears started to well up in Estelle's eyes.

'Now be off with you and have a safe journey.'

Angelique kissed her on both cheeks and then Rick approached.

'I sure appreciate everything that you've done for us, Ma'am,' he kissed her on both cheeks also then picked up the supplies packs, 'come on kids, let's go, Andy will follow, he has some business to finish.' The children and Rick marched off jauntily up the hill, which would take them past and beyond the now heavily boarded up cave.

Andy let them get some distance away before he turned to Estelle.

'I really don't want to leave but I know I must. I want you to know that I won't forget you and I will come back.'

'We shall see cheri, we shall see. I just want you to have a safe journey and that you come to no harm. If that happens, then I know there's a chance that we will meet again. That I would like very much.'

Andy took her in his arms and kissed her gently on the lips and continued to hold her close. He didn't want to let go but she started to push him away.

'Please cheri, you must go; otherwise I will cry and I want to remember you without tears, please now, go.'

Andy reluctantly turned away and started out following the tracks of Rick and the children. He never looked back.

Chapter 18

Rick and the children had passed the cave that had been the centre of Angelique's adventure and reached the top of the hill. They could see the farm below and also Andy approaching about halfway towards them, so Rick decided he would wait for him and take the opportunity for a rest. Anton had spent most of the time happily on Rick's shoulders and he thought that Angelique, although recovered from her ordeal, should not be pushed too hard.

'You okay, buddy?' Rick asked as Andy arrived.

'Yes, I'm fine, let's get going,' Andy said abruptly and started to walk in a northerly direction. Rick understood Andy's sadness and was unwilling to pursue his question further. He prepared to follow him but on reaching down to gather up the supplies, he turned to look at the farm for the last time when he saw vehicles approaching it up the track. There were two jeeps that appeared to be full of soldiers and they were German, he could just make out the swastika badge on the vehicle side.

'Hell Andy, looks like we left in time.'

Andy turned and saw what Rick was alluding to.

'You move on with the children Rick, I'm going back. I'll join up with you later.'

'Goddamn it man, no way, you can't go back there. There's too many of them and anyway, they're probably only going to stop for some food and water.'

'I can't leave her to handle them on her own Rick, I've already left one family to fend for itself and look what happened.'

'I'm telling you partner; you're not going down there because if you do, then you'll be abandoning these two kids. We've come too far for that and anyway, you'll have to get by me first.' Rick adopted a boxing sparring style with his fists. Andy was much taller than him but Rick was as strong as an ox and had spent most of his life having to physically defend himself and others, so he was well prepared.

Andy stepped forward and went to push Rick to one side but Rick sidestepped half a pace and sent a sidewinder punch to Andy's jaw. Andy body swerved away from the blow and grabbed Rick in a bear hug. Both men fell to the ground, rolling around and trying unsuccessfully to land blows on the other.

Angelique screamed out, 'Stop it, stop it, don't fight please.' She ran over to the men who were still struggling, 'you should be ashamed of yourselves, stop it this instance.'

The two men separated and lay side by side taken aback by the young girl's admonishment.

'I'm sorry Angel but I had to try and stop him from going down there, he would have got himself killed,' Rick said breathlessly.

Andy slowly stood up and said, 'I'm sorry too angel but I need to get back to the farm in case Estelle needs my help. You must go now with Rick; I will follow as soon as I can.'

'Just what the hell do you think you're going to do man, there are at least a dozen krauts down there.'

'I don't know but I guess if I get close without being seen, I've more of a chance of doing something if I have to.'

'I don't think you will need to go my friend; look.' Rick watched what was going on at the farm and pointed Andy's gaze in that direction. The troops had got out of their vehicles and appeared to be loading packages into them. Rick believed he was right that they were only there to collect food and supplies and after a short time, they were making their way down the track away from the farm and in a great hurry. Andy breathed a sigh of relief and was embarrassed by his overreaction.

'I am really sorry for the way I acted Rick; I should have listened.' He then walked meekly over to Angelique, who had been extremely distressed by the men fighting and pulled her towards him; wrapping his arms around her, he said, 'I'm really sorry to you too Angel, you've seen enough trouble in your young life without me causing more. Am I forgiven for being such a fool?'

'Yes, of course, I know you only wanted to protect your sweetheart,' she said with a knowing but coy smile.

Andy looked a bit shocked and was surprised by her precociousness. He looked to Rick who just grinned, winked and said, 'Let's move out now and get to where we are supposed to be and where is that kids?'

'Givet!' the children shouted in unison and with that the group moved off to the north. Andy didn't see Estelle waving to them. She had waited until the Germans were well clear of the farm then turned towards the hill that Andy and Rick had climbed with the children and looked to see if they were still there. Even if they were, she couldn't be sure if they could see her but she waved anyway just to let them know that she was okay.

When the Germans arrived, her main concern was that they would see Andy with Rick and the children walking away from the farm but fortunately, they were far more concerned about their own situation rather what was going on around them. They were obviously tired, hungry and battle weary, so all they wanted was food and water. She could understand some of what the troop commander was saying to his men and gathered that they were in full retreat from the advancing allies.

'My men will only take what is needed for our journey, so you have no need to worry Madame; you will not be harmed.' He promptly shouted commands to the men who raided the kitchen of all that they could carry. They were a bedraggled bunch of men who clearly hadn't slept or washed for many days and their only concern was the food. Some were eating what they carried, unconcerned by Estelle's look of disdain.

Thankfully, Estelle was relieved that they left almost as quickly as they arrived and fortunately the food stocks were quite low following the stay of Andy, Rick and the children, so not much was taken. She was certain that there would be more such visits and worried about her livestock, so she resolved to move all of them, except the chickens to a field further away from the farm and she would keep her food stocks as low as possible as she had no intention of feeding or being helpful to the occupying army.

They were gone for now and Estelle was thankful that Andy, Rick and the children had got away safely. She wondered whether Andy really would return after the war and hoped that he would but was doubtful and so decided to commit herself to working her farm and helping the Resistance.

The children had been walking for most of the afternoon and were very tired, so Andy decided that they should spend the evening where they were. They were still under the cover of trees and although it had been a very hot day, they had some shade from the forest canopy.

'Let's rest here, Rick and let the children get some sleep. We shouldn't travel once daylight has completely gone, given that we don't know the ground ahead and anyway, according to the map we should be coming out of the forest soon and into open terrain.'

'If that's the case Andy, we may be forced to travel at night or at least at dusk; moving in open ground in daylight aint going to be safe.'

'You're right Rick, it's a good point. Looking at the map and guessing on the kind of ground we will have to cover, I reckon that it would take us about an hour to get across the open ground to the next line of trees, so let's do it at dusk. That'll give the children about three hours sleep here before we have to move out.'

The children slept easily in the warmth of the late afternoon sun and Andy studied his map to figure out the next leg of the journey for tomorrow. Rick looked over his shoulder and followed Andy's out loud thinking. The terrain directly north looked quite severe and the more accessible route took them quite close to the main road.

Given the severity of the direct route and the possibility that the children may not be strong enough to manage it, they decided on the longer but easier path that ran adjacent to the main road. The men sat leaning against a stout pine tree and rested. There was nothing they could do now until the light started to fade and then they would make their way to the next wooded area.

They sat with their backs to each other against the tree and listened to the rumble of guns in the distance. Andy thought of nothing but Estelle and wondered if she would still be free when he returned. Rick broke the silence.

'What are you going to do after the war, Andy?'

'If I make it, I'd like to come back here.'

'You really are serious about Estelle?'

'Yes, I am, Rick, never thought I could ever feel this way about anyone again but now I want to get through this war more than anything else.'

'I hope it works out for you.' Rick paused and continued, 'me, I want to get back to Frankie, settle down, have a family and help Papa Frederici with his restaurant, which one day I hope I will take over. And hey man, if you and Estelle hook up after the war, you could cross over the pond, get to the Bronx and taste some of my great Italian coffee.'

'That sounds like a fantastic idea Rick and I'll look forward to it. I would really like us to keep in touch when this is all over.'

'Yeh, me too buddy,' Rick replied hopefully; he had some uncertainty about whether he would make it as he often thought of his dead brother and questioned why he should survive any more than his sibling.

The time soon passed and the air started to cool as the sun sank towards the horizon. Rick woke the children up and told them they should get themselves ready to move. Anton rubbed his eyes and complained to his sister.

'Why can't I sleep? I thought we were staying here tonight.'

'I don't know Anton; I shall ask Andy.' Angelique approached Andy who was gathering up the packs ready to go. 'Are we going to travel at night Andy, we thought we were staying here tonight?'

'No Angel, we cannot stay here because if we wait until morning, there is a very open piece of ground we have to cross and Rick and I think it might be dangerous to do so in daylight. So, we're going to walk across the clearing now when it's almost dark. We should be under cover of trees again in about an hour and then we'll be able to stay there tonight. Is that okay?'

'It's just that we are very tired and we would like to get some more sleep.'

'Angel, I promise that when we get to the cover of the trees, you will be able to sleep as long as you wish. Rick will even build you a shelter to sleep under, won't you Rick?'

As Rick was about to protest, Angelique screeched with delight and translated for Anton that Rick was going to build them a little house to sleep in. That seemed to placate Anton who stopped complaining. Rick however, nudged Andy with his elbow and tilting his head to one side said, 'Really?' Andy just smiled.

The party of four set out and quickly reached the edge of the clearing. Anton was hoisted onto Andy's shoulders whilst Rick and Angelique carried most of the supplies. After about an hour of steady walking, the new tree line could be seen in the near distance. It formed a dark shadow against the bright night sky and although it looked ominous, Andy knew they would be safer there.

He quickened his stride, knowing that everyone, particularly Angelique would need to rest soon. Anton, on the other hand, sat happily on Andy's shoulders chattering away in French. The party entered the tree line having crossed the clearing to what was considered its relative safety and quickly sought out an area to bed down for the night. Rick set about collecting small pine tree branches that he could weave together to form a small shelter for the children.

He managed to find a suitable spot where he could attach the branches and quickly constructed the accommodation. Rick announced:

'Your bedroom is ready, Mademoiselle Angel and Monsieur Tony.' He bowed low and waved his hand into the shelter entrance. Angelique and Anton laughed heartily and excitedly clambered inside the makeshift shelter and for a short time, played games of getting in and out of it. Rick was pleased that he had not disappointed them. It was not long before the two children were fast asleep.

'I think we should get some sleep too Rick, we'll need to be on our guard tomorrow being so close to the main road; we could be spotted.'

'I guess you're right partner but don't even think about me making a shelter!' Andy laughed and the two men settled down at the base of a tree, on the soft forest floor cushioned by decades of fallen leaves and lush moss.

It was about midnight when Rick was disturbed by the crack of a twig close by. He leaned over and nudged Andy, keeping his finger over his mouth to prevent him from making a noise. They listened for further sounds and could hear nothing and just as they were about settle down again, dark figures came rushing out of the shrubs screaming and shouting.

'Put your hands in the air, do not move.' Their warning was repeated several times. Rifles were pointing at Rick and Andy, so they did as they were told and laid stock still with their hands raised. Angelique had been disturbed by the shouting and instinctively knew there was danger. She grabbed Anton and held him close to her, she whispered, 'Quiet please Anton, do not make a sound.'

'Make yourselves known to us, who are you and what are you doing here?' The leader commanded.

'Goddamn it, you're Americans, thank God.' Rick shouted, 'well I'll be doggone.'

'Shut up and answer my question, who are you and what are you doing here?' Andy spoke first.

'Can I stand up and I'll be happy to answer your question, Sir.'

'No, you damn well answer my question or I'll as sure as hell shoot you where you lay.'

'Okay, okay, we're escaped POW's from a prison camp in Germany. I'm British and my friend here is American. We're trying to make our way back to our lines.' Andy realised that the children were hidden and had not revealed themselves, so for the moment elected to say nothing about them.

The soldiers were American and well camouflaged and Rick guessed that they were on an advanced reconnaissance mission. Rick thought there was about six of them with what looked like a young Officer in charge. He stood up but kept his hands above his head.

'Look, goddamn it, I'm an American soldier, ask me anything you like and I'll prove that I'm who I say I am. By the way, this is Sergeant Andy Miller of the British Royal Air Force and I am Private First Class Lucianno Frederici.'

'If you do not get back down on the ground and shut the fuck up, I'll ram this rifle butt down your throat.' The patrol leader announced. Rick was in no doubt of the seriousness of the threat.

The Officer turned to one of his men.

'Sergeant, go through their baggage, see if you can find out anything about them.'

The Sergeant emptied Andy's backpack and saw the various items that they had attained in their skirmish with the German General just after they had escaped; all of which, of course were of German origin and most glaring was the German map. He came over to the Officer and showed him the items. Two soldiers stood guard over the captives whilst the Officer and his Sergeant walked out of earshot to discuss the contents of Andy's bag.

After several minutes they returned.

'I believe you are German spies. We've been briefed on how good you might be in pretending to be on our side but I guess you weren't clever enough or perhaps you didn't have time to dispose of your German equipment. Anyway, we are going to take you in as our prisoners.' Rick was about to protest when the Officer said, 'Don't you say another fucking word, do you understand me? Just nod your head. I'm sure our intelligence guys will want to have a long chat, so get on your feet, keep your hands high and where we can see them and move out.'

Angelique had heard enough and decided to come out of hiding.

'Please sir,' she said as she gingerly approached the Officer with Anton, 'I can tell you that Andy and Rick really are soldiers and have been helping us for some time to get to our grandparents. They are not German spies, I promise.'

'What the hell! What are you two kids doing here?'

Andy answered, 'she is right, we are not Germans and I can explain why the children are with us, if you will let me.'

'You can do all your explaining when we get you back to our base camp. I'm not taking any chances that you may be krauts just using these kids. You can lower your hands but don't try any tricks. The kids will come with us too; our Commanding Officer will need to decide what to do. Now move out.'

The Allied soldiers herded Andy Rick and the children down the hill to the edge of the forest near a main road. Two vehicles approached slowly from a secluded area just off the road. Anton was crying and Angelique was shivering. Andy said, 'Don't worry Angel; these men are not going to hurt you. Isn't that right, Officer?'

The Officer stopped and stooped low to look at eye level with Angelique.

'No miss, we're not going to hurt you, I promise. We're going to take you somewhere warm and get you some nice hot food. Then you can tell us who you are and why you're with these men. Is that okay?'

'Yes but I want you to promise also that you will not hurt Andy or Rick. They are good men.'

'Yes missy, I can promise that they will not be hurt. You see, we do not hurt our prisoners even if they turn out not to be who they say they are. Is that okay with you?'

Angelique nodded her head and explained to her brother what the Officer had said.

The Officer spoke quietly to his Sergeant who then barked an order.

'Okay, let's load everyone up and get out of here. Move out.'

The two vehicle party drove for about half an hour without encountering any retreating Germans. Andy concluded that the German retreat east of the river Meuse must have been more rapid than he expected. They eventually arrived at a town that appeared to be an advanced headquarters. The town was historically heavily fortified, which could be seen from the thick walls that surrounded it.

American forces vehicles, some filled with soldiers others empty, scampered about moving at great speed in what looked like chaos but it was organised and had an element of swiftness, of hustle. There was momentum in that chaotic movement, yet in contrast soldiers could be seen resting wherever they could, some sleeping, others cleaning weapons and some blowing cigarette smoke into the night sky. There was no hurry here.

The vehicles carrying Andy, Rick and the children halted outside a building that looked like a town hall. An American flag waved proudly on a pole at the front entrance.

'Out!' bellowed the patrol Sergeant, gesturing to Andy and Rick. 'Come on kids, you need to come as well but don't worry, you'll soon have a warm bed to sleep in.'

The men and the children were guided into a small room and told to sit down. An armed guard stood by the door. An army nurse entered and spoke to Angelique.

'Hello, my name is Karen and I'm a nurse. I've been asked to look after you while you are here and first we're going to the kitchen to get some hot food. Would you like to tell me your names?'

'My name is Angelique and this is my brother Anton who doesn't speak English and we would like to stay with Andy and Rick please.'

'I'm afraid you won't be able to do that at this moment Angelique but I'm sure that if Andy and Rick are who they say they are, I'm sure you will be able to see them later. So in the meantime, why don't you come with me and get some nice hot food.' Anton was crying and wailed to his sister.

'I'm hungry and tired Angelique, can we please eat and go to bed?'

'What did he say, Angelique?' the nurse asked.

'Just that he was tired and hungry.' Angelique looked pleadingly to Andy and Rick for guidance.

Rick was the first to speak.

'You and your brother should go with Nurse Karen, Angel and we shall see you in the morning. I promise we'll be alright, won't we Andy?'

'Yes, we're going to be just fine, so don't you go worrying. Off you go now; we'll see you both tomorrow.'

The nurse led the children by the hand out of the door. Angelique looked back with some nervousness in her eyes at Andy and Rick as she was shepherded out of the door and out of sight. Her mind was racing. *We don't know these people, we don't where we are or where we are being taken, thankfully, at least they're not German,* she thought and there was a gentleness in the nurse's grip on her hand, which for her was reassuring.

Andy and Rick sat in silence for some time before the door swung open and an Officer and two armed soldiers entered the room.

'I'm Lieutenant Pinkerton and my job is find out what you are doing here and who you are. So, I will be talking to you separately until we find the answers to those questions. Guard, escort the short one to room two and stay with him until I arrive.'

'Yes Sir,' the soldier shouted out military style and pointing his rifle at Rick said, 'Up soldier and keep your hands where I can see them. Let's go.'

'Look guys, I could sure do with a cup of good old American coffee, any chance?' Rick asked seriously but with his inimitable cheeky tone.

'No chance until you answer a few questions,' the Officer responded. 'Now get going. The quicker I get some answers that I can believe, then you just might get a coffee.'

Rick was escorted out of the room whilst the Lieutenant paced the floor like a stalking cat. He looked directly at Andy and said, 'First off, I want your name, rank and number, what is your unit and who's your Commanding Officer?'

'I can give you legitimate answers to all of the questions, Sir but if you really think I am posing as an Allied soldier, don't you think we could have obtained that information from a genuine POW soldier under interrogation?'

'Don't get smart with me soldier, just answer my questions.'

Andy did as he was told and an assistant furiously took note of everything Andy said.

'Okay, we can check that out but as you say, you could have obtained that from a POW in one of your camps. So, I'm going to sit and listen and I want you to tell me everything from start to finish, which POW camp were you in, how you got captured and how long you were there. When or should I say, if you escaped, how did you end up where my patrol picked you up and what is your connection with the children?'

In the other room, Rick was being interrogated in a similar fashion. Their stories were identical except for Rick's excursion with the Resistance in Charleville Mezieres and Andy's previous escape attempts from the German POW camp.

When Andy described how Angelique had had to drag her dead father to the centre of the floor in their house and how they had watched their mother being dragged away by the Gestapo and then how they had met up with the children, saving them from a German deserter and promising that they would get them to their grandparents in Givet that the interrogating Officer seemed to soften his approach.

'So, you're telling me that before you met up with the children, you and your partner killed a German General and stole his car, driving it through several road blocks in Luxembourg. Is that correct?'

'Yes it is, Sir.'

The Lieutenant turned to his aide and said, 'Get a signal off to HQ, some of what this guy is saying can be checked out. In the meantime, organise a coffee for him while I go see his partner.'

Rick had described in detail his and Andy's encounter with the German General, his short time with the French Resistance and how he had helped destroy the German supplies. He described the battle at the town hall and how the doctor and nurse Celine had been killed. His interrogator was warming to this young soldier and was almost totally convinced that he was indeed an escaped American fighter. At that moment, Lieutenant Pinkerton opened the door and motioned for his colleague to join him outside.

'What do you think?' Rick's questioner asked.

'Pretty darned convincing, I would say. I'm of a mind to believe their story. It's the kids. I just don't buy them being conned by the Germans. The nurse has been talking to them while they were eating and they're in bed now but it seems that they are saying pretty much what I've been told by the Brit. I'm expecting a reply soon from HQ to see if these two are on their missing or taken prisoner register.

I suggest we give them the benefit of the doubt for the time being and get them some food and drink. Get them quartered away from the German POW compound for the moment and hopefully, we can get them in front of the Commanding Officer tomorrow morning.'

Rick and Andy were billeted separately and had been questioned for almost three hours but at least they had been given food and to Rick's eternal gratitude, a hot cup of American coffee. Both men were confident they would be believed and hoped the children were safe and resting. The morning would come soon enough.

Chapter 19

In the early hours of the next morning, Andy was awakened by one of his armed guards. Rick had similarly been aroused and both men were marched to the building they had first encountered on their arrival the previous night. Neither had had much more than two hours sleep and looked dreadfully tired. They needed a shower and clean clothes but what was going on around them suggested that there would not be time for any of those luxuries.

Soldiers were dashing about, loading vehicles, carrying boxes; vehicles were lining up and ready to move as a convoy. The organised chaos of last night was even more frenetic. It puzzled Andy; was this flight of retreat or a sudden advance, he thought. Whatever it was, he concluded, it was almost certain that this headquarters was moving house and he prayed it was not backwards.

Both men were to meet again for the first time since they were separated the previous night. Rick looked at Andy, winked and smiled in his usual way. Andy reciprocated. Lieutenant Pinkerton came into the room.

'Sit down men.' He gestured to the chairs. 'We have had confirmation of your story and we're glad to tell you that your units have been informed that you have escaped from the German POW camp and are now behind Allied lines. The record of Sergeant Andrew's capture was documented and reported by the Red Cross.

Unfortunately, your capture, Private Frederici, was much later than Sergeant Andrews and notification was not given to the authorities until now. So, you were listed as missing in action and your family was informed accordingly. That is being rectified as we speak. One of my men will escort you to the wash room to let you wash up and we will provide you with some clean uniforms.

For the moment Sergeant, you will be a guest of the American Army and will have to contend with wearing its uniform. We can't offer the luxury of showers because as you can see, we're on the move again and that's been the case since we landed on the Normandy beaches.'

Andy said, 'the uniform will be fine Sir, I'm sure and thank you. When you say you're on the move again, does that mean that the Germans are still in retreat? And by the way, where are we?'

'I'm not authorised to divulge too much to you but all I will say is that we are kicking German ass's big time, which means we're moving our HQ to keep up with the advance. I'm sure Colonel Harper will tell you more when he sees you. The town you are in currently is Rocroi, where we will go to next I can't say.'

Rick interrupted, 'Where are the kids, are they okay?'

'The children are fine, Private and are being looked after. You will get to meet up with them again after you've seen the Colonel.' The Officer turned to his aide, 'get the men kitted up and polished, Corporal and bring them to Colonel Harper's office in an hour.' He turned to Andy and Rick. 'I'll see you guys later.'

The Corporal left for a short time and returned with soap, towels and razors.

'While you're cleaning up, I'll organise the uniforms and any other equipment you might need, then we'll get some chow before I take you to the Colonel's office. So follow me, I'll show you the wash room.' On the way along the corridor, the Corporal spoke.

'We're lucky here; we have wash rooms and a roof over our heads. The guys out on the front line haven't seen water or clean clothes for weeks, sometimes months. They got a bit of respite when Paris was liberated but since then it's been push, push, push, all the way.' The Corporal opened a door and showed the men a wash room comprising of two wash basins, a broken mirror on one wall and a WC cubicle.

'I'll bring your uniforms and other gear back here in about twenty minutes.' He then left. Andy and Rick stood motionless, staring at their washing materials and for the first time since their escape from Germany realised that they no longer needed to run or hide. Both men adopted a position at a wash basin and filled it with warm water then proceeded to wash and shave and although they had started to get accustomed to their facial hair growth, they weren't too sorry to see the back of it. They were finished just as the NCO returned carrying uniforms, helmets and boots.

'Wow, you guys look very different without the fuzz. Here are your uniforms, I think I've got your sizes about right, tough if I haven't cos we aint got any more.'

Andy and Rick quickly set about getting into the uniforms and importantly making sure that the boots fitted; luckily, they did, just. Rick was admiring his reflection in the mirror and started to feel like a real soldier again. Andy's combat jacket was a bit short in the sleeves but he was glad to be wearing something clean.

'We have just about enough time to grab some chow but have to be at the Colonel's office in twenty minutes, leave your old clothes in this bag and let's go,' the Corporal announced as he held up a canvas sack. He stopped at the door and turned to Andy and Rick.

'I've heard your story and how you busted your asses to get back to your own lines. But what I liked most of all is the way you looked after those kids. Goddamn it, I just wanna shake your hand.' He held out his hand and took Andy's and then Rick's firmly in his.

'It's a great story and it makes me proud to be American; I won't forget that I met you two dudes.' The three men stepped out of the wash room and made their way to the mess area and then on to the Colonel's office.

Colonel Jack Harper was a highly decorated soldier; spoke with a strong southern drawl and still quite young for his current status. He had listened to Andy and Rick's account of their escape from the Germans and their subsequent adventures with the children. He had already been briefed by Lieutenant Pinkerton but wanted to hear it from the two men stood before him and insisted that they should sit down.

'So, men, tell me again about how you took out a high ranking German officer.' Andy obliged and made a point of saying that it was Rick who took the initiative. 'You then drove the General's car through roads packed with German vehicles and through two border crossings. I am surely impressed gentlemen. But what has impressed me most is your determination to see that the children reached their grandparents rather than you dumping them at some French orphanage. Tell me, what drove you not to do that?'

Rick answered, 'well Sir, we figured that given that the children were part Jewish that they would be vulnerable even in an orphanage and we knew what had happened to their parents. For kids so young, they had gone through enough and Andy and I believed they needed some help. So, Sir, as we were travelling west to get back to our lines, we thought that making a little shimmy north to Givet wouldn't be a big deal.'

'No, a little shimmy north wouldn't be a big deal I guess,' Jack Harper said with his eyebrow raised incredulously. The Colonel knew that they had taken on a great responsibility despite their own precarious situation.

He continued, 'I now have to make a decision, I can send the children to a local orphanage, they would be safe there now that we have reoccupied France and then I can get you guys back to your units, so that you can carry on giving the krauts hell. That sounds like the most sensible thing to do. Or, after I am certain the children are safe, I can send you back to England where you can get a well-deserved rest and recuperation at your base units.'

Andy and Rick froze at the thought of leaving the children in an orphanage but knew that if the Colonel chose to do that, they would be powerless to stop it.

Rick gulped and said, 'With respect, Sir, I would like to make a suggestion, I think—'

The Colonel interrupted, 'No, you may not suggest or think, Private Frederici, I will make any suggestions and do any necessary thinking because it will be my decision, is that understood?'

'Yes Sir,' Rick shouted in military style, standing up rigidly to attention. Both men looked despondent and Jack Harper knew why.

'Sit down Private.' His tone softened, 'you two have demonstrated incredible bravery, ingenuity and determination and I'm not going to let that go without recognition. I know what you want to do and that is to continue your journey with the children to Givet, am I right?'

'Yes Sir,' both men replied in unison.

'I will allow my heart to rule my head on this exceptional occasion and let you take the children to Givet. We believe that the Germans have vacated their positions there, so it should be safe enough, although there may be the odd straggler and you will have to be careful. Before you go anywhere,' he continued, 'I want to recognise your service to the war effort and your bravery. Although, I cannot make a direct award to you Sergeant Andrews, that will be down to your Commanding Officer as to what would be appropriate but I will write a letter of commendation to your C.O, highly praising your actions in getting this far.'

Andy stood up and said, 'Thank you, Sir.'

'As for you Private Frederici, I am using my powers to award you with a field promotion,' The Colonel paused, 'well done Lieutenant and congratulations.' Colonel Harper walked over to the men and warmly shook them by the hand.

'Lieutenant Pinkerton will help you with the requisitioning of a jeep and any supplies for your journey to Givet. When the children are safely with their grandparents, I expect to see my vehicle returned and you two on a plane back to your bases in England.'

Rick was stunned and couldn't believe what had just happened, he couldn't let go of the Colonel's hand and continued to shake it with his mouth half open.

'Well Lieutenant Frederici, are you going to let go of my hand and get on with completing the task you started some months ago. Or is this likely to continue to a point where I am prevented from getting my headquarters relocated?'

Rick shook his head to clear it, let go of the Colonel's hand and said, 'I'm sorry Sir, it's just a bit of a shock; from Private to Lieutenant, it's a bit much to take in.'

'You've shown me enough to know that you will make a good Officer Frederici; I know you will not disappoint me. Now, I suggest you and Sergeant Andrews collect your charges and deliver them to Givet as planned.'

Rick saluted the Colonel, turned and left the office with Andy. On the way to meet up with the children, Andy congratulated Rick.

'Well, Lieutenant, congratulations, you deserve it. I don't think we could have made it this far without your Bronx charm and bullheadedness.'

'Hey man, it was a joint effort and remember I probably would have been captured again if it weren't for you stopping me from going in the wrong direction. And don't forget how it was your navigation skills that got us here, so if you had been a Yank today in the Colonel's office, I probably would be calling you Captain now.' The two men laughed and put an arm around each other's shoulder just as friends or brothers would.

Lieutenant Pinkerton showed Andy and Rick to the door of the building where Angelique and Anton were being looked after.

'I'll be back in a few hours when I've got the vehicle and equipment pulled together, so go spend some time with them, I'll see you in a short while.

The men quietly stepped through the door entrance and could see Angelique and Anton sat in conversation with Nurse Karen, they looked relaxed. A hopscotch map had been drawn on the floor of the empty office and almost certainly Anton had encouraged Nurse Karen to participate.

Karen looked towards the door where Andy and Rick stood quietly watching. The children's eyes followed the nurse's and on spotting their friends, jumped up excitedly, running to them and shouting.

'Andy, Rick.' Anton jumped into Rick's arms and Angelique was swung around by Andy. They were so happy to be together again.

Angelique suddenly exclaimed, 'You have no beards anymore, you both look very handsome.' The look on her face suddenly changed to one of sadness and asked, 'what is going to happen to us now Andy, are you going to leave us here?'

'Why on earth would we be leaving you, Angel? I know we made a promise to take you to Givet and,' Andy deliberately paused before continuing. Angelique looked worried. 'That's exactly what we are going to do.'

Angelique squealed with delight before catching her breath to translate what Andy had said for a puzzled Anton. He was still hanging on to Rick and on hearing what his sister said demonstrated his obvious joy by throwing his arms around Rick's neck and squeezing him tightly.

'And we don't have to do any more walking, guys,' Rick announced with some difficulty, 'the Army is providing us with a jeep, so that we can take you to your new home in style.'

'Does that mean we will get to our grand-mere's house today?' Angelique asked.

Andy answered, 'we don't know that yet, Angel. We have to get the jeep and supplies and then when we do set off, we have to go very carefully just in case there are any Germans in the area. Then we have to find your grandparents house because I think it is a long time since you were there. But we will get there as quickly as we can, I promise.'

'But we will get there soon, won't we?' It was statement rather than a question.

'Yes, Angel, as soon as we can.'

Nurse Karen said, 'I have to go now, we still have many injured soldiers to see to and some wounded prisoners that have to be patched up as well.' She turned to the children, 'it's been a real pleasure talking to you, Angelique and I think you are both very brave. I hope you find your mother and that she is well.' She then turned to Anton, 'thank you for teaching me the game of Marelle Anton, it was great fun.'

She turned to go when Anton rushed over and kissed her on both cheeks, then said in faltering English.

'Thank you Nurse Karen, you are a very lovely lady.' Karen tousled Anton's hair, then smiling warmly at everyone, she left the room.

Lieutenant Pinkerton returned after an hour with a jeep and some supplies.

'She's all gassed up and ready to go. There are two carbines and some ammo just in case you run into any trouble and here are a couple of helmets for the kids, they were the smallest I could find.' He walked over to Anton and placed one on his head, stepped back and saluted. 'Okay soldier, you make sure you wear that all the time you're on the road and look after your sister.' He then gave the other helmet to Angelique, who giggled embarrassingly as she placed it jauntily on her head.

'I'll leave you guys to get yourselves ready to go. I hope we meet up again; I'd like to know how things went. Have a safe journey and good luck. Oh and by the way, some of the bridges have been blown by the Germans, so you may not have a direct route.' He shook their hands and left.

Angelique looked at Andy and Rick expectantly whilst Anton was busily hopping around on the hopscotch map. She waited and waited for one of them to say something and was bursting with anticipation. She finally exploded.

'Well, are we going or not?' She said in exasperation.

Rick winked at Andy and said, 'Do you think we should go right now or shall we wait until tomorrow morning? What do you think?'

'Umm, not sure Rick, perhaps we should spend some time over a nice cup of coffee thinking about it.'

Rick couldn't contain his smile and tried to hide it from the girl.

'Tell you what, let's ask Angelique, what do you think, Angel?'

'Now, we should go now, now, not tomorrow morning.' She stamped her feet and shook her fists, not realising Andy and Rick were teasing. When the two men started to laugh uncontrollably, she ran over to them and started to slap them around their arms. Still laughing, they feigned serious injury from Angelique's futile attack and it wasn't too long before Angelique started to see the funny side as well.

'Come on, let's load up and get out of here,' Rick said to Angelique's great relief.

Angelique turned to Anton and said in French.

'Come Anton, we are leaving right now. You must hurry in case Andy and Rick change their minds. Come quickly little brother, we're going to see our grands-parents.' Anton scurried over to his sister who took his hand and following the two men, led him from the room.

Outside was pandemonium, vehicles rushing in every direction, soldiers carrying large packs of supplies, vehicles being gassed up and bodies of men marching in single file out of the town. Then, marching in the opposite directions were groups of captured German prisoners guarded on their flanks by armed American soldiers.

They looked a sorry bunch, battle weary and tired with ragged, tattered uniforms. Some of the prisoners displayed wounds from their earlier battles and it was obvious from the clean bandages on display that they had been seen to by the American medics. Andy hoped that our boys, if captured, would be treated equally well.

'They'll probably be taken to a rear POW holding area,' Andy announced. 'Anyway, not our problem, so let's load up and see if we can leave here without getting tangled up in this circus.'

The jeep had seen better days but given the amount of fighting it had scraped through, it was in surprisingly good condition. Andy estimated that there was just forty miles to get to Givet plus some extra for searching for the grandparent's house plus some for detours if bridges were out. The two men checked the vehicle and its contents. Rick was particularly interested in the Jeep's controls that for the moment were unfamiliar to him.

Angelique and Anton stood patiently at the door, holding each other's hand, watching the preparations. Passing groups of soldiers cheered and waved at the children on seeing them standing there wearing their oversized helmets, one shouted, 'Hey cuties, you gonna help us win this one?' Angelique gave an uncertain wave back and smiled.

'Okay kids load up, we're ready to go.' Rick declared. The children got into the rear seats and Andy took up the passenger seat with his carbine and map on his lap. The two men looked at each other, both nodded and Rick, grating the first gear, pressed on the accelerator and moved off. They passed the lines of marching soldiers, the convoys of halftracks and command vehicles and then were on an open road heading north east.

They were to travel several miles before reaching a small town that straddled the river Meuse to find that both main bridges had been destroyed. There were lots of Allied military activity at both sites as they attempted to hurriedly build temporary pontoon bridges. They were not yet completed. Rick pulled alongside a small group of engineers.

'Where's the nearest crossing that is suitable for a single jeep, guys?' He shouted to one of the men. The soldier on seeing the single bar on Rick's helmet sprang smartly to attention and saluted.

'There is a small bridge further upstream Sir, it would just about take your vehicle.'

Rick was taken aback by the reaction of the soldier and for the first time became aware of his new status. Andy smiled and was pleased for him.

'Let's go then, Sir,' Andy said and not in any way mocking his friend's new rank, 'I believe I know the road that this bridge is on.'

The narrow bridge was a wooden one that led to a small country lane. It was clearly inadequate for any significant military traffic, which is probably why the German's left it intact. Andy could see that once on the other side, the road would head south before breaking north again and that would add twenty minutes or so to the journey. It was shortly after crossing the bridge that Rick suddenly swung the vehicle off the road into some dense shrubbery.

'What the hell are you doing man,' Andy shouted. He and the children were thrown to one side as the vehicle skidded and went sideways into the bushes.

'Tank, German panzer,' he said 'look, it's just come on to the ridge of the hill over there. I don't think he spotted us. Must be a loner because I would expect to see more than one. He may have been left behind to cover the German retreat.'

'So, what do you think we should do now?' Andy asked.

'Well, we should be okay under cover because I don't think he'll come down here, I think he's looking to attack the main bridges when our boys start to cross. We need to get a warning to the guys at the bridge; they can't see the tank from where they are.'

'Okay, I'll go,' Andy said. 'We can't break cover; so I'll make my way back on foot. You stay here and look after the kids; I'll get back as quick as I can.'

'Alright partner but be careful.'

Andy got out of the vehicle and taking his carbine with him headed back towards the main bridges where the engineers were frantically putting together the last pieces of the pontoon. It took him about twenty minutes to reach the work party and breathlessly he said, 'You have a major problem up ahead. There's a German tank just appeared at the top of the ridge overlooking this bridge crossing. You can't see him from here; we think he's waiting for the main advance party to start crossing before he starts to lay down serious firepower.'

The Sergeant in charge said, 'Thanks man, we'll get a message back to HQ right now. Can you show me on the map the exact grid reference of where this guy is?'

'Yeah, sure.' Andy gave a precise reference of the tank's location and then said, 'for God's sake, don't drop anything short, my buddy and two children are under cover in a thicket just over the wooden bridge.'

'Don't worry friend, our boys will take the kraut tank out, no problem.'

'Fine,' Andy said, 'I'll go back and join up with my friends.' He started to retrace his steps as the platoon commander radioed the coordinates of the tank to his HQ, 'good luck,' he shouted to the platoon leader as he raced back to Rick and the children.

Another twenty minutes went by before he was able to reach the well camouflaged jeep. Rick sat at the wheel staring at the German tank on the ridge whilst the children lay flat on the back seats. Andy made his way through the bushes and gasping for breath said, 'Well, we should see some action soon. Is the tank still there?'

'Yeah, he's still there and he's in a great position. If we hadn't spotted him, he could have wreaked havoc on the main convoys that are going to be crossing soon.'

Andy added, 'he may still do so if they don't take him out soon.'

It was as soon as Andy finished speaking that artillery fire screamed overhead and started to pepper the tank position. One shell landed in front, another behind, a billow of smoke appeared from the tank exhausts as the Commander realised he had been spotted and instructed the tank driver to reverse away from the ridge out of sight and out of danger.

As the tank lurched backwards, a shell hit the vehicle causing a massive explosion, a direct hit had destroyed the tank instantly. Andy's coordinates were obviously very accurate. Rick gave a triumphant fist in the air and held out his hand for a high five with Andy. The children cheered and Angelique grabbed hold of Anton in a bear hug. It was a bizarre scene that two young children could be in the thick of a battle and yet seem so unfazed by it.

Rick said, 'alright, we should wait for half an hour before we set off, just in case that last panzer had any friends in the area.' Andy agreed and they waited, securely hidden in the shrubbery. After the allotted time, the group set off again following the road south east before reaching a main road that ran north to south.

Andy thought that there was a strong possibility that the river would have to be crossed again and therefore every likelihood that the necessary bridge to do so would be out of action. They should take a chance, he thought. After about ten uneventful miles, the river crossing they would need to take appeared. The German's had attempted to blow it up but had only been partially successful.

Nevertheless, an attempt to use it even with a light vehicle such as theirs was extremely risky. The bridge was lop sided and had lost some of its upper structure. It was decided that Andy and the children should walk across keeping to the sturdy side. Andy went first and showed that it was safe to walk over.

He went back and guided the children over retracing his earlier footsteps. It remained for Rick to decide whether he wanted to risk driving the jeep over. He decided to take the chance.

'Take all of the supplies out of the vehicle and leave them with you on the other side just in case it doesn't make it, Andy.' Andy returned to the jeep and started to remove the essential provisions. Rick moved the vehicle to the edge of the bridge and helped Andy unload and carry the goods to the other side. Angelique and Anton helped by taking what they could handle from the men and stacking them neatly on the road beyond the bridge.

'Okay, that's it; I'll go back and get the jeep,' Rick said.

'Rick, you be careful, if there is any doubt that the bridge can't hold up, then get clear and to hell with jeep. Colonel Harper will just have to get used to the idea that he is minus one beat up old jeep.'

'Yeah, yeah but just remember it's my commission that'll go with it, buddy.' Both men laughed. Rick got into the jeep and started it up, gently easing it forward. His aim was to keep as much to the left as he could, avoiding the broken part of the structure. The vehicle slowly edged forward and was leaning quite sharply to the right.

Rick urged it on but was mindful that every foot of bridge in front of him was ready to give way. About three quarters of the way across, a loud creaking noise could be heard coming from under the bridge; the supporting structure was starting to collapse. Rick decided against continuing in slow and steady pace and pressed heavily on the accelerator, causing the rear wheels to spin furiously.

The creaking became loud cracks and the bridge started to buckle as if in slow motion. The four wheel drive kicked in as Rick eased off the accelerator and then pressed down again, shooting the vehicle forward off the bridge and onto the road, almost crashing into a wall on the other side. As the jeep came to a stop, the bridge disappeared into the river below.

Andy and the children had held their breath up until that moment and were mightily relieved to see Rick safely on this side. They gathered around him as he stepped out of the jeep and engaged in a group hug. After loading up the vehicle again, they set out on the final leg of their journey, one that would take them into Givet where, hopefully, the children would be reunited with their grandparents.

Chapter 20

It was early September when Andy, Rick and the children entered the outskirts of Givet. It was quiet with no sign of any German military activity. Rick slowly edged the jeep further into the town and saw two women approaching from the opposite direction. They were unaware of the jeep as they were busily in conversation until suddenly one of them threw her hand to her mouth and said:

'My God, American, it's the Americans,' she shouted. Her companion stood motionless, stunned. The vehicle pulled up alongside the ladies.

'Morning, ma'am,' Rick said, smiling his large Italian smile, 'can you help us, we're looking for—'

The women started jabbering away in French and Angelique needed to interrupt them to explain to the women what information Rick was asking for. She explained to Rick and Andy what they had been saying.

'They cannot believe that you have finally arrived, they have waited for this moment for nearly four years. They want to know where the rest of your Army is.'

Andy said, 'Angelique; ask them if they know whether there are any Germans still here.'

Angelique obliged and Andy noted that the women shook their heads.

'Tell them that the Allies will be here very soon, in days not weeks. Now, do they know where your grandparents live?' Other locals started to gather around and soon there was quite a gathering. Many just wanted to shake the hands of Andy and Rick and pat them on the back; the people were overjoyed.

One woman passed a bunch of flowers to Andy, another gave them some bread. The two men now had some idea of what liberating a population meant, albeit in this case quite a small one; what Paris must have been like was unimaginable, Andy thought.

There was much chattering and pointing going on between some of the townspeople and Angelique, until finally Angelique was able to extricate herself and describe roughly the direction Rick should drive in. It transpired that old Mr

Soliman and his wife lived in a small house on the outskirts of town. Angelique and her brother had not visited them for some years, so they had no idea where the house was nor did the local people recognise the children as being related to them.

Rick edged the jeep away from the crowd that had gathered who were waving and clapping their hands; some were crying. The party made their way through the town and were accosted every time they stopped or slowed down. Some people ran alongside the vehicle cheering, smiling, patting Rick and Andy on the shoulder.

They were being treated like a victorious liberating army and whilst it was quite flattering, the men knew that the real heroes were those men who had forced the Germans to retreat towards Germany; many of whom had paid the ultimate price.

As they reached the edge of the small town, Angelique became quite animated.

'I remember this road, I remember. grand-mere's house is at the top of the hill; I'm sure of it. Look Anton, we're nearly there. Perhaps our mother is there waiting for us,' she said excitedly. Angelique never forgot her prayers every night before she went to bed or even when she laid down in the forest and each prayer was the same; that her mother would have somehow found her way to Givet and was waiting for them.

The vehicle pulled up alongside the small house and Andy said, 'Rick and I will stay here for now Angel, go and see your grandparents and when you have reintroduced yourselves, perhaps we'll come in for cup of coffee before we return to our units.'

Angelique and her brother stepped out of the jeep and made their way to the front door. She knocked, gently and tentatively at first, then a little louder. The door opened just a couple of inches and a face suspiciously peered through the slit.

'Who is it, what do you want?' It was an old man asking the question when suddenly the door was flung open and an elderly woman pushed herself to the front.

'Stand aside you stupid old fool, can't you see who it is, it's Angelique and Anton, our grandchildren.' She started to cry and held her arms out to embrace the children, 'my word, haven't you both grown up, it has been so long since we saw you last. Where is your mother and father?'

The children didn't get a chance to answer; they were being hugged, lifted up and swung around. Mrs Soliman was overjoyed seeing her grandchildren again but was now breathless, Mr Soliman looked on bewildered. It was at this point that Rick spoke to Andy.

'Perhaps we should introduce ourselves, I don't think we should leave it to Angel to explain what has happened to her parents, do you?'

'No, you're right Rick, let's go and talk to them.' They both got out of the jeep and approached Mr and Mrs Soliman. Angelique saw them and said, 'These are our friends, grand-mere; they have looked after us and helped us ever since we left Sedan. This is Andy, he is British and,' pointing to Rick, 'this is Rick, he is American. They are both very brave.'

'What has happened, Angelique?' The grandmother said, her brow furrowed by concern of what she intuitively felt she was about to be told. 'Where is your mother and father?' she repeated the question asked earlier.

Rick interrupted, 'do you want us to explain what has happened, Angel?'

'No, it's alright Rick, my grandparents don't speak English, so I would have to translate anyway. I will tell them.' She turned to her grandparents and said, 'can we go inside please grand-mere, I will tell you everything that has happened.'

'Of course, of course my child, please come inside, all of you.' She turned to her husband who was still a little bewildered, 'Manny, please help me get our guests something to drink.'

Inside the cottage appeared quite austere and also dark. The windows had been covered with heavy dark curtains but Angelique could see photographs of her parents and some including, she assumed, her and Anton when they were younger, dotted around the room. The photographs upset her greatly but she suppressed any emotional reaction as she knew that would emerge when she told her grandparents that her father was dead and probably her mother too.

Andy was deep in thought, how on earth does an eleven-year-old tell her elderly grandparents that their daughter had been taken away by the Gestapo and may be dead; that their son-in-law had been murdered by the same people. He watched Angelique speak slowly and quietly and with great maturity. He raged inside at the thought of what this war was doing to young children and especially for those that may survive it, how they would cope with their memories. It just wasn't fair and he was frustrated that he currently had no way of expressing his anger.

Mrs Soliman sobbed and her husband held her close to him. His face was racked with the pain of what he had been told by his young grandchild. *How could this be,* he thought, *why am I being told by a young child that my daughter is most likely dead and her husband has been murdered?* He held his hand out to bring Angelique and Anton close to him and he held them tight with all of them now weeping quite freely.

At last, Andy thought, Angelique was releasing some of the pent up emotion she had bravely concealed since her ordeal had begun. Andy and Rick stayed in the background and allowed the family time to release their grief. After a time, when their cries subsided Rick decided that it was best that he and Andy should leave and let them continue to comfort each other in the privacy of their family home without strangers looking on.

'I'm afraid we must leave you now and return to our unit. I'm sorry Sir, Ma'am that we have had to bring you such bad news but at least your grandchildren are safe and with you. So, we'll bid you goodbye.'

The two men stood up and turned to leave when Angelique shouted, 'No, no, please don't go yet.' She turned to her grandmother, 'please grand-mere, don't let them go this soon, please make them stay a little longer.'

Mr Soliman stood up and said, 'Just a moment, messieurs.' He walked to the corner of the room, lifted the carpet and started to remove some of the floor boards.

Mrs Soliman cried out, 'No, Manny, don't.'

'Hush woman,' he said forcefully, holding his hand up to prevent any further interruption.

He removed a silk shawl known as a tallit, which he placed around his shoulders then placed a black skull cap, a kippah, on his head. He then reached back under the floor boards and retrieved a bottle of what looked like a very old cognac.

'Messieurs,' he said, 'we have hidden these items along with our faith for four years and they will be hidden no more.'

'Manny, you know what will happen if we are found with these things, they are not allowed,' Mrs Soliman said, her voice quivering.

Angelique was simultaneously translating the conversation of her grandparents for the benefit of Andy and Rick.

'My love,' he said, 'after what we have been told tonight, do you really think there is anything else they can do to us.'

'Yes, you old fool, they can harm our grandchildren.'

Andy interrupted, 'No, that will not happen Mrs Soliman, the Germans have left your town and are being pushed back into Germany. It is unlikely that you will ever see them again.'

Given what Andy said, Mrs Soliman suddenly realised that it was right to celebrate and went over to her husband and kissing him on the cheek saying, 'You carry on Manny, let us pray together as a family and I hope our friends will join us at supper.' She turned to Angelique. 'Please ask our guests to sit with us and have dinner.'

Andy and Rick did not hesitate accepting the offer.

Whilst Mrs Soliman with Angelique's help was busy preparing the meal, Manny Soliman opened the bottle that he had carefully hidden away for many years and said a short Hebrew prayer before pouring large measures into three glasses. He raised his glass and proudly shouted:

'Shalom.'

That evening, the group sat at the table and ate their meal, a simple one of vegetable soup and bread while Andy and Rick retold the events of their meeting with the children in Sedan and the adventures that followed. Mr and Mrs Soliman who were fascinated by the story, expressed great pride towards their grandchildren and frequently looked at them with loving smiles on their faces.

They were naturally deeply saddened by what they had already been told by Angelique about her mother and father, so Andy avoided any reference to the events leading to the children being left on their own. The story took much longer than would have normally been the case because of the need to translate and to answer the many questions that came from Mr and Mrs Soliman.

Suddenly Angelique's face paled and she looked worryingly at Andy.

'My grandmother wants to know what happened to my father's body, was he buried? Andy, please I don't know how to answer,' she said with a note of desperation in her voice.

'Don't worry Angel, just say that I saw to it when I went back to the house to collect your clothes. You don't need to explain what or how, okay?'

Falteringly, Angelique did as Andy advised and was relieved that it seemed to placate her grandparents. Mrs Soliman then looked directly at Andy and asked, 'Do you know where they took my daughter?' Angelique translated the question.

'No, I'm afraid I do not know Mrs Soliman but Rick and I will try to find out when we return to our unit.'

Rick said, 'I'm sure ma'am that the authorities in Paris will have a record and if my Commanding Officer will allow it, then we will return with any information we can obtain. But now I'm afraid we must leave. Thank you for the excellent dinner.'

Mrs Soliman thanked the soldiers and wished them a safe journey. The two men got up from the table and started to make their way to the door. Angelique and Anton rushed after them.

'Don't go yet, please,' Angelique pleaded. Anton clung on to Rick's arm, saying very much the same thing but in French. Mrs Soliman watched on tearfully and then urged the children to say goodbye.

'Your friends must return to their duties my children; they cannot stay any longer.'

Andy hugged Angelique and then Anton.

'I'm sure we will see you again, so for now look after your grandparents and enjoy the peace of this lovely place without the Germans here.' Rick also hugged the children, kissing them on the cheeks French style and with his beaming smile said.

'Goodbye Angel and you big fella,' he said, picking Anton up, 'your sister and your grandparents are going to need a strong man around the house to help them, you do that for me, okay?' Anton understood Rick better than anyone and nodded with tears in his eyes saying, in French.

'I will grow up strong just like you Rick and will care for my sister and grandparents just as you ask.'

Angelique translated what Anton had said and Rick turned away quickly as a large lump formed in his throat.

'Come on Andy, we need to go.'

The two men clambered into the jeep and waved to the family who stood at the door of the house as they drove away. The children waved and cried and Mr Soliman put a comforting arm around his wife who dabbed her tear-filled eyes.

Before Rick had chance to shift gears, Andy shouted, 'Rick. Stop.'

Rick braked sharply and said, 'What, what's wrong?'

Andy reached into the back seats and retrieved the two helmets that had been given to the children to wear on the journey here. Rick understood and smiled his approval and reversed the vehicle back to the house. The children were still there and their faces brightened on seeing Andy hastily making his way down the path.

'We thought you might like to keep these as a memento, something to remember our time together.' He passed the helmets to them and turned away once again. Rick avoided looking towards the children as he found it difficult to hide the emotion that welled up inside him. As soon as Andy got into the vehicle, Rick sped away as quickly as he could.

The two men sat in silence as they made their way back to where the HQ was but they knew that Colonel Harper had moved his command centre and therefore would have to trust that they could find the new location.

They decided that they would make their way back towards the last known location, mindful that they could still hear the sound of gunfire and artillery in the distance. It was therefore possible that they could run into retreating Germans. As they approached a crossroad, a group of American military policemen were setting up a traffic control point. One held his hand up to stop Andy and Rick.

'Where are you guys headed, you aint going in the right direction.' He pointed to a scrawled wooden sign by the side of the road saying, "Berlin and Hitler this way". He noticed the single bar on Rick's helmet. 'Sorry Sir,' stood smartly to attention and saluted.

Rick was still getting used to people calling him Sir but liked the idea somewhat.

'We're trying to get back to Colonel Harper's headquarters having completed a mission on his behalf. We left him at Rocroi but I know he was moving. So, which way soldier?'

'That way Sir,' he said pointing to the way of the sign. 'The new HQ is over the Belgium border in Dinant. We're making ready for other units coming through here shortly.'

'Well good luck soldier, we'll see you in Berlin,' Rick said, saluted and drove off.

Andy studied the map and concluded that they had come about seven miles east and that Dinant was twelve miles north of Givet.

'Assuming we have no major detours or hold ups, we should reach HQ in less than an hour,' he said. That was the first words spoken between them since they left the children and apart from some directions from Andy, the rest of the journey was made in silence.

Both were lost in their own thoughts and both of their feelings were focused on the children. A strong attachment had been made between them and it grieved both men to see their sad, tear-stained faces as they left, so neither of them were in the mood for conversation.

They were eventually close to the HQ and were abruptly stopped by a patrol. A platoon commander pointing his carbine at Rick said, 'Identify yourselves Sir and where are you headed?'

'I'm Lieutenant Frederici, we have completed an assignment for Colonel Harper and need to return to his HQ.'

'Do you have any I.D. Sir?'

Rick showed the letter of authority given to him before they left the last HQ location and the platoon commander was satisfied.

'Sorry to delay you Sir, just doing our job Lieutenant, head on down this road for about a mile and then take a left into the town. The Colonel's set up is in the town hall.'

'Thanks, Sergeant, keep up the good work,' Rick said feeling just a little smug with his new found ability to give out praise.

Rick pulled the jeep up outside the headquarters building and the two of them marched briskly to the Colonel's Command centre. They were met by Lieutenant Pinkerton, who instantly recognised them.

'The Colonel will be pleased to see you guys, he heard about the kraut panzer you helped take out. If it hadn't been for you, then we could have lost a lot of men. Follow me, please.'

The men were led to the Command Centre where Colonel Jack Harper was busily issuing instructions for the next phase of the advance. He looked up and saw Andy and Rick and immediately dismissed the men that were gathered around the maps on the large table.

'You guys go and get yourselves ready to move out at first light.'

He bounded over to Andy and Rick and shook their hands.

'Did you complete your mission and by the way, thanks for the job you did identifying that kraut tank, it could have caused us a mess of trouble. Come into my office and we can chew fat some more. Pinkerton, can you rustle up some coffee?'

'Certainly, Sir,' Lieutenant Pinkerton replied. Pinkerton didn't mind being asked as he was extremely impressed by the actions of Rick and Andy.

'So, take a seat Lieutenant, Sergeant,' the Colonel continued, 'tell me did you get kids to their grandparents?'

'We sure did, Sir and we're sure they'll be happy there. But there is something we still need to do.'

'And what might that be, gentlemen?'

Wesley Pinkerton re-emerged with the coffee and was glad he was able to sit in on the conversation.

'Andy, you know more about what happened in Sedan, would you explain to the Colonel the situation regarding the kids mother?'

Andy recounted what he knew of Mrs Wilder being taken by the Gestapo after her husband was shot and that they had told Angelique that if we could find out where she was taken to, that there might be hope that she is still alive. And if we did find anything about her at all that we would return and tell her and of course the grandparents.'

Jack Harper stroked his chin thoughtfully.

'I'm afraid you're not going to be able to do that gentlemen. At first light the day after tomorrow, you are both being taken to the nearest airfield where a plane is standing by to take you back to England. This was arranged in your absence and cannot be undone.'

Rick stood up.

'Sir, with respect, we have made many promises to those children and never broken one of them. We would prefer not to break one now. Is there any way we can delay our transport?'

'Sit down soldier, no there is no chance of a delay but I'll tell you what I will do. We will get a message to the French authorities in Paris to see if there is a record of her being taken and if so, where to. If and I emphasise if, there is any news and it comes in time before you leave, then we'll see if you have time to get the news to the children. I must tell you that if she is Jewish, then the chances of her still being alive are extremely slim.

The news that is coming out of Poland and other occupied countries of concentration camp atrocities is damned sickening. I will do my best to find out as much as I can.' Jack Harper turned to his aide. 'Wesley, get the French liaison officer in here as quick as you can.'

'Thank you Sir, we appreciate your help,' Rick said.

'Okay, you guys, go and get some shuteye, we'll talk again in the morning after my battalion have moved out.'

It was late morning before Andy and Rick were summoned to the Command centre.

'Colonel Harper has some news for you and wants to see you right away guys, let's go.' Wesley Pinkerton said as he ushered the two men from their sleeping quarters.

Jack Harper had his back to them as they entered the room and on turning, both Rick and Andy saw that he was in a very sombre mood.

'Gentlemen, the advance is going according to plan I'm pleased to say but what I'm not pleased about is what I have to tell you. Please sit down. The French have informed me that Mrs Wilder when taken by the SS was moved to Natzweiler-Struthof. That is a Concentration camp near the French German border in the Alsace district.

They cannot say whether she has survived but are almost certain that she would not have done so. There were very few women taken there, some were gassed and others were transported to Auschwitz or Dachau. That's all they know and we must wait until the camp is liberated to find out more.

But they are certain in their view that even if they survived the journey to whatever camp they were sent to, it would be extremely unlikely that they would survive for very long there. I'm sorry men but I don't think it's something you will want to tell those children, so I am asking the French Liaison officer to go to Givet to tell the family what I have told you and anyway, you don't have time to get there and back.

Your transport to the airfield is ready now, so you can go early; it's possible that your plane is waiting for you. Now, I've got a war to fight, goodbye and good luck.' He shook each of them by the hand and turned away.

Andy and Rick took off earlier than planned and said little during the flight; both had a feeling that their task was unfinished but now they were on their way back to England and could do little about it. After a short time, Rick said, 'I hope you and I will keep in touch buddy because after we land, we will be sent in different directions and we're not likely to see each other again until after this goddamned war is over and that assumes we survive it.'

'You're right Rick, who knows what will happen next. But I make you a promise; if I survive, I will seek you out.'

Upon landing in an airfield somewhere in Kent, the two men left the aircraft and were directed to a nissen hut where they were to be allocated their onward transport. They sat and waited until eventually an orderly approached.

'Lieutenant Frederici?'

'That's me,' Rick said. He stood up and faced Andy who was also now standing. 'Good luck buddy, maybe I'll see you in New York when this thing is over.'

'Maybe, my friend, maybe. I hope so.'

They shook hands then threw their arms around each other possibly for the last time as friends and brothers in arms.

Chapter 21

Three months earlier

When Emily was dragged out of her home having watched the murder of her husband, she was horrified not only by the murder but also terrified about the danger her children were in. She knew she couldn't reveal their location and prayed that Angelique would protect herself and her young brother. Emily wept openly as she was pushed forcefully into the back of a military truck.

There were many people already sitting there, some silent, some sobbing and others shivering with fear. The faces that she could see were all the same, hollow eyed, pale and full of fear, it was difficult to imagine what terror they each foresaw could befall them.

Questions tumbled through their minds, why have I been arrested, where are they taking me, what will happen to me? But most knew the answers as some had been suspected of helping the French Resistance and others like Emily had Jewish connections, so in their minds their fate was sealed.

After over four hours of travelling, stopping only once for the guards to take a toilet break, the arrestees were not allowed that privilege and some had soiled themselves unable to contain the need. One woman cried with shame as a puddle formed at her feet, shaking her head in distress at the humiliation of it.

None of the travellers felt the need to remonstrate with the woman as they knew they would all have to face far greater indignities than that. A German guard screamed at her and slapped her across the face with back of his hand. The woman slumped to one side as the guard took up his seat at the tailgate of the vehicle, he laughed and called the woman a filthy pig.

They eventually arrived at what appeared to be their final location, the only indication of where it might be was a sign above the wooden gates on an arched entrance, "Konzentrationslager Natzweiler-Struthof" it said. Little translation was necessary and the arrestees had realised their worst fears.

The vehicle stopped outside one of the nissen huts, of which there appeared to be many and the guards shouted, pushed and dragged the prisoners from the truck. Some fell off the tailgate unable to move quickly enough to satisfy the guards. They were ordered to get in line whereupon the guards separated women from the men.

A solitary female German guard appeared, carrying a large baton and ordered the frightened women to follow her. They marched past the line of men, most of whom had their heads lowered staring vacantly into the ground at their feet.

The female guard stopped at one of the huts and stood on the wooden steps that led inside.

'Remove all of your clothes and leave them here,' she said in very good French, 'you will be given special work uniforms once you are clean.' A sardonic grin appeared on her face, 'in the interest of hygiene, your heads will be shaved and then I shall take great pleasure in hosing you down to remove any filth before you get dressed again.'

Some of the women started tentatively to remove their clothes and Emily followed suit. Some would question why they would do it and just obey an order that would be considered reprehensible in most circumstances but most would not feel the malevolence from the place they were now in. The why was soon to be explained as one of the women demanded to know why she was here and why she should remove her clothes.

'It's degrading, I have done nothing wrong,' she said. The baton wielding guard stepped forward and rammed the baton into the woman's stomach and then crashed it into the side of her head as she doubled up in pain. Blood gushed from the side of her face as she fell to the ground.

'That's why.' The guard said with venom in her voice. 'Now, if anyone else wishes to question why they need to do as they are told now that they are here, then please speak now.' She nodded to two German soldiers who stood in the background, leering at the now undressed women. They stepped forward and dragged the injured woman away.

The remaining partially dressed women quickly shed their clothes.

That night, Emily lay on a thin straw mattress in her black and white striped "uniform" her head shaven with her thoughts only for her children. The humiliation of what she had endured today paled into insignificance at the thought of her children, alone, frightened, hungry. A tired, weary voice from the next bunk broke into her thoughts.

'Be very afraid of what you have seen today, believe me there is worse to come.'

Emily turned to face the voice.

'How long have you been here? I really can't comprehend the cruelty of these people.'

''I'm one of the lucky ones, I've been here for three months and trust me when I tell you that to survive this, you will have to demonstrate that you are strong. If you do that, you just might be allocated to the work parties in the munitions factories. They badly need workers to make ammunition and weapons. Just be prepared to work up to fifteen hours a day, every day.'

'And what is the alternative?' Emily asked, half-knowing the answer.

'Look, I am very tired and need to get some sleep before they wake us up but you will find out what the alternatives are soon enough.'

Over the following days, Emily got to know the woman she spoke to on her first night in the camp. Her name was Rachel. Emily was shocked at first to see how frail she was. Her black striped clothes hung loosely on her thin frame and her face was gaunt, her eyes black and hollow.

Fortunately, Emily was given the task of working in the munition factory some miles from the camp, so each day they would be transported to their workplace at 5.30 a.m. Her job was to load finished goods onto a wheeled basket and push it to the loading bay. It was back-breaking work with few rest periods and very little food but she had heard about the alternatives and counted herself lucky.

She was told of medical experiments being carried out on some inmates and how some were selected to be transferred to Dachau, never to be seen or heard of again. The full horror of what went on in the camp was not be exposed until the camp was liberated later that year. In the meantime, Emily worked hard and did as she was told, knowing that it was the only way to stay alive and then hope to be reunited with her children.

As usual in the early hours of a particular morning, the German guard came into the hut shouting and screaming at the sleeping and still exhausted workers. Emily gathered what little strength she had and roused herself. Rachel remained still and Emily went to her.

'Rachel, Rachel, come my friend, you must get up or the bitch will thrash you, come let me help you.'

'No, Emily I have had enough now, I cannot do this anymore, just leave me or you will get in trouble,' she said, her voice weak and trembling.

'I can't leave you; you know what will happen, please get up, you must keep going.'

Most of the hut inmates had gathered outside of the hut as was required each day with the exception of Emily and Rachel. The guard returned having discovered their absence.

'What is the meaning of this? Get outside now or I will kick you there.'

'I'm sorry Corporal,' Emily said meekly, 'I'm trying to get this woman out of bed. I don't think she is feeling very well.'

'Isn't she now, well we'll soon see how well she is.' She turned to Rachel. 'You get up now or I'll drag you outside myself.'

''You can do what you like because I don't care anymore. I shall stay here,' Rachel said defiantly, yet her voice was barely audible. Rachel knew that she was dying.

The guard turned to Emily.

'You get outside and join the others.'

Emily did as she was told and wept as she heard thud after thud of the guard's baton, knowing that Rachel would have breathed her last breath.

It was now late into August and the days had melded into weeks. Each day got harder for Emily but she gritted her teeth and thought only of her children. She had to stay alive for them, she kept telling herself.

Strangely, one morning the guard did not arrive to wake the workers and although some, Emily included, woke without waiting for the dreaded shouting, many others just slept on. Emily was about to move and try and discover what was happening when the female guard came into the hut.

'Your services will not be required today, instead you will help clean the camp up.' She left as quietly as she arrived.

Internees who had just woken up staggered from their beds bewildered, others like Emily ventured outside into the early morning mist and queued up with others for food, which was always nothing more than water with a few oats. Nevertheless, it was better than nothing.

What on earth is happening, Emily thought. The smell of death in the camp was now stronger than ever and for the first time, Emily was able to see the chimney stack that billowed foul-smelling black smoke. She was able to guess what it was and prayed for those that had entered that building.

It was several days later that they were told that they would be leaving the camp. German soldiers scurried about loading vehicles with boxes of documents and supplies and ordered the internees into a line of three abreast. They were not to know that they were about to embark on the notorious "death march" to Dachau.

The internees were herded out of the gate, some already finding it difficult to walk. For many miles, the prisoners were brutally treated, given no food or water and some collapsed, only to die where they lay. Emily had regained some of her strength during the previous days of light work and helped as many as she could but many were beyond help.

It was late in the evening and she could see the sun setting behind the slowly moving trail of marchers and deduced that they were heading east and therefore, towards Germany. She couldn't understand why they had suddenly vacated the camp and why they were being taken to Germany but then realised that it could only be because the Germans were losing the war and needed to get out before the Allies arrived.

Her heart skipped a beat at the very thought of that being a possibility but then she could not figure out why they would force march thousands of people and treat them so brutally. When someone collapsed, unable to walk any further, a guard would shoot them dead and then just leave them. To Emily, none of this made sense.

For the next twenty four hours, the prisoners were force marched without being able to stop while the guards would be replaced every five or six hours by fresher men who had rested in the vehicles that brought up the rear. The numbers falling down and dying or being shot increased and Emily knew that she had to find a way to escape or meet the same fate.

At one point on the second day, she noted that the guards were not bothering to shoot the stricken marchers anymore and just left them to their ultimate fate. Emily watched one marcher fall to the ground and a guard rushed to him and was about to shoot him when another guard shouted, 'Save your bullets Hans, he'll be dead in a few hours anyway. We'll need all of the ammunition we have for when the Americans come.'

Emily didn't understand the German but guessed what had been said when the guard lowered his weapon and just kicked the stricken individual in the stomach and rolled him into the ditch at the side of the road. Perhaps this was her chance of escaping, she thought and would wait a little longer to ensure that there were no more shootings.

After several more hours, she decided to instigate her plan. Although she was very tired anyway, it didn't take much to feign complete exhaustion so, making sure she was in view of a guard, she fell to her knees. Before the guard could respond, she got up and staggered onwards with the help of one of the men alongside her. Over the next hour, she did the same twice more and each time, she pretended to be less able to rise up than before. The man next to her said, 'You must keep going or they will leave you to die, come give me your arm, I will help you.'

'Thank you,' Emily replied 'but I intend to be left to die. I may need your help though.'

'How can I help?'

'The next time I fall, I would ask that you carry me for a short distance and then help me to walk for a short while. I will then collapse completely and you must leave me. Can you do that?'

'Yes of course but you are risking that they will shoot you.'

'Yes, I know but I'd rather that than be marched till I die. So, help me please.'

'Yes okay but be it on your head.'

They walked on for some distance with Emily half-dragging her feet and half-being carried, making sure that they were visible to the guards. She was making a good show of someone who was about to finally give up. She lurched forward, forcing her helper to use what little strength he had to hold her upright.

She retched and spluttered as she fell to the ground, banging her head in the process and losing consciousness. Her friend stooped down and tried to lift her but she was now a dead weight. A guard shouted, 'Leave her, move on.' Her companion didn't need to understand the words but understood the gestures and slowly carried on walking. He watched the guard approach Emily and place the barrel of his rifle under her body to turn her over. He saw the blood seeping from a gash on her forehead, her face was pale and her eyes closed. He kicked her hard in the side and pushed her into the ditch at the side of the road. Her companion had watched as he walked on and was relieved that he didn't hear a gunshot.

Emily was on her face in the ditch, which fortunately was dry and she resisted moving. She could hear the scraping of tired feet on the road above her and held her breath for as long as she could as the guards footsteps faded into the distance with the marchers. Several supply vehicles then went by and again she lay perfectly still, continuing to play dead.

Emily waited for what she thought was about an hour, although she had laid there for only thirty minutes before making any effort to move. Her head was painful but had stopped bleeding, her side hurt like hell from the kick she received but now it was time to see whether her ruse had worked. She slowly turned to one side and then raised her head to see that the road was quiet, no vehicles, no people.

Her heart skipped a beat, she had made it, she had escaped, now she must find her children but she had no idea in what direction she should go to get to Sedan nor indeed how far away it was. Emily was exhausted but knew she could not stay where she was, so she moved further into the wooded area. Each step was agony and she thought at one point that she really would collapse and die but once she was in the thicket of shrubs, she felt a little more secure and lay down to rest. She was quickly asleep.

It was the sound of birdsong that awakened her and she lay there without stirring, listening to them. All the time she was in the camp, she never heard a bird sing or any other sound of a summer morning. The place was bereft of life completely. It was cold and dead. Yet here, it was as though she was in a different world, she could smell the freshness of the grass, listen to the birds and hear the rustle of leaves in the trees as they swayed in the breeze.

She was suddenly invigorated. If it weren't for her shaven head, her gaunt features and grimy black and white striped pyjamas she was forced to wear, she could have been an ordinary French lady on an ordinary French summer's day. Emily staggered onto her feet, cautiously looked around and on seeing that it was clear of any immediate danger, she started to walk.

Initially, each step was excruciatingly painful but that pain eased as she stepped out, keeping the sun either on her left shoulder or behind her in the hopeful knowledge that she should be walking west and back to France.

After several hours, she came to a clearing and a road that appeared to run north and south. Emily wondered whether this might be the road that runs along the French German border. She of course could not be certain but decided to cross over it and continue her walking. She was becoming very tired now through lack of food and water and each step became more leaden as she drove herself forward.

She could just make out a building in the distance, it was shimmering in the haze but she was certain she wasn't imagining it, so pushed on through the pain.

She was gasping for air with each step, her throat parched, her bruised body screaming out for her to stop but she thrust herself forward.

Just a few steps from the front of what looked like a small farm, she fell forward, unable to take another step and lay in a crumpled mess on the ground.

The door opened and a man came out, ran to Emily and shouted to his wife who was still inside the farmhouse.

'Come quickly Colette, bring some water,' he said as he cradled Emily's head in his arms.

Colette came rushing out without the water, confused by her husband's shout for help.

'My god,' she said clasping her hand over her mouth, 'who is this, where has she come from?'

'Never mind the questions woman, get some water and some clean towels, I will bring her inside.'

Emily could hear voices, they were vague, distant but she was certain they were French. She felt the coolness of water against her parched lips and started to grab at the vessel that was held close to her mouth.

'No Madame, not too quickly, just a little at a time.' The voice said. His was a gentle voice as he let her sip some more. At that point, Emily slipped into a deep, exhausted sleep.

'Colette, I will carry her to the spare bed but I think you will need to undress her and get rid of these filthy clothes. When she wakes, we will find out more. The poor wretch looks as if she has been starved.'

For three days, Emily slipped in and out of sleep and whilst awake, was fed with warm soup and plenty to drink but had not yet spoken nor had her hosts asked any questions. It was almost a week later that Emily awoke fully.

'Where am I?' she asked Colette who had brought some food.

'We are a small farm near the town of Colmar, my child. We guessed that you had been held by the Germans, is that correct?'

Emily nodded and while she ate some more solid food, she explained what had happened to her, how her husband had been murdered and how she had been taken to the concentration Camp at Natzweiler-Struthof and had then escaped. She had been bathed and was now clean, her hair was starting to grow just a little and the farmer's wife had provided her with a nightdress.

Some clothes were folded up on the dresser for her to wear. Her husband, Alphonse, had knocked on the door and entered to listen to Emily's story. Her description of what went on at the camp horrified them.

'We heard rumours of what was happening there but couldn't believe them,' Alphonse said. 'At least you are safe now, the Germans have gone and we hear that the Americans are not far away. Let us pray that they chase them all the way to Berlin.'

'Monsieur, I truly thank you and your wife for helping me, I believe I would have died had it not been for you but I need to get to Sedan to find my children. They will be alone and helpless. Can you help me?'

She added quickly, 'I know you have already helped me more than I could have hoped for but please, is there any way you can help me get to Sedan? I will find a way of repaying you, I promise.'

'There will be no need for repayment, child,' the old man said 'I will get you to Sedan. But first you must regain your strength, so stay just a couple of days more.' Emily agreed. She sat and talked with Colette while Alphonse went to visit some of his farmer friends to obtain fuel for his car sufficient for the journey.

After hearing the story of Emily, they were only too glad to donate as much fuel as he needed for his 1930s Peugeot. The vehicle had hardly been used but was his pride and joy. He had kept it covered up in the barn and regularly uncovered it just to admire it but he rarely used it.

The following week Emily announced that she felt well enough to make the journey. She was still painfully thin and her hair was now a fine fuzz but the change was in her face, it was fuller, less strained and full of hope.

'Okay,' Alphonse declared, 'let's leave first thing in the morning.'

Emily couldn't sleep that night and waited impatiently for morning to arrive.

The next day, Emily prepared to leave and thanked Colette for the clothes and her help and kindness.

'I shall not forget what you have done for me, Madame.' She waved goodbye as she and Alphonse drove off towards Sedan. Alphonse estimated that the journey would take about four hours, assuming that there were no hold ups. Emily was soon to find out how rough the journey would be as she felt every bump through to her fleshless bottom.

After five bone-shaking hours with only one stop, they finally reached Sedan. Emily was shocked at the sight of the devastation and even more horrified after directing Alphonse to her former home. She sank to her knees on the realisation that her children could never have survived such destruction. She buried her head in her hands and sobbed, 'My children, my children.'

Alphonse had joined her and put a comforting arm around her shoulder.

'What do you want to do now, my child? I will help if I can but there's nothing we can do here.'

'The only place I can go is to my parents who live in Givet.'

'I'm really sorry Emily but I can't take you there. I only have enough fuel to get back to Colmar. Why don't you come back with me?'

'No, that is alright, Alphonse, I will find a way of getting there. You and your wife have done enough for me already and I will never forget it. Please have a safe journey back. I want to stay here for a little while.'

Alphonse bade his farewell and left.

Emily knelt down and was praying for the souls of her children when a vehicle pulled up behind her.

'Excuse me ma'am, are you alright, can I help you?'

The sound of the vehicle frightened Emily at first but then she recognised an American voice. She understood English as it was she who had been responsible for Angelique's skill in the language.

'No thank you sir, I just want to stay here for a little while.'

'Okay,' he said, 'but if you need any help, I'll be happy to assist if I can.'

'Just a minute officer, is it possible for you to help me get to my parents in Givet?'

'Well, I'm sure,' he paused, trying to figure out if it really could be her, 'Do you have two children, a girl named Angelique and a boy called Tony, I think?'

'Yes I do, well I did until this happened, how do you know about my children?'

'Ma'am, my name is Lieutenant Pinkerton and I know that your children are safe and well in Givet with their grandparents and boy are they going to be goddamn sure as hell to be happy to see you.' He went on to explain what he knew about the situation with Andy and Rick and how they had got the children from here to their grandparents.

'You sure as hell should be proud of those kids ma'am, they never gave up and still believe you are alive and we are going to get you to them as soon as I have spoken to Colonel Harper.'

Emily broke down on the news and couldn't contain her tears but this time they were tears of joy.

After Pinkerton's conversation with Jack Harper, he said, 'We're good to go ma'am, we should be there in about two hours.'

As they pulled up outside the Soliman's house, Emily paused to catch her breath. Inside, they were all were celebrating Angelique's twelfth birthday and were unaware of what was about to happen.

Lieutenant Pinkerton asked, 'Would you like me to go and prepare the way, so that it's not too much of a shock?' He explained that the French liaison Officer had already told them that their mother's survival was extremely unlikely, so apart from losing their father, they had already been through a significant period of grief.

'Yes please,' she said, still dabbing the tears from her eyes which were now full of happiness rather than despair.

The lieutenant knocked at the door, which was opened by Mrs Soliman. After he explained who was in the jeep, she almost collapsed and the Officer had to hold her up.

Gathering herself, she shouted to the children and her husband.

'Come Angelique, Anton, Manny, quickly I have someone you need to meet.'

The children rushed to the front door to see a woman standing on the path, waiting for them with arms outstretched. At first, they did not recognise her because of her hair or lack of it and her thin frame but it didn't take long before they knew and ran down the path to greet her.

'Mother,' Angelique asked incredulously, 'is it really you?'

Emily nodded her head.

'Yes my child,' she said.

Angelique threw herself into her mother's arms and was quickly followed by Anton. They were all overwhelmed with joy and Angelique thanked God for answering her daily prayer. They hugged and kissed and cried and as the grandparents joined in, Lieutenant Pinkerton—who had been watching the blissful reunion with his steel helmet under his arm and a large lump in his throat—quietly left.

Epilogue

Andy and Rick were given special duties in England after their ordeals as POWs and then as escapees, so were not asked to return to active duty. Neither Andy nor Rick were happy with the idea but could see that the war was coming to an end and were content to have played a part in it. They each received a letter from Colonel Harper telling them about the discovery of Mrs Wilder and the reunion with her children.

For both of them, it was the closure they had sought ever since they had left the children in Givet and they were both overjoyed by the news. They would now see the war out happy in the knowledge of what they had achieved.

Andy was promoted to Flight Lieutenant and was given the task of training new navigators. He and Estelle regularly exchanged letters and their relationship appeared to be holding up as they talked constantly of when they would meet again.

Rick was returned to America to his home base unit and for a short time also took on a training role, which bored the hell out him. When the war ended, he decided to take his discharge papers, return to his family home in the Bronx and marry his long standing sweetheart. His father, as expected, retired from his Italian coffee shop business and passed it on to his son Rick, who had grand ideas about expansion into a full on Italian ristorante. It turned out to be a great success.

Mrs Wilder had almost fully recovered from her concentration camp ordeal, her hair had grown again and she had put on quite a bit of weight. She would probably never fully recover from the emotional scars or the memories that would haunt her. But she was happy with her family now.

Manny Soliman openly practiced his Jewishness whilst Mrs Soliman revelled in her grandchildren. As for the children, Angelique was growing up into a very pretty young lady and training to be a teacher. Anton, whilst also growing up, still liked to play his hopscotch, or Marelle as he liked to call it.

For Andy, the war ending meant he could try and get back to France to see Estelle and hopefully continue where he left off the last time they were together.

After almost two years of exchanging letters, he decided he would return to France and surprise Estelle. There were many uncertainties in his mind, the most prominent being whether Estelle would feel the same towards him when he presented himself.

What if their long distance relationship was as far as it could go, he thought. *What if their perception of each other had been idealised by the war and the environment that it created.* He personally felt that their relationship was stronger now that time had passed but the war was now over and perhaps the passion, the urgency of the time when they were together would not be the same.

He certainly had no desire to stay in England anyway, with all of its inherent unpleasant memories. So, with those thoughts and doubts swirling around in his head, he left for France and the farm in the Ardennes where he hoped he would be reunited with Estelle.

After a very rough ferry crossing and several different train journeys, Andy arrived at Charleville de Mezieres. On leaving the station, he could see the hills in the distance that he, Rick and the children had climbed on their way to Estelle's farm. The river that ran through the town was running freely and the bridges had been repaired.

There was much activity about the place, with houses being repaired or rebuilt, roads being re-laid and people going about their business. But now, there was now an air of normality instead of the fear that prevailed during the war time occupation. He scanned the ground in the distance to see if he could spot the shepherds hut that had been such an important part of their journey. He couldn't see it but was tempted for a moment to retrace the gruelling steps they had taken but on reflection decided against the idea.

Perhaps another time, he thought. On this occasion, he would take a taxi.

The journey to Estelle's farm was to take less than thirty minutes and Andy remembered the almost full day it had taken on the previous occasion, over the hills and through a vicious storm. He recalled the massive efforts that Rick and the children made in their desire to reach this place of refuge.

Andy recognised the track entrance to the farm.

'Stop here please; I'll walk the rest of the way,' he said to the taxi driver.

'Are you sure, Sir, I don't mind driving up the track, this old bus has travelled over worse roads than this,' the driver replied in good English but with a very strong French accent.

'No, this will be fine, I will enjoy the walk after all my travelling.' Andy smiled, paid the driver and carrying his large travel bag walked towards the farm. As he approached the farm, a small sheepdog ran towards him and Andy was surprised that it hadn't barked. He remembered what the dog was called.

'Come here, Enzo, there's a good dog.' The dog loped towards him and brushed up against Andy's legs, wagging his tail frantically as Andy stooped low to stroke him. There was no doubt in his mind that Enzo had remembered him. 'Come now, boy, let's go and see your mistress.' Andy strode on with Enzo by his side and quickly came upon the front entrance to the farm.

He waited to see if Estelle would come out of the front door to greet him but there was little sign of movement. He turned towards the barn and saw Estelle scattering some chicken feed from a basket. She turned and saw Andy with Enzo quietly at his feet. She dropped the basket and clasped her hands over mouth.

Estelle was stunned, rooted to the spot, until she recovered her senses and started to babble away in French and ran to Andy. She launched herself into his arms, frantically kissing him on his face and neck while still chattering in French. Suddenly, in English she asked, 'What are you doing here, how did you get here, why didn't you tell me you were coming? Look at the state of me, I am not ready, I have no make-up on, my clothes are a mess.'

Estelle hardly took a breath until Andy asked with a sullen look on his face, 'Whoa there, slow down. Are you not glad to see me, should I have warned you that I was coming?'

'Of course, I am glad to see you and yes, you should have warned me then I would have been better prepared. But I am so happy that you have come, so happy. Come, come inside, you must be tired after your journey. I will make some coffee.' Estelle had gotten over her initial shock and embarrassment and was deliriously happy. They walked hand in hand to the farmhouse with Enzo following on dutifully behind them.

The following months saw their relationship grow stronger with each passing day and there was little doubt that they were truly in love. Andy's fears that the war had distorted their emotions and had somehow clouded their judgement were clearly unfounded and so he quickly settled into life on a French farm with Estelle.

It was now 1950 and Andy and Estelle been living together for almost two years. On one evening over dinner, Andy plucked up the courage to ask Estelle to marry him and although it was initially a shock, she accepted. Invitations were sent out to Patrice, who had survived the rest of the war, and also to Angelique, Anton and the family from Givet.

Unfortunately, the children's grandparents were now too frail to travel but their mother had fully recovered from her ordeal and was happy to join her children at the wedding. Angelique was now eighteen years of age while Anton had just become a teenager. Both of them had matured significantly in the preceding seven years and neither Andy nor Estelle had seen either of them since their visit to the farm in 1944.

Angelique and her brother had spent most of the last few years making the most of their time with their mother and particularly their grandparents who were not in the best of health. There were moments of sadness for all of them and Angelique felt it most when she remembered her father and that terrible day back in 1944. But now, she was a little happier and training to be a teacher while Anton had set his sights on becoming a soldier, which was heavily influenced by his time with Rick.

In the intervening period, there had been the occasional letter from Rick, who was now married to his longtime girlfriend and was very involved in running his "Ristorante". Andy missed his friend and often thought about him. Rick also often thought of Andy and the children but wasn't a great one for sitting down and writing letters.

'Why don't you write to your friend, Rick?' Frankie would regularly ask in a chiding way. 'You must make the effort to answer his letters, and what about those lovely French children?'

'I will, I will, I just have to find the time, honey.' His response was always the same but he never found that time.

So for Rick, in New York, it was all about working tirelessly on making his restaurant a success. He would get up early each morning to buy the fresh produce from the local markets and would accept nothing but the best quality. He spent many hours choosing the materials he would need for his kitchen. The restaurant occupied most of his waking hours leaving little time for anything else.

He did finally write to his friend Andy but only to apologise for not being able to attend the wedding. He was mortified that he had to turn down Andy and Estelle's invitation but he was convinced that the business his father passed on to him had to come first. Rick had agonised for many days and nights before he made the final decision to decline their offer, torn between loyalty towards his best friend and promises he had made to his father.

Andy, Estelle and the children were constantly in his thoughts and particularly so at the time of the wedding. Of course, he sent a congratulatory telegram and a gift but remained not only embarrassed but also regretful.

Shortly after the wedding, Rick was working hard in the restaurant serving Italian coffee for just a few customers. It was a quiet day and there were just a few customers slowly sipping their espresso and eating small pieces of Italian cake. His favourite music was playing in the background and remembered how he and Frankie danced to this very Glen Miller record on the night of their wedding.

Remembering his wedding brought sadness to Rick for not attending that of his best friend. Rick looked around his restaurant and wondered whether he had done the right thing putting this place first before his loyalty to his friend. It was at that moment that a new customer entered the restaurant.

'Hey, morning Ricky, see you've got some crazy people outside doing crazy things on your sidewalk.'

Rick came from behind his bar and said, 'What crazy things, they'd better not be messing up out there.'

'Na, man, they're just having a game, I think. Just hopping around on one leg. Crazy but they're having fun,' the customer replied.

Rick's face suddenly lit up and as he tore off his white apron, he shouted, 'Frankie, look after the store. I think I've got visitors.' He dashed outside.

He was greeted outside by a smiling Andy. Angelique and Anton had now stopped playing Marelle and waited for Rick to recognise them. Estelle stood to one side with the children's mother and let the group that had been through so much together finally reunite.

Frankie arrived at the front door of the restaurant to see her deliriously happy husband playing hopscotch with Angelique, Anton and Andy. She finally saw that unique beaming smile on his face that she hadn't seen in a long while.